Mrs Mulvaney

Hilary Bailey was born in 1936. Educated at ten schools and Newnham College, Cambridge, she has written many short stories and articles for newspapers and magazines. She is the author of several novels including *Polly Put The Kettle On*, *Hannie Richards* and *All The Days Of My Life*, which is also available in Pan books. At present she reviews fiction for the *Guardian* and is working on an historical novel about the building of the railways in Britain.

Also available in Pan Books by the same author

All the Days of My Life

Hilary Bailey

Mrs Mulvaney

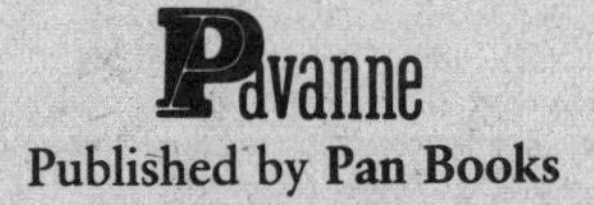

Published by Pan Books

First published in Great Britain 1978 by Constable and Company Ltd
This Pavanne edition published 1987 by Pan Books Ltd,
Cavaye Place, London SW10 9PG
9 8 7 6 5 4 3 2 1

ISBN 0 330 29622 1

Printed and bound in Great Britain by
Cox & Wyman Ltd, Reading

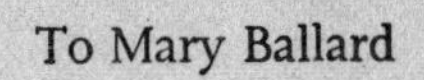
To Mary Ballard

The picture which comes back to me now, when I remember that time before anything changed, is of the garden, two acres of trees and grass. It is a small London park, private, enclosed, overlooked by the back windows of the tall houses around it, and always filled with the noise of the traffic roaring, day and night, beyond them on all four sides.

It was in the garden that, each afternoon, when the cold amber sunshine filtered through the browns and yellows of the trees, I, Joseph Coverdale – Joe – used to walk my dog along quiet gravel paths and over the chilling October grass scattered with fallen leaves. In some places the eternal rattling and belching of the traffic muted to a low roar, like that of an approaching wind. Walking under the trees, over grass, you might think you were in the country.

I remember the near-silence, half-solitude of those autumn afternoons. The freshness and clear light.

All around, the back gardens of the houses led on to the square. Here is one with white trellises, a pool and marble statues. I see a tabby cat slide across the paving round the pool and head for the cover of the trellis against the wall, where a few roses still hang among the drying leaves and petal-dropping blooms. In another garden the axle of an old motor-bike grows out of weeds and long damp grass studded with thrusting baby sycamores. Next door, a red-eyed white rabbit sits up, a carrot in its paws, on a billiard-table lawn. And, as I pass a high, yellow-brick wall, two Alsatians leap up barking. Their heads and paws appear over the top. They yelp. They thud down again. They are comic and frightening, with their red lolling tongues and yellow fangs, like cartoon wolves. My spaniel, Philip, toffee and white and curly, stands and growls at them, runs away down the path, comes back and growls, runs beside me as I pace on, staring up with rolling brown eyes, in search of my strength. A little, cool wind begins to blow.

Imagining that time, the time of my slow, numbed walks in the autumn garden, dazed even by the circling, racing, leaf-chasing dog, always aching the dull ache of an old wound, the healed bone, I see, suddenly, the picture of Mrs Mulvaney's long garden with its trees, the rusting seesaw, the spade abandoned in the patchy grass, and of Mrs Mulvaney, framed in the window of her upstairs sitting-room, on her knees, very still in prayer, quite visible through the long windows.

There she kneeled, in profile from above the waist, and staring blindly towards the right-hand wall. To the left of her I could see part of the old sofa. On it was a pair of wellingtons and one of the mistreated but beautiful, rich, needlepoint cushions – Aphrodite rising from the sea was one I remembered, and Salome, presenting the head of John the Baptist – all done in rich reds, blues and greens, the loving creation of some old aunt or spinster cousin. Behind Mrs Mulvaney was the shape of the small battered grand piano, with its green velvet piano stool. Behind that, the open hatch looked, I knew, into her cluttered kitchen where the wall-cabinet doors usually stood ajar and the counters were laden with many unsorted domestic objects – a seaside bucket full of shells, an odd sock, an unused bowl of flour, a book.

The sun was beginning to get lower as that small cool wind began to blow. Mrs Mulvaney knelt there without moving. She wore a navy-blue jersey. Her blue arms hung by her sides. Her head, topped with its bouncy, frizzy, light brown hair which always gave her face the soft look of a young Edwardian postcard beauty, leaned slightly back as if the object she looked at were a little above her.

I knew the statue to, or at, which she prayed. It stood alone on a high white-painted bookshelf against the wall. Above it was a green-spined set of Balzac. Below was a shelf of lopsided pieces of pottery, made at school by the older Mulvaney children. There was a large jug, a bowl, a couple of mugs and a rabbit painted black and red with pencil-point jabs for eyes. The statuette, alone on its shelf, was about a foot high, ivory-coloured, showing the Virgin Mary, eyes closed, head bowed, and hands, below long trailing sleeves, placed together in prayer. It was, in short, that statue which is in the windows, along with the holy pictures, cards of medallions, crucifixes and prayerbooks, in any Catholic repository, from London to Lourdes.

At first I felt concern. What, I asked myself, could be so badly the matter that someone, a neighbour, a friend, should be praying, out of church, on a weekday in the middle of the afternoon? Was the child, Ajax, who was said to have measles, in fact gravely ill? Was Mrs Mulvaney's mother, who now lived alone in the large crumbling house in Dublin, and still terrorized her seven children by the fact of her existence and her uncannily-timed long-distance phone calls, suddenly dying? Had Julian Mulvaney actually left, instead of staying on with his wife and children and ostentatiously pining after his former personal assistant, the dull-faced Glenda MacFarlane, now transferred to the dust and infernal heat of the Department of Trade and Industry?

Ah, not so, I thought. Katie Mulvaney was not the sort to turn to God in a crisis – or to his mother either. No, she would not ply her God, or Goddess, with requests on her own behalf and would be sparing in her requests for others. It would be for more love, more faith, more compassion, that she appealed. That banal little statuette on the shelf was just a focus for her outpouring of faith, love and energy, a way of connecting with a more abstract object, the font and source of goodness, warmth and light.

Such love, I thought, standing in my parched, self-regarding state on the rocky bed of a dried-up river. Such love. Such strength. If, I thought morosely, as a dried leaf drifted gently down and settled on the shoulder of my jacket, if I had a God in whom I believed, I should ask for what I really wanted. Continually. *Dieu me donnera, c'est son métier*. But Katie, humble, proud, perverted, blasphemous, absolutist Katie, would not.

It had grown much colder. The light was fading fast. The numbness, the distancing of my surroundings which were now a permanent condition with me, came down like fog. As I was, without thinking, beginning to move back across the grass to the house, in the corner where I lived, I saw the boy, Ajax himself, wearing a green-and-white-striped jersey and jeans, pounding across the carpet towards his mother, evidently shouting something. She looked round and held out her arms. With his round face, brown, small, beady eyes, his jet-black hair cut in a fringe and his ruddy cheeks, Ajax, in repose, always looked to me like a large Chinese doll. Undressed, he looked like a little, tiny man. He had shoulders like a chicken-hut door, miniature biceps on his arms, a deep chest and wee, heavily muscled legs. He was deeply frightened of King Kong. As I watched he ran full on into his mother's extended arms. She jolted, hugged him, rose slowly to her feet, said something to him and started to walk into the kitchen. She pushed a hand through her wavy hair. She wore green trousers. Ajax, tugging on a khaki forage cap, swaggered after her with the air of a child who may begin to feel the menace of boredom at any time. Soon, I knew, he would be rocking to and fro on top of the kitchen cabinet.

Sighing for my friend I started off, back across the grass. Did Julian, I wondered, know that his wife prayed in the afternoons? With any luck he would never come home unexpectedly and catch her at it. Kate Mulvaney's religion was one of the things Julian seemed most to dislike about his wife. In the old days I had spent more than one bad half-hour at their dinner-table, as he attacked her for religiosity, superstition, subservience and, rejecting the sabre for the sharp kitchen knife, for loving God instead of focusing her attention and concern on the people around her. Naturally I could not say whether this was true or not. Probably his attacks on her faith were just shorthand for whatever else it was he objected to. Sexual frigidity perhaps, or disorderly children, or the peculiar blind stare which would come down from time to time, seemingly arbitrarily, over her eyes like a fog. Or was it her housekeeping, or her flea-prone mongrel bitch, Lady, or her righteousness, or just the fact that she was his wife?

Philip, who had been running ahead of me back to the house, stopping short from time to time, feathery ears flapping, to make sure I was still behind, reached the path, pulled up short and gave a barking howl. My mind dulled, drifted away into numbness. I turned back. In a flash Jessica Lombard's two Cairn terriers were up to him, yelping.

'Would you kindly call your dog off?' cried Mrs Lombard, appearing through the misty dusk, pulling a wheeled shopper. What a voice to call the cows home, stop a horde of fuzzy-wuzzies dead in their tracks, bring the hound of the Baskervilles creeping on his belly. Already poor cowardly Philip was trying to leap into my arms. Seeming to ignore this demonstration of canine love, Mrs Lombard, in the gloomy forest, allowed the phrase, *Like master like man*, to escape from her head like a comic strip bubble.

She called, 'Rufus! Danny! Here!'

The basket contained, I noticed, a bag of courgettes and a packet of Sainsbury's meringues. Mrs Lombard, a thrifty housekeeper, must be entertaining tonight.

'Turning cold,' I remarked, offensively drawing myself to her attention.

'I must get on,' she announced.

'There's always summat to do,' I said, broadening my accent.

She was away. Her fast feet and the wheels of the shopper rattled on the gravel. The cairns ran yelping round as she and her basket disappeared down the path in the gathering mist.

How right she looked, I mused, burning holes in her straight, departing back, as she crunched along the path with her barking dogs. In the past she had been the light-stepping prefect running on the chill playing-fields of a country boarding-school. Move her into the future and there was an old lady wrapping a parcel for a grandson at Oxford, carrying it through autumnal lanes to the post office. For she would return to where she came from – that big semi-rural house near the golf course, with its lawns, hydrangeas, tennis court. I had been to the Lombard's cottage, too, a place of low ceilings, scant food and damp, too near the estuary, and borne the whole burden of the myth of the town-dwelling middle classes, always believing in their secret and wholesome link with a douce, unchallenging countryside where they were, of course, landlords rather than tenants.

How she drove about, I thought, dazed at the idea; how Jessica drove about so resolutely, ferrying her children with the air of a social worker taking them somewhere for their own good – one to a child-guidance clinic, another to the magistrates' court, and the remaining two to a GLC home where they would be properly looked after. I had once opened a bedroom door by accident at the Lombard's. There was Jessica, bare-shouldered in front of the mirror, wearing a clinging sage-green evening dress, determinedly applying scent to wrist, neck and shoulders like someone putting Dettol on some nasty spots. The contrast between that slender sapling body in green, the white of her shoulders, the column of her neck and the pile of ruddy blossom that was her hair, and the nurse-like application of Arpège, arrested me.

'Bathroom's next door, Joe,' she had said, without turning round.

All this was, of course, in the old days.

Now she hated me, did Jessica Lombard. Oh, how she hated me. Well, it was a hard life, in spite of the au pair, Monique, the daily, Mrs Waddell, and the automatic washing-machine. For where the wife of a building worker might spend an hour with mop, bucket, screaming toddlers and a heavy period, washing all the floors in the flat, and then straighten up groaning for a cup of tea and a moan with another woman, Jessica, in solitude, would spend the same time driving the children to school and fetching them back, delivering them en route to the maths coach, the art class, the recorder lesson and tea in Kensington with a cousin. Then would come the reassembling of the children, hand-over to Monique, quick change, dart-round with the peanuts and olives before the arrival of Hugo Lombard with some business friends, chat, cheer, flatter, an anxious eye on the cassoulet in the oven, mental note to Monique to keep the noise of the Western down upstairs and never, never for an instant let anyone, least of all herself, know for a moment that she was not one of the civilized, one of the wonderful women of the world, or how she, Jessica Lombard, was giving herself cell by cell, corpuscle by corpuscle, to the lives of others.

No wonder she hated me. I had to allow that, as a moral being, Jessica had a perfect right to legitimate moral objections about my behaviour. But in my position I had become used to being at the other end of plenty of legitimate moral objections, and I knew what the real ones felt like. Katie Mulvaney, for example, really disapproved of me, but she regretted, rather than condemned, grieved, rather than reproached. She wanted to help me. I suspected that more than one candle, every drop of wax an anxious wish, had, lit by Mrs Mulvaney, gone up in incense-laden darkness on my behalf.

No, it was not moral objections, I reflected, but hatred I aroused in Jessica. That – and her green-eyed half-sister, envy. Six million, countless millions, including poor turned-off parlourmaid Fanny, bearing her baby in a ditch, had died because people felt about them the way Mrs Lombard felt about me. She feared me in case my weaknesses were contagious, in case I contaminated her with my desuetude, lust, sloth, and accidie. Or in case I infected society likewise, was part of a secret movement which might make all her efforts worthless, even in her own eyes, reducing her to nothing but an Horatio, suddenly realizing she stood on a bridge no one wanted any more, the Tuscans having ferried themselves across the river higher up some hours previously. And she envied me – why? Well, because I was wrecked, ruined, done in, washed up, finished by my own vices, my uncontrollable appetites, my total failure to think ahead. And, having enjoyed the splendours and miseries of my evil acts, here I was – free. Free for bugger-all as it happened, but there is nothing to equal the aching green of the grass when you see it from behind bars.

Now it was dark. The birds were nearly silent.

I opened my iron-barred gate, walked through my tangled garden, where weeds dropped among the sprawling roses and seeding plants. A rotting child's ball, with water in the hollow where it had deflated, floated on my choked pond. The grass, uncut for a year, straggled damply over bald patches on the lawn. From where the apples lay bruised and rotting under the tree I heard a child's voice call 'Daddy!'

And so into the still house. Over the rough concrete of the children's playroom, full of planks, half-built shelves and cupboards. A wooden rocking horse, covered in builder's dust, had been hopefully placed there for the day when the room would be ready. On into the kitchen, where the dim light of evening filtered through gaily patterned blinds, not raised that morning, where the new oven with its spaceship controls lay disused yet filmed with London grease, where the formica counters lay, raw, chilly and bare. A Marks and Spencer's bag, a pound of apples, a broken alarm clock, an empty can of dog-food. A wooden salad bowl containing small bags of peanuts and three bananas.

I put on my slippers, which were standing side by side in the middle of the floor. I put my shoes under the round pine table. On it, in the half-light, lay the *Guardian* and an empty coffee-cup.

Up the stairs, hand trailing up the dusty banisters, hearing my slippers flop on the stairs like an old man's. Into the sitting-room. The Sunday papers, a sock, a fallen brocade curtain on the floor under the window. Beer cans in the grate among the nine-month-old ashes of the last log fire. I sit down, so tired, in the armchair by the fireplace and play high, clear music out into the brown and yellow leaves on the trees. The room is dark-panelled. There is a tapestry sofa against the wall, an old picture, heavily varnished, and half a dozen prints. What am I doing in an old man's study in the dark, hearing old music and the wind shuffling the dry leaves on the trees? The dog sits beside me, thumping his tail hopefully on the floor, waiting, as usual, for the flames to leap, lick up and make us light and warm.

I can hear the children's voices, echoing from wall to wall of the dusty room.

Still hearing them, I pick up the phone.

'Joe? It's me – Elmira,' screamed Elmira in her great Antipodean parrot's screech. 'Why don't you come over for a drink? It's not good for you – sitting on your own there, brooding. Anyway,' she added threateningly, 'I'm lonely.'

'We're all lonely, Elmira,' I told her.

'Well, let's all be lonely together,' she cried encouragingly.

'Who's that behind you, singing *The Wild Colonial Boy* when you're so lonely, then?'

'Just some cousins of mine from Perth. Joe – you've got to come and help me get rid of them.'

'No. No, Elmira.'

'I need you, Joe.'

'No, Elmira.'

After that, for a while her healthy voice overbore the voices of the children. Then they came back.

On the next day light streamed through the windows of the church, shining on the cream of the walls and all the glitter. Beside me in the pew Katie Mulvaney sat quietly, her eyes fixed on the golden figure of Jesus, hanging on the golden cross of the altar. On either side of the altar were baskets and boxes decorated with coloured crêpe-paper and satin bows, containing apples, bunches of greens, packets of tea and cornflakes and bunches of bananas. Below the steps leading up to the altar was a decorated table on which was set a giant loaf a foot wide, made of plaited bread, more baskets, a pile of apples, a melon and two cauliflowers. The beautifully white centres of the cauliflowers, full of a hundred curled flowers, were like twin eyes. Beside them, stood vases of mighty, ragged, orange and white chrysanthemums.

Mothers and fathers shuffled in, edged into their pews, dropped down and said their perfunctory prayers.

Above, Jesus hung on his cross.

I looked sidelong at Katie, whose lips now moved in prayer, whose breathing, I heard, came steadier, slower and shallower at every breath. She sat a little higher in her seat, her attention caught. Following her eyes, I saw nothing. There was the altar, covered with its gilded embroidered cloth and the golden, hanging Christ. Below there was the harvest-laden table. Mrs Mulvaney was staring into the space behind the altar rails, the red-carpeted chancel – that platform, so to speak, without an actor, lying in front of the altar and behind the heaped food of the harvest.

I turned my head, now, to look at her. Her face was intense and eager, yet she wore a certain air of consideration, of critical intelligence, as if a loved and trusted friend had just brought her good news, but good news which had to be thought over and evaluated.

I glanced along the pew, to see if Katie was observed. At the end, on the aisle, sat Mrs Greenwood, the vicar's wife, in her old green winter coat. She was sited so as to be able to spring out and put a stop to any mayhem which might develop during the service. She looked straight past Katie's rapt profile and smiled me the wan smile of Christian hope, charity, forgiveness and total incomprehension of who and how I was. Her long pale hair lay limply on the worn collar of the faded green coat. Her long, pale face was drawn tight as a drumskin. I smiled back, and saw nothing in her eyes but fear.

I turned to face the altar again, thinking of Jesus, and of the great, dark-gold plaited loaf, the green and white cauliflowers, the heaped-up apples. I wished Katie would not stare at that empty space behind them as if she had just, in a crowd at a railway station, found the face of a dear friend she had come to meet, as if the nurse had just handed her a new-born baby, as if she had fallen in love.

The children were led in by their teachers. They came, shuffling and banging, from the little ones hurrying in on short legs, hair in bunches, socks falling down, to the big ones with their long, winter-chilled legs, huge shoes, long trousers, ladies' dresses, hair already awry and expressions of vacuity, fear and intelligence, childishness and maturity flickering like a light-show across their faces. Suddenly these older children became ruffians, professors of physics, plumbers, doctors, tired mums, air hostesses, MPs. Equally suddenly, they were children again. As they marched down the aisle Katie's eyes left the altar and her eyes took in the features of her surroundings – the lectern with its brass eagle, the back of the heads of the men and women in front, the stained-glass window at the top of the altar. She smiled to herself, turned to see her eldest daughter Siobhan, at the head of a column of marching, staring tots, holding the hand of a small red-headed bad boy, who was obstinately clutching a big leek in his other hand. Katie detected her son, Patrick, shambling in with his class, wearing a T-shirt saying *QPR Rule Forever*, winked at both, glanced at the numbers displayed on the hymn board and composedly found the first hymn.

I was confounded. If not actually seeing visions, Katie Mulvaney had certainly been receiving some revelation not open to the rest of us. Katie's broad, clear-complexioned face was as readable as a child's. Looking into her big blue eyes was like looking into a toddler's at a birthday party, where doubt, fear, good cheer and delight can be seen chasing each other in rapid succession. She had not, that crisp, sunny morning, been working out the meals for next week, listing unmade telephone calls or just worrying about Julian. What had she been thinking, receiving, seeing?

The children, their solid legs all chilled with cold, still came marching in like a dwarf army. An air of confusion hung over them as they sat down, scraping their feet and coughing, and stared at the boxes, packed by themselves and their impatient mothers in a fluster of crêpe-paper, kitchen foil, old cans of emulsion paint while packets of Indian tea and Italian tomatoes spread themselves all over the kitchen table. They certainly knew shopping when they saw it. They knew that the boxes and baskets would go to hospitals and old people. Harvest and God were, on the other hand, fairy stories to the young ones and mere concepts to the older children. What did they, or any of us, know about the desperation of the old harvest, with man's own efforts and the weather tipping the balance between life and death in the winter, making the life of God, simply structured between Easter and Christmas, and all foreordained, seem such a simple matter, without so many of the elements which cause us pain down here, below? A bit of a doddle, in fact, lacking in that specially human struggle to maintain and satisfy the flesh, keep body and soul together.

All be safely gathered in,
Free from sorrow, free from sin,

We sang, children and grown-ups, in all that cream and gold, as dockers unloaded our Israeli oranges, sugar from Barbados and New Zealand butter, as trains rushed up from the coast with our French sweetcorn, our aubergines and our courgettes.

Katie Mulvaney sang beside me in a surprisingly deep, husky voice. And Roy Greenwood, small and husbanding the vagueness which I always felt hung between him and the world the way a net curtain at a window mutes and dulls the big, bright, noisy world outside the house, went up the steps into the pulpit and began his address. It was a confusing and hesitant series of recollections of a Norfolk childhood, of long golden fields, horse-drawn haywains and light, sunny nights. But I thought it was the recollection of a brief wartime stay in the country, observed by a town child from the outside, for the benefit of children whose own real landscape was made up of streets and buildings, whose experience of growing things came from parks and small gardens, whose food came off heaped stalls or, packeted in foil, cardboard and cellophane from shelves, into wire baskets and through the checkout to the kitchen.

Outside the church, crisp bright sunshine fell on to the street, the trees, over the roofs of the church and the houses round about it.

The children were led in a long crocodile back to the school. Patrick Mulvaney winked at his mother. Beth Lombard grinned at me, admitting the farce of school, church and family, for an anarchist's heart beat under the narrow chest of the Victorian print dress worn by Jessica's eldest daughter. There was Faith Greenwood, pale, in a kilt too long for her, clutching the hand of her older brother, Mark. He had fainted during the service and spent its duration sitting in the church porch with a teacher.

The sunshine shone down on the column as it wound through the fallen leaves round the church.

'Lift home, Katie?' called Jessica, leaning out of her car.

'I'm walking with Joe,' said Katie. And Jessica pulled away from us.

'How are you?' Katie asked me as we walked along.

'As well as can be expected,' I said, sorry for myself and guilty that I was so sorry for myself. 'And you?'

'The same,' she said.

'You seemed to be in a trance there, in the church.'

'I was,' she told me. 'Father McGrath is very worried about me.'

'Why's that?'

'I have,' she said, 'visions. Experiences, they are, really. He suggests I ought to have a job, or more sex, or a holiday.' She spoke quite naturally, but with an effort. She glanced at me, sidelong, to gauge my reaction.

'He won't accept the validity of these experiences?' I said.

'The Church will not encourage married women with children to have such fancies,' she said. 'Not that they're very keen on them in nuns, or anyone, for that matter.'

'What's it like?' I asked. Neutrally, for of course I did not accept for a moment the idea that Kate Mulvaney was in touch with God.

'I don't see anything,' she said, stopping by the pillarbox to rummage in her handbag for a letter. 'There, that's the Gas Board satisfied. It's just a feeling of closeness, of being near to the source of goodness.' As she posted the letter she said, 'There's something there, greater and better than me. Father McGrath's thinking of calling the Bishop to me.'

We were at her gate. Ajax who had been minded, with a friend, while Kate was at the church, burst out, wearing one shoe, and as I went off up the street I heard his gradually diminishing howls of complaint about the friend and demands for a Coca-Cola, a honey sandwich, a new bearded Action Man.

I went home, dry-mouthed and tired, unable to think. I dragged myself upstairs to my unmade, aching bed, stared at the dusty dressing-table where the surface of an open pot of face cream grew gradually greyer and the level of the scent in a bottle near the window grew slowly lower and lower. Sleep, slow walks, slow wakings and sleep again. Like an invalid, that was the shape of my days.

Sometimes the phone would ring and a thin voice, often a woman's, would come to me down the foggy telephone line. They all wanted something, help, support, love, a commitment, friendship. I did write the cheques, I did help mend the car, fix the fence and mind the baby, but the rest, I could not do; I was numb; I had run out of feeling.

I soon slept again. That sleep and wakefulness should be the same – that was my intention; and that was the shape of my days.

By November the streets around the houses were littered. Black plastic bags lined the gutters and lay sprawled in heaps round all the lamp-posts. It seemed that a chill, damp wind always blew over the tall houses, down the littered basements.

Sometimes, perhaps because of the wind which howled through my sleep at night, I dreamed I was a small boy again, in Yorkshire, running home in short trousers through the straggle-grassed graveyard on dark evenings – running home to a clean cloth, pilchards on toast, toasted teacakes, parkin, a bright roaring fire, to Mum, to Dad, to Uncle Joe, sitting in his chair by the fire, to Susan and Mary with their rosy, scrubbed faces and bright hair in short plaits. Crossword puzzles, the Goons, homework with the cat on my knee, a cup of tea with the grown-ups when I'd finished and the girls were in bed. Those were the long evenings when it was too dark to work outside, when the wind roared over the hills and round the house and Mum knitted, Dad listened to the radio and Uncle Joe, in his chair, read and told me what he had been reading. He was nearly always in pain, was Uncle Joe. 'He puts up with it well,' the women in the shop used to tell my mother. 'There's nowt to do but,' she would reply. It used to anger me, as I stood by her, holding the basket, and anger me more, because I knew, and the other women knew, that she was bearing her brother's pain as well. 'It shouldn't be like that, mother. They should give him something for the pain.'

'They do what they can. There's some things folks have to

bear.' Well, I thought as I walked over my flat pavements, through the market, littered with boxes and blowing paper, through Woolworth's, where they were already selling tinsel and playing carols, well, I thought, I had got away from a world where a man could lie pinned down on wet grass with a tractor on his smashed chest until people noticed he hadn't come home for dinner; I had escaped cutting the lambs out of dead ewes while a blizzard blew over the yard; escaped mending a wall with frozen fingers in the half-dark on a frosty winter's morning. I had escaped pain, labour, fortitude and manliness and now I, Joe lad, walked through a flat and alien land amid strangers.

Perhaps my lust, my sloth, my hidden anger, my secret pride, would vanish, away from the high buildings, the people, these flat, dirty pavements, would vanish if I went home to my cold inhospitable hills? I could not go. I had brought myself into this misty tunnel and I had to go on, step by step, on to the oncoming locomotive, or to the light at the end, dim or bright. Worse, I had to go on, and on, and on, in silent darkness, my fingers forever brushing its sooty sides, my feet stumbling on the tracks.

The sound of carols filled the air. Outside the record-shop an old man scraped on a violin. Surely the children looked pinched? Was it only the children of wealthy Jessica Lombard who were hungry?

In Tesco's I saw one of Olivia's brothers knock a tin of cat-food off a shelf into his old red waterproof shopping-bag. His thin, black hand clutched the stranded handle, the arm of his jacket did not reach his thin black wrist. A man in a green nylon coat was coming towards him up the long, brightly lit perspective of food. I took the cold hand, took the cat-food from his bag and put it in my own wire basket. The man passed us, staring hard, not daring to meet my eye, the eye of an Englishman, perhaps homosexual, perhaps a solicitor, perhaps a doctor, banker, branch manager of a building society.

'What would Olivia say if you got into trouble?' I demanded of the boy.

'Olivia sent me,' he said.

They lived in a big, crumbling flat in the far corner of the gardens. Their door was light blue, their window-frames bright red, rock and reggae boomed out night and day. While her mother worked, tall Olivia looked after her brothers and sisters and a cousin or two. All summer long the gardens were pierced by their cries, tearful, 'O-livia – I'm hurt' or enraged, 'O-livia, he hit me.' Tall, shabby Olivia would hurry up, conscious of the stares – condemnatory, from the older inhabitants, sympathetic from the wealthier, liberal newcomers. There was no difference to her. She knew that to onlookers she was an oddity, an object of pity, reproach, a problem, a blot on the parkland landscape, a dark stain on their vision. Under their gaze she would sort out the issue, lead one off for elastoplast, cuff another, walk away, outcast.

'Is the cat hungry?' I asked.

'Yes.'

'Are you all right at home?'

'We managing.'

So I bought the tins of cat-food, the bread, cheese, butter, hamburgers, tea, cartons of milk and gave my thin charity to him, walked away into the noise of the market with my own drinking chocolate, my apples, my pork chops, my tomatoes, my aspirin, my bottle of whisky, my peanuts, my bag of sugar, my biscuits, my cornflakes. Two young girls, pale and unkempt, approached me. The bigger one was supporting the smaller.

'My friend's ill. Can you lend us the money to get home?'

Twenty pence. It was odd how I, who really gave so little, was giving so much today. A boy offered to sell me a pair of worn tarot cards.

How chill the wind struck on those exhausted streets. Suddenly snow began to drift down. A small child in a hooded anorak held out his hand to catch a snowflake. An old woman shuffled home faster. Two women at the bus stop looked up at the sky in disgust. Soon a thin carpet of snow covered the pavements and the tops of the cars and the bags of rubbish. It sprinkled itself over the tops of the tired laurel bushes in the front gardens.

Beth Lombard and her brothers were ringing my bell as I came up the path. Skinny Beth, in her long yellow dress, held her brothers' hands. She looked like a Victorian child sent to beg for crusts and old clothes. She turned as I came up the steps and said, politely, 'Hullo, Mr Coverdale. We thought we'd come to see you.'

'Come in,' I said, 'and have a drink.'

'Can we watch *Blue Peter?*' the boy, Ben, asked eagerly.

'We went to see Elmira – Miss Toomey – but she wasn't in, Beth remarked as we went along the hall. She spoke up bravely, almost expecting a reproach.

'It's a little bit cold in here,' said little Sam, who was seven. 'Have you got any more of those Victory V lozenges?'

'Sam,' Beth said, reprovingly, ashamed of his bluntness.

The Yorkshire lad I had been felt sorry for these well-brought-up, polite, cold, hungry children.

I said, 'Would you like a snack? Come into the kitchen and I'll put some stuff on a tray. You can carry it upstairs. Does Jessica know where you are – more or less?'

'More or less,' said Beth.

Jessica knew all right. Why didn't she forbid her children to visit a moral wreck like me? Wasn't she afraid I would go a little further along the line and molest them? How did she know I hadn't already, and sent them home believing if they said a word a huge slithering thing would come through the bedroom window at midnight and suck them dry, leaving only flattened little figures, just skin and bones, behind? Was she so mean that she was prepared to let them visit a haunted house just to get peanuts? How shrewd she was, Jessica – she knew I was safe, so safe that I was not only to be trusted not to put my hot hand on her children's thighs, but would not even fill them with tooth-destroying body-corrupting sweets and cakes.

In the kitchen, as I put apples, nuts, glasses of milk on the tray Sam said, 'We have very good food in our house – wholemeal bread and organically grown vegetables. And mackerel,' he said with a scarcely perceptible wince, straining his loyalty to the uttermost.

'You'll grow up healthy then,' I said. I looked down at the three pale brown heads as they hovered round the tray.

What was I, a grown man, doing as the year died? Standing in a disused house, my head stuffed with cottonwool, my legs like jelly, feeding children not my own, that was what I did as the year died. As my phone rang they carried the tray upstairs, singing, 'We three kings of Orient are, bearing gifts we travel afar – '

'Joe, how are you?'

Cottonwool in my head, stuffed in my ears, up my nose, cottonwool lined my throat.

'Very well.'

'Still on the pills?'

'Still taking the tablets.'

A pause. 'It's Christmas – Joe,' said Naomi, my wife.

I was an old man in slippers. 'Yes, yes,' I said. 'Well – shall I come?'

'It would be better.' I felt the steel again, familiar as my razor and less to be trusted. There was the real, hard cutting edge of the woman who knows what is due to her from a man. Suddenly, like putting your hand on a piece of cottonwool concealing a razor blade, the blood starts. That was how women had always had to survive, weak and powerless, in Manland, tireless entrepreneurs between man and the world. Lacking themselves the necessary skills, they had learned to achieve their objects by conjuring flattery, coldnesses, warmth, and induced guilt so quickly into such complex patterns that no wonder we say, 'I don't think I'll ever understand them.' The light of the candles over dinner, the flash of white bosom over the low-cut dress, the sudden fainting fit, glitter of tears, sound of laughter, scream of rage all conceal motive.

As I started up the stairs the telephone rang again. Another voice. I said, 'I'm sorry. I can't come. I can't come. No – I'm sorry. He's done it before, hasn't he? I can't keep binding the same wound. You must do something yourself. I'm sorry. No. No.'

Pills, the window, the bathwater running pink under the door. I thought: in their weakness they were tougher than me, these women. Now I could only fight them with their own weapons – passivity, shamming dead, waiting for the other person to act, commit himself, take responsibility.

Then I thought of my mother, not gilded, scented or decked out, who laid food on the table for us, clothed us, nursed us and kept the house warm for us. What man in this situation does not secretly hate the women he has used, and who have used him in return, does not turn to the idea of his mother, who gave everything and took nothing – and who, childishly, he has wanted ever since. These scented Jezebels, Delilahs, would, no doubt, look the same to their sons in future. I had a vision, suddenly, of a woman's face, the lines of tension sweeping over the slackness of fatigue, as she climbed out of bed in the early morning on to the torturing floor and walked over knives to the screaming cradle. Of the same woman putting make-up over those same lines in the mirror that evening, so that, even later, eighteen hours after she had dragged herself out of bed, she could grimace and smile with a smooth face into my face, or that of some other man, so that I, or he, twenty hours after she had first dragged herself to the cradle, could put his seed into that womb, so that it could swell and swell and then burst and that fruit go again, red-faced into the cradle – and did they make us what we are to them, or did we make them what they are?

And so I walked, heavily, up the stairs again.

Jessica's children sat in front of the television.

'We could make you a lovely fire,' Beth said wistfully, gesturing at the empty grate.

'You'd better not settle in,' I said. 'You'll have to be off soon.'

'My recorder lesson,' Ben said suddenly.

'Oh, my God, Ben,' Beth said in her mother's voice. 'How could you? You'd better go now. Come on.'

Ben got up reluctantly. The three pale faces stared at me.

'I could stay,' said little Sam.

'No, Sam, mummy wouldn't like it,' Beth said firmly.

How Jessica had managed to insinuate that it was all right for three of her children to stay with me, but not for one to stay alone, I shall never know. She must have been as subtle and penetrating as radio waves and they as sensitive as geiger counters. Nothing can, in that household, have been said, for in enlightened homes, where frank replies to questions are always given by parents, the art of the game is to prevent the questions from being asked, and the signals, consequently, are more complicated than in those poorer and simpler homes where the parent answers an awkward question with a request to the child to mind his own business, or an unambiguous slap on the side of the head.

So Beth rushed the children into their coats and took Ben to his lesson and Sam home to his mother.

Oh come, oh come, Emmanuel!
Redeem thy captive Israel

came Patrick's sweet voice over the sound of his sister Siobhan's uncertain piano playing. I walked over the worn apple-green carpet and, suddenly weak, for I had not been in anyone's house for some time, sat down on the sofa by the window, looking out on to the bare trees.

That unto exile drear is gone
Far from the face of God's dear Son.

I was alone in the long room with the children. Siobhan's long, pale brown hair drooped forward as she bent over the keyboard. Patrick leaned beside her, reading the words. The room was still. There might have been no one else in the house. I sat, looking at the patch of carpet where Katie must have been kneeling.

Julian had let me in, saying nothing but, 'Hullo, Joe. Upstairs,' and disappearing down the passageway to what was called his study, where he played Beethoven on his expensive stereo, read the newspaper, or history, and, presumably, sometimes worked on his papers. From this deliberate lack of welcome I deduced that I was in greater disfavour at DNPD, who had given me what was being variously described as a sabbatical or a period of extensive leave due to ill health, but which was, I knew, really a breathing-space for them while they decided whether or not to sack me. From Julian's flustered manner I also concluded that he was probably annoyed that Katie had invited me – because of my moral turpitude, because I had gone further than he would have dared, and had had a good run for my money, because I was in such bad odour at the Department that association with me might reflect badly on him and spoil his chances. For Julian was ambitious and careful. When my sorry tale first came out he had covered me over quickly, the way a cat covers a turd. If the official view of me had now become even harsher, Julian would be even more embarrassed about having me in the house.

When I stopped to consider it, Julian had never liked me personally anyway. He had accepted me as a neighbour, and a colleague, and as the father of his children's friends – someone, too, it might be useful to know; but not only had he never liked me, but every betraying gesture – his snake-like leanings back from me in conversation, the rapid flicker of his eyes as he spoke – revealed him, in retrospect, as a man who had actively disliked me. He had, as the chilling phrase would now go, had me in for drinks occasionally. Now that I had revealed myself, done my deeds and been disgraced, now he could acknowledge his dislike for me. Not only was I no longer anyone Julian Mulvaney would care to have in for drinks, I was someone he would repudiate, would blacken, if necessary, to make himself look whiter. I could hardly complain – I had not even allowed him the dignity of being anyone I might like or dislike. I had ignored everything about him except his actual presence, when he was physically there. Nevertheless, it is a blow, almost like a punch in the stomach, to realize suddenly, you have been hated by someone to whom you have done no actual harm. And I was vulnerable, in no emotional condition now to be able to accept it. So it was not agreeable when he came into the room, looked at the children, said, 'Get up to bed now. It's past your bedtime,' and then said, 'Drink, Joe?'

The children, sensing a mood, left the room quietly and it was not until they were halfway upstairs that the usual noises of the Mulvaney children – the accusations, giggles, thumps and rattlings of the banisters – were to be heard. At these sounds Julian without remark, stiffened, effortlessly projecting the persona of an intelligent man whose nerves were being lacerated and sensibilities rent by the manifestations of the coarse, mundane and indifferent world in which he lived. I remembered doing that act myself – it is easy to perform if you are a father engaged professionally in brain-work. There he stood on his own green carpet, producing the effect of an eighteenth-century gentleman and scholar, time-traveller in his own home. He must have created this self-image very early, finding himself a child, a bright displaced person in his semi in Bognor Regis, while his father, no doubt, was producing things from under the counter of his high-class grocer's shop for the retired gentry of the South Coast, was being pleased by the praise of the bankers' widows and colonels. How cheered Julian had been, I recalled, when I talked about my own family and he found out that I came from humbler stock than he did.

In the meantime I mumbled something about only drinking soft drinks, a remark lost as Katie added her own bellow to the uproar on the landing. Then I heard her heavy tread on the stairs. She came into the room saying, 'Did you turn down the gas under the stew, Julian?'

'I'll do it now,' he said distantly, and retired.

'Well, Joe,' Katie beamed. 'Let me get you a drink, now.'

'Tomato juice,' I said.

'Oh yes – the pills. How do you feel?' she said, going over to the kitchen hatch where, unwisely, I thought, bottles and glasses stood. While pouring the tomato juice she of course knocked a glass through, on to the counter behind.

'Is it broken?' she asked Julian.

'No,' he said flatly.

'Can you pass the Worcester sauce,' she said. 'I think it's in the bottom cupboard.'

I heard him start to rummage as Ajax, in stars-and-stripes pyjamas, burst into the room holding a box of paints, followed by Siobhan, in tears.

'He won't give me back my paints.'

'My paints. My paints.'

'Not in the cupboard.'

'I'll drink it without.'

'Will you go upstairs.'

'Hullo, Katie. You're looking well,' said Hugo Lombard, crossing the floor with a firm stride and pecking her on the cheek. He was a tall, blond man in well-faded denims and a well-washed Arran sweater, bearing about him the mixture of health and seediness of a sedentary man who stays in good shape, as if the week in the office followed by a fishing weekend, followed by another week in the office, chased by an active weekend in the country cottage, created such instability in the cells of his body that they themselves could never be sure if they were fatty tissue or solid muscle.

Behind Hugo came Jessica in a soft, pleated woollen dress, reddish in colour, which swung against her shapely legs as she walked. 'Hullo, Katie,' she said. 'What's going on, Siobhan?' Then she caught sight of me, on the sofa, and looked startled. She appeared not to know how to look at me.

'It's to do with some paints,' Siobhan said, embarrassed at being caught out in a childish wrangle.

'Come on, Ajax,' Jessica said. 'Give Siobhan her paints and you can have some bubbles.'

Ajax, without looking at Siobhan, held out the paints and gazed at Jessica, who clicked open her handbag, found the drum of soapy water and made sure it was operating by taking the ring from it and blowing a cascade away from the door. As the bubbles floated in the air she handed the little drum to Ajax, who began to blow.

'Perhaps you'd better take him back to bed, Siobhan,' Jessica suggested. 'Don't blow the bubbles in bed, Ajax, in case they go over your duvet.'

'Thanks, Jessica,' Katie said gratefully. 'You're an angel. What do you want to drink?'

'Gin and tonic,' suggested Jessica. 'If there's any tonic. Or some sherry.'

'Gin,' said Katie. 'Julian pass me a bottle of tonic, will you? It's on your left.'

Julian's face appeared in the hatch. He handed Katie a bottle of Worcester sauce.

'Do Joe's first,' he said wearily. 'I'll come out with the tonic. Casserole's all right.' He looked at me suspiciously, as if I were planning to stay to dinner.

I took the tomato juice and the sauce from Katie. 'I only came in for five minutes to talk about tree surgery. But while I'm here I ought to mention something about Schell's visit. Is it still on?'

'Yes,' Julian said, after a hesitation.

'There's something not on the obvious files. And a possibility, as they say, of embarrassment to the blushing virgin, HMG.'

'All right,' said Julian. 'But of course we really came to discuss the trees.'

'Well – I agree with Joe about them,' Hugo said. 'I was walking round the gardens with a friend of mine the other day. He works at Kew as a matter of fact. He said that the big birch, in particular, was very dangerous. One gale, he said, and it might easily fall.'

'Well, if you all agree with me,' I said, 'and since the next garden committee's meeting isn't for another month. I'll call Wallace in immediately and see what he says. There's no point in hanging about waiting to put it on the agenda when the chances are that the next windy day will bring down heavy branches at least.'

'Not to mention the elms,' said Hugo.

'Quite right,' said Julian.

'I think, between us,' Jessica said, 'we must be a quorum.'

As the others talked I walked over to the window to examine the trees, wintry and sturdy, silver and brown-trunked. Beyond them lay the lighted windows of the houses opposite. Julian joined me at the window.

'What's this about the Schell visit?' he asked.

'Oh – ' And I grappled for the information which now eluded me. 'Oh – Christ. Give me a minute. I think it's these bloody pills.'

Julian's careful patience, his doubt and cynicism made a wall between us. Suddenly I saw the page in front of me. 'That's it. It's in some eight-year-old report from Rumania. That's why it's not on the relevant files, or only if you track it back through a student visit made in 1968 – it came from Packard – it seems he and Schell got drunk together when he came over here on some British Council study tour – Schell was quite junior at the time, and at the time he was carrying on to Packard about the unrealities of a communist economic system, putting facts and figures on to a set of fairy-tale co-ordinates and all that – they were both drunk at the time. The matter was never mentioned between them again and Schell probably didn't remember what he'd said. But Packard left a record behind. It occurred to me that if he thought it important enough to put on paper you should know. In case Schell decided to do a dash, claim political asylum – that's all there is to it, really.' A reflex, a final twitch of the corpse, made me add, 'The report's on GTO 603 – something or other 25, if you're interested.'

Julian held steady in the face of my uncanny memory. 'Not,' I added, to cheer him, 'that I give a bugger. They'll be firing me soon.'

'I think they weren't going to,' he said carefully. 'Until they found out about Pascal.'

'Pascal who? Françoise Pascal? – Ah,' I said tumbling to it. 'Well, I don't expect you to believe me but all that happened was that we got trapped in a hotel in Lyons while her car was out of action – we talked about baroque music, the French economy and ate a lot – those are her main interests. Satisfied?'

'Why don't you explain – ?' he said.

'Balls, Julian,' I said. 'They're trying me behind my back. Anyway, it's what I did do that counts, and that's enough. Plus the fact that they can fire me today, tomorrow and from a cannon for ever and ever if they want to.' I flagged, looked at him and said, in despair, 'You do see that, don't you?'

He flinched from my contaminating gaze. From me he could catch the diseases of disloyalty, indifference and loss. And there was Jessica, saying, 'I hear you're going to Stonebridge for Christmas.' She had decided, perhaps, that she could forgive me. And she needed to see me redeemed – my redemption would make her safe. But in my despair I could not respond, either to Julian's desire that I should struggle for my job at the Department of National Planning and Development, or Jessica's, that I should struggle for my marriage. At that moment – I did not know why – I had no grip on those lives, no interest in them. Somehow, my lack of concern frightened them.

'Yes,' I told her. 'I'm going there. Have you spoken to Naomi recently?'

'She rang me up.'

I thought I could hear Naomi's voice, 'It seemed better to ring and ask *you* how Joe is. He doesn't get in touch with me any more, which is a blessing in many ways, but when I do talk to him I don't get much impression of how he really is.' And Jessica would sit at her little table, with one eye on Sam doing a jigsaw-puzzle on the rug, in front of a pile of engraved postcards headed *Mrs Hugo Lombard* and would say, carefully, 'Well, I think he's very low.'

Both of them, I thought, with true childish depression, hated me anyway. Neither would ever really forgive. In another society Naomi's four brothers would come, crowding me on the step, backing me into the hall threatening me. 'Heh – what you doing to our sister – huh?' Naomi, behind them would come in in a ragged dress, crying, 'Joe, Joe – I can't stand it any more – ' She would pour tumblers of wine, sob and dance.

But Jessica saw me at Stonebridge in Staffordshire in a room with a fire and a Christmas tree, with the children going up to bed in their slippers and dressing-gowns, and with the Trents, later, easing themselves out of their chairs by the fire, going into the kitchen to make their Horlicks, putting cups and digestive biscuits on a tray and with a, 'Well, we must take ourselves off,' the strong couple would go upstairs leaving lovely Naomi, my wife, their only child, in her chiffon gown, gazing at me softly in the firelight. Would I be wearing a dinner jacket? Even that was possible, for the Trents dressed, put the silver on table and dined determinedly on special occasions. So there we would be, a handsome young couple in the firelight, while upstairs the parents hoped, without discussing it, that downstairs I was seducing their daughter, just as, in bygone days, they had hoped that I was not. They would wait for the feet on the stairs, the click of the bedroom door – we, downstairs by the blazing log-fire just like Barbara Stanwyck and Gregory Peck, would know they were waiting.

Truly, I had married out of my class and out of my region, married from a hill-farm into a prospering factory in the Midlands, married from high, open places down into the lowering flatlands, badlands. And now, for society, for married love, for Queen and country, for the threatened security of the Lombards, the Trents and the whole doughy lot of them, I was going to the big house at Stonebridge, standing at Yuletide in its soggy plains, and would be left, a dinner-jacket on that Yorkshire back handed down to me by generations of ancestors who had carried sheep up hill and down dale on their shoulders, and a glass of good malt whisky in a hand more suited to the sheep-shears, I would be left in the firelight, where the presents lay in piles around the tree, to apologize, deny, and explain that I must have been mad at the time and, finally, to be allowed off my knees, kissed on the cheek and welcomed back to matrimony, my job, good dinners, a pony for Harriet, a rifle for Paul and all the warmth of the family hearth. And they had me, the Trents, the Lombards, the decent people of the world, smiling, talking in comforting language, had me with their *better-for-everybodies* and *least-said-soonest-mendeds* because they had my children and they could keep me from them unless I toed the line. They held my children for ransom, and the price was my conformity, that I should assent to their decent-job, good-holiday, reasonable-dinner, well-kept-home philosophy. And if I put a bomb under the White House, Stonebridge and blew it up, flying out of the rubble would come teddy, and locks of Harriet's brown hair, and Paul's green jumper, a red bridle, pieces of wood with black spots painted on them, fragments of Old Rocker himself.

So I just looked at Jessica and said, 'Yes, yes, I'm going there,' and Jessica, only too keen to accept me back into the great club of sensible people of goodwill throughout the world, gave me a smile very reminiscent of Her Majesty's on Christmas Day. There was an odd look behind that regal smile, though. What was it?

Meanwhile Julian disassociated himself from all this. He knew in detail what I had already done and he was not the man to give a bad dog the chance of a second bite.

'I'd better be going now,' I said, and felt their relief. But there was Elmira, ruffling my hair with a muscly hand, saying, 'Oh no, Joe, stay a bit.'

'Must go,' I said.

'I might see you later,' she said, meaning that she would cut out of the Mulvaney's dinner as soon as she could. She was a real tonic, standing there, tall and skinny in her glittering green dress, just like a Christmas tree.

And in the hall Katie Mulvaney gave me a kiss and said, 'See you soon, Joe.' Women – mother, daughter, sisters, wife, lovers, friends – have always been indulgent to me, although then I was too sorry for myself to realize it.

And it must be obvious that at the time about which I am writing I pitied myself excessively. I was also lazy, solipsistic, gloomy and lacking in self-control, self-discipline or any proper sense of direction. This was because my wife had left me, after fourteen years of marriage, taking with her my two children. Then, I did not know what was happening to me, or why.

The reasons for it all go back over the years of our marriage, back to our childhoods, probably back to the early years of both sets of parents. There is Henry Trent, for example, coming out of the army in 1946, back to the wife and the small daughter he had hardly seen, back to his father's scrapyard which seems, after five years of fighting in North Africa and waiting in India to invade Japan, a very small, ill-run and dark place. Here is Irene Trent, who had married Henry just before the war, had borne and reared a child in her mother's house, faced with a new desperate young man, her husband, who starts going to night-school to learn engineering, and, helped at first by the post-war need for scrap and then by the post-war need for a better life, chivvies his father into ambition, and slowly, working long and hard, starts his firm, chiefly making kitchen ranges, and makes a fortune. On the other hand there are my mother and father living on their remote rented farm, living as their parents and their parents' parents always have. There is Naomi, barely remembering poverty but reared very much by her mother because father is always so busy. There am I, eldest child and only son, heart of a warm, poor family. And we married in 1963.

That we met at all, at Oxford, was a tribute to the great post-war release of energy, which got Henry Trent into the bourgeoisie and me, through socialist education policies, into Oxford. In those days, we all thought anything was open to us. By the time I reached Oxford that enthusiasm, that sense of possibility, were already declining. The barriers were being thrust back into place. My father, my uncle, all those hopeful old-time socialists from the Dales, did not know it, but I did. Although I hope incidentally my present tone is not assumed to be entirely the accent of a man trying to sound other than he is – to sound posh. The way I speak or write, is, like much of my ensuing story, to be accounted for by the fact of my being a gifted mimic, a parrot, an echo. It made me a good linguist, but in everyday life it continually tempts me to use the language, the dialect, the accent of the person I am speaking to or of the person I am trying to be at that moment. What appears, to the other person, like mere sympathy, understanding and attention is, on my side, a terrifying assumption of his or her attitudes, a temporary *becoming* of the other person. It can make me seem, and sometimes be, passive and indecisive. It can make me look, and sometimes be, a hypocrite and a turncoat. It can make me likeable, sympathetic and successful, if that is the word I want, with women, who suffer more than many of us would care to think from the inattention and rampant egotism of men. And like all blessings, which I do, at bottom, believe it to be, it still sometimes seems more like a curse.

But, coming back to where we, Naomi and I, were, as the 'fifties became the 'sixties, here I am with my partial view of what happened. To me, an ambitious, insecure and successful young man, with no predetermined pattern for his future, everything about Naomi, from her smooth checked skirts to her cashmere sweaters, from her evening taffetas to her tight suspenders, spoke of plenty, security, unquestioning affluence and cheerful complacency. Remember, we are in Harold MacMillanland, dominated by the solid upper-middle-class grandfather and Prime Minister, whose whole being radiated the assurance that he was Lord Palmerston, leading a nation which would remain as rich, strong and powerful as it had been under Queen Victoria if only we all kept our places and made no disturbance. Was it the intense snobbery of those days as the upper and middle classes fought their battle to keep things as they were, and fought all the fiercer because they no longer, in the main, had the resources to maintain their position unthreatened, which led me, perversely, to court Naomi, to fight my way through her protective clothing – the billowing skirts, nylon petticoats, the iron suspenders, the nankeen bra, the undergrowth of snapping elastic, straps and buckles – into her most secret places like a pirate sneaking aboard at night to plunder the hold of a well-rigged ship? I have often wondered.

England was full of young men like me – products of an educational system begun, after a war, in hope but now backtracking rapidly. We were intelligent enough to see that after that first bound towards success we were entering a world much as it always had been, where the medals and diplomas went to the meritorious, and the jobs still went to first cousins and the sons of old friends. I suspect, now, that my siege of Naomi was an effort to ally myself, in my insecurity, with her class and income. Nevertheless, my courtship at dances, in college rooms at tea-time, by river banks in summer, at cinemas and parties, was successful. How shoddy it now seems – the fumblings and the muttered arguments, the love speeches, reproaches and blackmail – and what a black triumph it was, as she lay, finally, trembling in my arms on narrow bed in my lodgings. Worse than that, only that morning I had been given the Holt Scholarship for Economics, and so proved myself, in my eyes and hers, to be a man with a future. Even then, naive as I was, I sensed that her submission was not altogether to the lover, but to the provider, the successful man. And yet I loved her and our final year at Oxford, when we were engaged, had moments of passion, peace, satisfaction, the sense that we were beginning to create a good life for ourselves. But there was always a stiffness between us, and a lack of ease. The situation was that I, over-anxious, over-trained and ambitious, had seduced her, a rich and guilty virgin, and that in the welter of my lack of confidence and sexual inexperience and of her guilt and flinchings back to a secure girlhood from the heavy weight of the demands I laid on her, somewhere and somehow, love was lost. Even during our engagement I nagged about money and security, she was anxious about getting pregnant and where and how we should live, and each of us concealed half our feelings from the other. In spite of all that I wanted to be a good husband, she to be a good wife. To that end I refused the hoped-for offer of a Fellowship from my college – Naomi and her parents had a healthy disrespect for academic life – and made her pregnant just to be on the safe side. To that end she got in touch with house agents. To some extent that is what we were for each other – the means to an end. Just think, when we married she was twenty-two and I, twenty-three. We had spent our lives at home, school and university. I knew about work and life from my farm – and any real knowledge I drew from there of human affections, troubles and joys I, curiously, regarded as local and specific to the Dale. Naomi's information all came from her mother and from boarding-school. And what we saw ahead of us, and wanted, was a perfectly standard, prosperous, contented, safe and predictable life.

At any rate, our friends all envied us. All, that is, but my room-mate, Edward, who never told me so directly. But without ever altering his expression he managed to convey mistrust and disapproval either of my devotion to Naomi or of the motives behind it. Night after night I would come racing in, flushed, reeling, perhaps a bit drunk and throw myself on the worn maroon sofa at our lodgings, while Edward, who had been hard at his books during the evening, with the gas fire economically switched off, would light it dourly, put the kettle on the gas ring and get out the Nescafé.

'Cheer up, Ted lad,' I'd shout. 'Life can be beautiful.'

'Not for the workers.'

'She said she loved me again.'

Edward, kneeling by the gas ring, would shoot me a sidelong glance and say something like, 'Take care, man. You'll be getting yourself wed.'

'The sooner the better. I know – that's what your Uncle Albert said before he killed his wife with a pick-handle, ran away, got caught hiding in your granny's back entrance by the coal and was hung in Durham Gaol on Christmas Day – '

'There's no way to warn a man bent on getting himself into trouble. Where did you go then?'

'For a cold walk down by the river.'

'In a couple of years' time you'll be wanting to throw yourself in it,' Edward would say, handing me the cup.

I thought it was envy, and indeed it was. I thought it was his innate conservatism urging me towards a canny lass with a good nature and a strong pair of shoulders on her, the sort to see you through a two-month strike without complaint, to pawn her wedding ring for bread and not mention it, bear a child in the back bedroom, get up and go back to the wash-tub. Because I never said this he could not tell me that if he had liked Naomi for her qualities, envy and class consciousness would not have come into his reckoning at all, even if she had been the Queen of England and Brigitte Bardot all rolled into one. But all that would have gone beyond the limits we set to our friendship. So Edward merely wore on his face the same expression I saw on the faces of my parents when they met Naomi – a barely detectable expression indicating reserve, doubt, an optimism tempered by fear for both of us. I ignored these looks, although to me, accustomed to the long, expressionless looks of the North, they were as legible as the headlines in a tabloid reading: COVERDALE MARRIAGE – LITTLE HOPE NOW, SAY RELATIVES.

And so we married in August, from Stonebridge church. Naomi suggested that Roderick Glennister, her childhood friend, son of the local big landowning family, would make a suitable best man. I knew the Trents all thought that six-foot, hunting-man Roderick was a better deal, would look more impressive in the wedding photographs and be suaver at the reception than short, dour Edward, who was my choice. They were right, but I stood firm. I spent the two weeks before the wedding at the White House, as Naomi grew tenser and more anguished over fittings for the wedding dress, guest lists and the presents which arrived continually. It was very hot. I felt unwelcome. I knew the Trents were hoping Edward would get ill or die so that they, who were paying for everything, would get the best man of their choice. I knew that by standing out against them I was being ungrateful – they were paying for the wedding, putting a deposit on the house in London and giving me, quite free, their only daughter.

Meanwhile I spent hot, anguished night after hot, anguished night in their guest bedroom. Naomi, tense, tired and secretly pregnant would not sleep with me. At midnight in the rhododendrons beyond the lawn I fell on her, tumbling her to the ground and throwing up her dress saying, 'Naomi – just once. Please, please – Naomi,' and she struggled against me – oh, how well I recall the scratching of the dry rhododendron stalks, the heat, the burning rage as I stalked up the garden, back to the house, doing up my fly, and the sound of her feet dragging behind me, and her muffled sobs. After that I was quieter, acknowledging the total hegemony of the Trents and my own insignificance. I was done up in white satin, stuck all over with engraved invitation cards and put in a corner until the day of the wedding. Of course, I nearly ran away one night and, of course, I stayed.

It was sweltering in the church, as I stood, with Edward, feeling my back exposed to the massed Trents on one side and the fewer Coverdales on the other. My side of the family had not proved quite so vulgar as Irene Trent had feared – the dough, as it were, of farmers smelling of manure was leavened by my mother's brother, the Mayor of Scarborough (how near Naomi's mother had come to asking him to wear his chain of office), by a cousin who was a solicitor and by my sisters, Susan, a teacher of science at a grammar school, and Mary, engaged at the time to an MP. A Labour MP, admittedly, but an MP nevertheless.

The smell of the flowers was overpowering – hundreds of roses which because of the heat had reached their peak and were on the very brink of decay. The sweat poured down my back, the organ sang in my ears. I was, although I had never fainted before, ready to drop. Behind the heady scent of the roses the pews were giving out the resinous smell of hot wood. With that, and the mingled perfumes of the women, I had the sense of being trapped in an olfactory nightmare. And now I could not leave.

Edward, at my side, gripped my arm, making the act of holding me up physically look like friendly moral support. He was like a man bearing up a pit-prop during a cave-in down a coal-mine.

I heard Naomi's dress swishing up the aisle behind me as I stared blurrily at the vicar. 'Man, she looks lovely,' said Edward and I turned my head. There she was, looking at me uncertainly, my wife and carrying my child. I felt mortality. I could have dashed from the church to avoid the responsibility which the child and the home would place on me, to avoid fatherhood, ageing, a place in time. She had no such doubts, and I felt, perhaps for the first time, lost and betrayed because she could not share my feelings. How could she? Our feet were now planted on the two separate paths which disunite two people in marriage. For the first time I felt that tug of tenderness and protectiveness and that resentment of the chain they create which afflicts so many married men. When Edward handed me the ring he could not help, by his gentleness, reminding me of the male relative who picks up the clod of earth and hands it to the widow to throw, first, on her husband's coffin. As I put the ring on Naomi's finger I felt a despairing love for her, tainted with fear. The choir sang and the flowers released that scent, made all the headier because it verged on decay, and we walked out of the church into a blinding August heat.

And, of course, I forgot all this in the early years of marriage, when we lived in the little house in Battersea. I began my career and the children were young.

Then came the house in the square. It finished me. I had been happy in the narrow Battersea house in its narrow Battersea street and had quite gladly turned to and worked on it. I believed, I think, that it was to be our last home, but Naomi, who had to manage in it, pointed out that it would soon be too small for us, that the kitchen was inconvenient, that congenial neighbours lived too far away and that the garden was too confining for growing children; whom she therefore had to trudge to the park more often than she wanted. So came the larger house, in the big enclosed square in a gentrifying area of London. And, as I say, that house was the end. In Battersea Naomi had run the playgroup, sat on the committee of the PTA, been secretary of the local Labour Party, had Reuben, Cassandra and their mother in for tea, made Harriet's dresses, stared at herself disbelievingly in the mirror as the children's birthdays marked, for her, the passage of time and had been snug as a bug in a rug, reading Habitat catalogues, studying Spanish at night-school and having dinner parties. What else did I want her to do? Take to the bottle? Leave the children and run away to Katmandu? Of course I did not. I liked the comforts of home and she, so far as I knew, had what she wanted. As far as I knew – but even I knew I could not read her at all, had no idea of her discontents, if any, or of her secret fears. Probably because all the time we were working – working as, by God, only the middle classes know how to work. She wrote the minutes as I wrote a book on nineteenth-century children's fiction, those books of my uncle's which had shaped me as a child in Yorkshire and became a passion later. The book financed the conversion, which I did myself. In the meanwhile we swam, went for walks and flew kites with the children, Harriet cooked gourmet meals for friends, I knocked down a wall, she made twenty pounds of plum jam, I catalogued my library. It was a fine example of hard work and the Protestant ethic. It was effort producing measurable results. In the end, I maintain, we had less actual freedom than a docker doing overtime to pay the mortgage while his wife, with three young children to rear, had a part-time job cleaning the local doctor's surgery. Moreover, we had not the excuse of needing the money. And we certainly did not know each other. To manage like that we had to produce for ourselves the fairly simple joint self-image of a cheerful, competent, tolerant, nice young couple, with happy well-adjusted children. Small wonder that in the end, someone – me – collapsed for want of a genuine private life. On the cross of DIY, service to the community and cheery, well-disciplined children – early readers, too – we crucified ourselves. We sat, like fakirs, so long in the same position that in the end, without noticing it, other parts of ourselves began to atrophy.

The move to West London, the heavy work needed on the ample, but neglected mid-Victorian house, Naomi's assumption that once again she would locate straight away the nearest compatible neighbours, youngish professional couples with children, and form a group with them, and that she would join the local Labour Party, while I, equally naturally, would take over the Habitatization of the house and do a few ILEA classes to bring in extra money, frightened me suddenly. But I was tired and secretly worried about the large mortgage we were paying and the extra costs of making alterations to the house. There was no obvious reason for this fear. We were only balancing on the edge of the same precipice which most ambitious young couples balance on, but the extra factor was my fatigue which, after the move, became chronic and unshiftable and which led me to doubt, quite without my realizing it, whether I could go on taking the weight I had assumed. I tried to tell Naomi what I felt, but she could not understand. She pointed out to me, quite reasonably, that the debt was manageable and all I felt was my aching back, my scratched hands and the painful muscles in my legs. As I worked on that house I felt it was consuming my body into its fabric. Naomi's delight at the improvements made me bitter. Her forays into central London for wallpapers and curtain materials, her accounts of triumphs at sales and gems snatched from under counters, only made me think of letters from the bank. She was all sympathy. She made me see a doctor and put me on a high-protein diet but these efforts began to look to me like a man's attempt to keep an ageing horse alive to pull the cart.

And in the meanwhile, in fact within a week of our arrival at the new house, she and Jessica Lombard, like two magnets, had found each other. In no time at all Naomi was privy to all the details of the neighbourhood – which couples got on well, who was having trouble with their children, where to pick up bargains. Naomi's unqualified admiration for her friend, Jessica, disturbed me because, suddenly, there in flesh and blood, in the person of Jessica, whom I privately considered snobbish, ambitious and unlikeable, was the woman Naomi most desired to be. Poor Naomi, I realized, had never felt secure since the position of heiress to the Trent factories had failed to impress her friends at boarding-school as much as it had the children she knew at Stonebridge. Poor Naomi worried eternally about her looks and popularity with people who counted with her in a way which made me wonder if, in spirit, she had ever left that school. As she and Jessica rattled on it always reminded me of the Head of School and the Captain of Games in earnest conflab over the cheeky manners of the Lower Fourth. I could not see, then, why they had failed to grow up and I could see no way of jerking Naomi, stuck perennially in the Sixth Form, clever, anxious to do well and worrying about her looks, into the world in which I lived. I talk as if I would have dared to try but the truth was that I relied too much on my comfortable well-run home and my domestic peace and quiet. I could not face the results of wounding Naomi – the back turned on me in bed, the slightly poorer food, the more frequent returns to Stonebridge with the children to see mother and father. But the truth was that I needed her because I felt weak and desperate, and the more I needed her strength, the more frightened she got at my weakness and the more she pretended not to notice it and raced back, led by Jessica, to the certainties of the prefects' room. In the end I felt locked out, banging weakly on the door and crying, 'Let me in. Let me in,' while from inside came the high, sure voices of the girls with their giggles, bitchings and small enthusiasms. A stronger man might have solved the problem, but I was not a strong man. I was a man who feared his bank statement, went to work knowing that half the floorboards on the landing were up and that the family would have to edge their way past the exposed beams to the bathroom until I nailed the new ones down, and that Mr and Mrs Fraser and the Pattens were expected for dinner that night. Exhausted, it was as much as I could do to get past the day-to-day problems.

I went on trying until, without making a conscious decision, I stopped. I began by failing to drive the children to the coast on fine winter weekends or take them to the park on Sundays. Instead, I left Naomi to do these things alone. Meanwhile, instead of employing myself constructively I sat about the house reading thrillers in my pyjamas and enjoying the silence. I went to the cinema straight from work, attended unnecessary functions at night, often coming back the worse for drink. In short, I committed matrimonial offences, from the most minor – the missing Sunday-morning cup of tea in bed – to the more serious – the fist banged on the dinner-table, the broken plate, spilled gravy and weeping children. It was only in bed that I knew how much I loathed Naomi. My flesh crawled at her touch, and finally, overmastered by a silent, raging depression, I declared that because of insomnia I had to sleep in the spare-room. Finally, it was only in there, under the flowered duvet in that room which needed decorating, by me, home from a reception and drinking a nightcap from the whisky bottle I kept in the wardrobe, that I ever felt peaceful and at home.

Naomi's rage was deep and concealed. She began to frighten me more than ever before. The marriage contract is like the Hobbesian social contract, being based on the notion that if everyone stays in his place and does his job, anarchy and civil war will be prevented. Naomi had kept what she saw as her side of the bargain and when I began to show signs of breaking mine she, child of the self-made industrialist, was as indignant as she was grieved. When she said, 'Joe you must tell me if there's anything wrong,' the words barely covered an outrage as deep as that of a man whose wallet has been snatched. When she drank half a bottle of brandy and fell, sobbing, on her knees on the rug beside the sofa where I was sitting, pleading to know if there was another woman, I could still feel the rage of the deprived child and the deceived businessman. If, months before, she could have put me to bed with a cup of cocoa, taken me for a week at the seaside, told me I was ill and should not do anything for a few days, had, in short, babied me, I might have pulled myself together; but we were too far gone now for that, and all I said was, Naomi, I'm tired.'

'Perhaps we shouldn't have taken on this big house,' she said. 'Let's have a holiday, together.'

I was too tired. It was too late. She was too late. I had drifted too far from land now, to be got back. I did not want to go back

'Joe – Joe,' she wept (the first of Coverdale's weeping women) and her sobs followed me upstairs, to the spare-room, where I poured myself a stiff drink, drank it, got into bed, stared at the damp patches in the dark old wallpaper, very much as the old man must have, the old man, I mean, whom the vendors of the house had displaced to induce us to buy. Then I fell into a deep sleep, heavy as a stone.

Naomi became a heroine. She resigned from the Labour Party, laid the stair-carpet herself, cooked me chops and roasts, changed her hairstyle, was cheerful, resolute and friendly. Unfortunately, ungratefully, all I saw was Henry Trent faced with a full order-book, a wage claim and a stoppage, pulling himself together, rolling up his sleeves, taking a hand in the work and, still with the marks of toil about him, going to the negotiating table in a cheerful, compromising and comradely manner. A more humane or a more practical man might have accepted the gesture, forgotten about the motives and rebuilt from there. I might have begun negotiations and made sacrifices, produced a compromise and come to a settlement satisfactory on both sides. But at that time I did not want a settlement. Instead, bent on destroying the firm, I went to an office party and back that night to the flat of Joy Cross, of the Information Department.

I will not go into the details of my relationship with that tall, gangling coarse girl, describe her red hair, like a lavatory brush, or her skin, which had the texture of the plaster I should have been applying to my own walls, nor will I tell of her joy in her own sexual behaviour, the delight of someone who keeps a fierce and uncontrollable Alsatian which is forever attacking the postman and leaping up at small children; nor her squalid glee at being the first to capture me, the brilliant, the impeccable, the respected, the successfully married man, J. E. Coverdale.

Joy's curiosity about my married life was insatiable. I lay there one night as she cross-examined me, and gave her helpful answers to all her questions, as she, the Peeping Tom, and I, the exhibitionist, thrilled to the pornographic delights of lifting up the curtains to reveal the inside of that private room, my marriage. The privacy of marriage is a shocking thing. We try to present our own, particularly if we are women, in a good light, or, if men, in no light at all. We struggle not to listen to the secrets of other people's marriages. Thus marriages live in isolation, sometimes becoming, for want of compassion and criticism, more bizarre, more cruel, more wild or more eccentric, than any of us can possibly imagine. Joy, listening to my tale and returning anecdotes culled from the lives of the other married men she had slept with, made me feel less alone, less anxious. And there was something cheering, I found, about having an absolute bitch for a mistress. She sharpens the wits and dulls the conscience – wives often have the opposite effect.

Nevertheless, I ditched her and then found, to my complete surprise, that I had jumped on to an adultery and fornication roundabout at the Department, the existence of which, in fourteen years, I had never suspected. Up to that point I had never known that George Rogers, the decent statistician I sometimes had lunch with in the canteen, spent more weekends in Brighton with Alison Jenks, of Accounts, than he did at home with his wife. I discovered the real reason for Ursula Naismith's visits to Brussels – her husband was there and the man I often saw her with in the pub next door was, in fact, her lover. I learned of the long-standing, and very sad relationship between John Fadley, whose wife had muscular dystrophy, and Cecilia Lindstrom, his assistant, who had even borne his child, which was being reared by her parents in Wiltshire.

After only a few weeks with Joy, I was suddenly welcome in this hidden hell's kitchen of clandestine love affairs and intrigue, becoming part of the fellowship of the lowered voice and significant glance. There were unnecessary visits to my office, invitations from people I had not known well, and I even felt the typist's breast brushing my back as she stood behind my chair.

After Joy came Jacquie; after Jacquie, Veronica – it was like learning to swim, or ride a bicycle. In the early stages it seems impossible, later, you are amazed to find you can do it, and, not long after, you cannot remember what it was like not to know how. I learned something about women, too, about their lack of confidence, their generosity, their pain – things which I had not known because, as I found, they hide themselves so cleverly. In our world they cannot afford to be vulnerable. What they show us is a weakness which has nothing to do with their real weaknesses. I heard tales of the cruelty of men to women, all told in the neutral accepting tone which women use to speak of past batterings – how their fathers maltreated their mothers, how their brothers were favoured, how their husbands used them. 'I don't think he knew what he was doing.' 'He didn't really want to do it.' 'I think he regrets it now,' they said. It was an education, one I did not know at the time I was receiving that long year of lust, clandestine meetings, secret phone calls and experiences which now, looking back, seem to me like pictures in a what-the-butler-saw machine – jerky flickers showing women climbing into bed and climbing out, flashes of gartered leg, startled expressions, faces peeping over backs, ruffles and smiles. All without any coherence, intention or, indeed, feeling. The emotions I sometimes stirred up seemed to have nothing to do with me. It was gross but at the time I thought it was normal. I had simply passed from despair to desperation. I had been low. Now I was high. I moved fast and felt no pain, my own or anyone else's. My world had altered as it does when we are in love, or bereaved or even when we come back after a trip, or a holiday, with a changed perspective.

That year I gave up making excuses for coming home late and Naomi gave up mentioning that my dinner had dried up in the oven while she waited for me. Later still, she stopped cooking dinner. She turned to and produced food for me when

I did arrive home. I nearly always ate alone. During that year I also worked with great brilliance, producing, almost single-handed, what I now see as a fundamentally new approach to our way of balancing imports from the Common Market countries on the one hand, and Eastern Europe on the other. Half the time, indeed, when I said I was working it was true. I simply went straight from the House of Commons, or wherever it was, to a mistress's flat.

Naomi laboured on, keeping the house clean, the larder well-stocked, the children quiet when I came home. When she spoke to me her voice was calm and her face tranquil. She treated me like someone she had just met and quite liked as far as she knew. I came home once and found her at the stove, stirring a large pan of jam while Harriet and Paul and two friends played Monopoly on the table in the kitchen. As I came in behind her she was just telling a joke and the children were laughing. Then, her head turned towards the table to the right, she half-saw me in the doorway, started a little, stopped smiling and turned to say, 'Hullo, Joe. You're early.' Harriet and Paul both looked at me.

'You throw, Harry,' cried one of the little girls, still enjoying the excitement of the game.

'All right,' said Harriet and slowly took the cup with the dice in it from her.

I went upstairs and sat down in the living-room. It was fragrant with roses. Naomi's sewing stood on a little, highly polished table next to her chair. I sat there for a while, looking out of the window until Paul came in and said, 'Mum says: do you want some scones and hot strawberry jam and a cup of tea?'

'Sounds fine,' I said and sat there until Harriet brought up the tray, with one cup on it, and a plate, and some scones and a little pot of steaming jam.

'Mind the jam,' she said severely. 'It's boiling hot.'

'I shall.'

I drank the tea and ate the scones and slowly mounted the stairs to pack for the trip I was taking to Geneva, but not alone. I came back into the kitchen doorway carrying my case to find Naomi studying the row of jampots on the kitchen table.

'I've got to go to Geneva tonight,' I said. 'Do you know

where my sunglasses are?' 'Where have you put my sunglasses?' was what I would ordinarily have said.

'I think you must have broken them last year,' she said. 'I found the pieces in the wastepaper-basket.'

'That's right,' I said.

She went on staring at the jam, wearing, suddenly, such an expression of tiredness and resignation that I pitied her, as a stranger might, for what I was doing to her. I could hear the cries of the children playing in the garden. On that civil, guarded face, the face of a well-trained servant, I read what my sulks and rages and undiscussable arrivals and departures had done to her.

'I'd better go now,' I said lamely. 'Get some more sunglasses at the airport.'

'Yes,' she said.

'Good-bye,' I said, going over to kiss her. She seemed to brace herself for my arms going round her like a patient who knows the doctor is going to probe a painful spot. I kissed her on the cheek and left.

Standing in the hot, wide street, waiting for a taxi, I had a vision of the girl who was waiting for me at the airport, a pretty, good, honest and intelligent girl, and then of Naomi, who suddenly seemed much more than a girl. Then I flagged down a taxi, threw myself on to the hot plastic seat and called myself an idiot. I told myself it is a form of egotism in men to go rushing back to the woman they have made suffer the most, an egotism amounting to sadism, and both vices built on the shifting sands of lack of self-confidence, as if we had to have proof of love, not wanting a cheerful dog, an affectionate dog, an obedient dog, a useful dog, but a dog guaranteed to starve itself to death on our graves. Nevertheless, there was no joy in Geneva, either professional or emotional and I was pleased, in the end, when they cabled me to go straight on to Berlin and I could send the girl home. My attitude had been so dull and unfriendly that she was relieved to go.

On the flight to Germany I thought that in the fortnight's leave I had coming after the trip I would go first to see my mother and father, whom I had also neglected, and then ask Naomi if she could not leave the children perhaps at her parents' home, for a week, while we went away together. I had put all this in hand, and sent the letter to Naomi, when I knocked over a woman, Eva, in a street during a thunderstorm, or, rather, she met me and allowed me to knock her over. Lying on top of her on the wet, greasy pavement, with torrential rain pouring over my back, I saw her smile up at me with the open, dazed smile of a gratified woman. I was rising when a great clap of thunder arrested me. I crouched over her with my knees on either side of her legs, and a shaft of lightning dazzled me.

'Phew,' I said, and 'I'm sorry,' and I scrambled to my feet.

I offered her my hand and she pulled herself up. She was rosy and blonde. I bent down, for she was short and said, 'Are you hurt?' as I would have said it to Harriet and she said, 'No, I'm fine,' in English. Perhaps it was this feeling of false familiarity, based on her resemblance to my child, which gave me the ease to suggest that we went to sit down in a café to recover from the shock. She offered to take me sightseeing. We had dinner. The next morning I cabled Naomi to say that I was detained on business in Germany and spent the fortnight's holiday I should have spent with my wife, my mother and father and my children – in bed with a blonde Hungarian in a hotel in Berlin. She told me she ran a restaurant in Budapest.

I returned to London with a sweater Eva had knitted for her brother in Bayswater. I believed that I must leave Naomi. And, as I went up my own front steps thinking about this I turned my ankle and fell on the steps, dropping my suitcase, so that I lay alone for minutes on the steps, surrounded by spilt clothes. I remember somehow getting Eva's parcel back into the case, and the first drops of rain falling on my face. No one came past. In the end I heard a car door slam, then Naomi's voice, then a cry and she ran to me as the car drove off. She laughed at me and put out a hand to help me to my feet.

'I don't think I can,' I said. So she called the postman, who had just arrived at our gate, and together they got me upstairs and sat me on the step. Naomi, quickly and carefully taking off my shoe and sock, said, 'There's no point in going inside. We need an ambulance.'

And so it was that after arriving home with the idea of leaving I was, four hours later, lying in the matrimonial bed with my leg in plaster up to the knee, sipping a before-lunch sherry from a glass on a silver tray on which stood a single rose in a crystal vase. A pair of National Health crutches lay neatly across the end of the bed. I was deeply contented and the main reason for this contentment was that I had no more decisions to make, or none that I could implement, and the other was that I recognized that I was mad. I had decided to go back to my marriage in Geneva, had, only a week later decided to abandon it completely in Berlin and, a week after that, was lying in my bed at home in London with no desire to do anything. And, symbolically enough, each decision had been reached by falling over. Too far gone for conscience, I just leant back and enjoyed the comforts of the home I had betrayed. Making up a plausible story to explain it away, I got Naomi to post the jumper to Eva's brother in Bayswater.

I listened to the radio and the birds singing in the garden, read thrillers and practised on my crutches. I invited Naomi to join me in the big bed at night.

'I'll only make you uncomfortable,' she said.

'It'll be all right,' I told her.

'No. I'd keep you awake,' she said. 'I'll be better in the spare bed.'

I asked her up in the evenings to join the children and me as we watched TV, did jigsaw-puzzles and made model aeroplanes.

But she, carrying out a tray, said, 'I'll come up sometimes. But I enjoy the peace and quiet – being on my own.' I, who had, when it suited me, dismissed her prattle about relationships and marriage as a right-wing, self-centred bourgeois heresy, a way of selfishly shutting the door on the world, now felt rebuffed. I also reflected that she must have spent many an evening with the children, the TV and the aeroplane glue – was it six months, nine months or a year? I did not care to examine it all that closely.

One evening I said to Paul, 'Pop down and ask your mum to make me a cup of tea.'

He said, 'I'll do it. She's out.'

'Mind the boiling water, Paulie,' Harriet warned him as he went out.

'Shut up,' he said from the landing.

'Where's she gone?' I asked Harriet.

'She might have gone to the Labour Party,' Harriet said. 'Or the cinema. I don't really know.'

I watched the television until Paul came back with the tea. On the tray he had some orange-juice and biscuits.

'Only two each,' he said severely to Harriet.

Harriet looked at the clock and said, 'Half an hour. Then we've got to go to bed.'

'Just to the end of the programme,' he said.

'Yes,' she conceded.

There was something practised about the whole operation. A suspicion grew in my mind. 'Does mummy sometimes go out and leave you alone at night?' I asked.

'Sometimes,' said Paul. 'Sometimes we have Maria to babysit.'

'Doesn't she leave a phone number.'

'Well. We've got a few people to ring if we need them. Like Jessica. Mum finds out if they're going to be in.'

'We don't need them, though,' said Harriet.

'Who puts you to bed?'

They began to catch my outraged tone.

'We do,' said Paul. 'We know what to do. Check the stove and unplug the telly and that.'

'Make sure the doors are locked,' said Harriet. 'After all,' she added. 'We're old enough to look after ourselves by now.'

I was shocked. I felt that Naomi had let me down. I had imagined that all this time, while I was out, Naomi was in the house. Buried always at the back of my mind, as I dined, or lay in bed in flats from Earl's Court to Winchester, was an image of Naomi in a sweater and trousers, sewing, talking to the children, taking them up to bed, reading to them and then turning out the light, going downstairs to watch television or read, walking the dog round on the paths of the enclosed gardens at the back of the house, turning out the lights and going to bed. I had assumed that, administratively speaking, my home was secure, taken care of, that things and people were in their proper places. Occasionally I had found Maria there when I came in. On one occasion Naomi had come in just as I was going upstairs to bed. But what about all the other times, when I had come in to find the hall light still on and had assumed that Naomi was upstairs in bed, asleep? Had that bed been empty, with the sweater and trousers she had taken off when she dressed to go out, flung across it? Had the dressing-table been disordered, as it was when we came back from parties? Did the air still smell of scent? Suddenly, irrelevantly, I saw her, in jeans and a woolly hat, her hair whipped round her collar by the wind, pushing Paul in a pushchair and leading Harriet by the hand, coming back at dusk from the Battersea Park on winter afternoons. As the memories vanished, other thoughts took over. Where was she going to on those nights when she left the children unattended in the house? What did she think she was playing at anyway? Anything could happen – a fire, a serious accident, the arrival of an intruder, a burglar, a rapist –

'What would you do if fire broke out?' I demanded suddenly of Harriet.

'Go through the front door, or the back door or down the balcony steps into the garden,' he recited.

They were sitting now with their faces turned towards me, hovering between loyalty to their mother, whose methods I appeared to be criticizing, and trust in my judgement.

'What if you don't wake up?' I persisted.

'Get burned to death,' giggled Harriet.

I looked at them. Harriet was twelve and Paul, ten. After they had taken themselves off to bed with experienced calm I lay in bed, shifting my plaster cast to and fro restlessly, burning with rage and discomfiture.

At eleven I heard the front door open and the taps running in the downstairs bathroom. A little later Naomi came up and put her head round the door.

'Fancy a cup of cocoa, Joe?'

'Where have you been?'

'Cinema,' she said.

'What did you see?'

'*Casey's Ride*,' she told me. 'Are you all right?'

'I'd like to have seen that,' I said.

'Oh – well – ' she said. 'I suppose it didn't occur to me. I'm not used to going out with you any more.' She spoke perfectly naturally. That morning she had brought me up another letter from Hungary addressed in Eva's spiky foreign hand. The day before she had lifted the phone downstairs and heard me talking to a woman in German, which she did not understand. 'Sorry, Joe,' she had said, and put the phone down.

'And what's all this about the children being left alone when you go out?' I demanded.

Gently, with the obvious air of someone dealing with a crochety invalid, she said, 'Sometimes Maria can't come. Do you want some cocoa – or a nightcap?'

I lay crippled in bed. She was standing on her two sound, straight legs in the doorway, wearing a loosely woven, striped jacket and skirt in red and cream, and a small round matching cap. She looked energetic and springy, full of fun. Once I had helped her choose her clothes. Now, I thought, I just paid for them.

'I think it's dangerous,' I said.

'I think they're old enough – they're very sensible,' she said. 'And I always find out which neighbours are in and leave the numbers for them. Of course I know there's a risk but there always is with children. They could be run over on the way to school, but that doesn't mean I should take them every day. They can fall off their bicycles, drown in the sea – but I can't manacle them to my wrist twenty-four hours a day just in case.'

She was not just refusing to have a row. She was avoiding one.

'I think I'd like a whisky,' I said. My leg was made of solid carved mahogany, a collector's item, I had no genitals, all was dead until I got to my one, living leg.

She came back with two glasses, a bottle and a jug of water on a tray.

'Are you sure you'll sleep? What about a pill?' she said, handing me a drink. It tasted of dust.

'Sleep? I'll never sleep again if I know the children are left alone at night,' I bawled. I had given her enough openings to score some domestic runs. And even now, as I evoked the image of myself lying uneasily in the bed of another woman, unable to sleep for fear that the house where I should have been was going up in flames, she merely said, 'Well, I thought about it and it seemed all right. A lot of people don't bother with babysitters when their children reach this age. They're very expensive. And Harriet's nearly thirteen now.'

She lit two cigarettes and handed me one. She sat down in the armchair by the fireplace and turned on the electric fire. She said, in the most level of tones, 'I've been sitting alone for a year, Joe. You were seldom there. The year before that you went away in spirit. I realised none of it was doing me, or the children, any good. At first I got babysitters. A few months ago I decided that sometimes I didn't need them.'

I had been lying in bed for a week. I was like a housebound woman who starts a row with her husband when he comes in from work. Naomi, like the husband, with enough on his mind as it is, was avoiding trouble.

'There's another man, isn't there?' I said.

She turned and looked at me. She bent down to turn off the fire. She stood up and said, 'Have I asked you, Joe?' and went out of the room.

'You come back!' I cried and, breathing fast, hauled myself out of bed and got my crutches. I went out on to the landing. She was going down the stairs.

'Come up here, Naomi,' I shouted. 'I want to talk to you.'

She still went down. I bumped down on my bottom, to find, on the hall floor, that I had left my crutches at the top.

'Naomi – I want my crutches,' I shouted.

'What's going on?' said Harriet, leaning over the banisters in her nightdress.

'Bring my crutches down and get back to bed,' I called.

Naomi was in the living-room doorway, holding a library book.

'You bitch,' I said, from the floor of the hall.

She took the crutches from Harriet and for a moment I thought she was going to hit me with them. Then she helped me up and said, 'Go back to bed, Harriet. Dad's fed up because he has to lie in bed all day.'

'Mr Pearson mended the garden fence when he broke his leg,' observed the child.

'Get back to bed and mind your own bloody business,' I said.

Harriet went upstairs, with an understanding and self-righteous glance over her shoulder at her mother.

'You'd better come in here, Joe,' said Naomi.

I flopped on to the sofa and put my crutches beside me. I was shivering. She went out of the room and left me. I was at her mercy. I couldn't talk to her because she could get away from me. She could go upstairs and lock her bedroom door. If I banged on it and shouted the children would get up.

But all she did was come back into the room with my dressing-gown and give it to me, observing, 'I've often tried to talk to you but you wouldn't listen. Now you've broken your bloody leg, and you're housebound and bored and helpless, I can't avoid the kind of scene you always tried to dodge. Because I'm sorry for you. But I just feel bored. Like you used to, I suppose.'

'Too bad.'

'I'm tired,' she said dreamily.

'Yes?'

'Yes.'

'I suppose you've been out with your lover.'

'Yes.'

'And I suppose it was his car you got out of when I was lying on the step with a broken leg?'

'There've been a lot of times when I could have broken my leg and you wouldn't have found out for a fortnight,' she said.

'I wouldn't have thought it of you, Naomi,' I told her.

'I don't know why not.'

'Who is it?'

'I don't have to tell you. It began when I rang the office to find out when you were coming back and they told me you were on holiday. What was I supposed to think? We'd only met before that – he hadn't been my lover. But after you promised that holiday – '

'Who is it? You owe me that, at least.'

'No, I don't.'

'Look. It'll cost you nothing to tell me. I don't want to go to the doctor with my nerves and wonder why he's so quick on the diagnosis – '

'Oh – him,' she muttered. 'What a funny thought. No, it's not Fraser. In fact it's Roderick Glennister.'

I breathed in. 'God!' I said. 'I might have known. Oh – it's obvious isn't it. Good old Roderick. Well, I must say I'd have credited you with more taste – that upper-class, stupid, empty-headed twit. My God – he's been standing there for fourteen years with his hands open, waiting for you to drop off the tree. Couldn't you have found anybody better than that? What do you talk about – his falling dividends or the transmission on his new Mercedes?'

'I knew you'd be like this if I told you.'

'I could have taken anything but that. That creep, a poor woman's Mark Phillips if ever there was one – '

I saw her flinch. She said, 'Joe – you haven't been at home for a year – '

At least I had shaken her, which was what I wanted.

'I thought he was in the Midlands, making his pile?'

'He's at Head Office, now.'

'Nice for everybody. Mummy and Daddy must be pleased. A bit of class at last.'

'Oh – shut up,' she said. Her head drooped. 'I've been very lonely. And I've had to face everybody – they all knew you were never around and why.'

'How did they know that?' I interrupted.

'Julian Mulvaney kept on hinting, of course. And so I did my best, but in the end – even Jessica said it was time I found somebody else.'

'She would,' I said.

'She's been a good friend to me, Joe. Better than you, over the last few years.' She was silent, remembering what it had been like. 'Even when Paul went into hospital to have his appendix out – ' she said.

'I was in Brussels.'

'I know,' she said. 'But it was always the same.'

I began to cry. 'I was coming home, Naomi. That's why I sent you that letter from Geneva – about the holiday.'

'What about that woman, all those letters, and the phone calls from Hungary?' she demanded, but her voice was unsteady as she handed me a tissue.

At least I had cracked that quietness, that resigned and accepting calm that follows storms of feeling. Men are brought up to fight for their homes and whatever the threat, even when it comes from inside that home, they can generally put useless emotion to one side and muster the speed and ingenuity of primitive man faced with primitive beast. They are so trained. Naomi thought she had faced the worst, reconciled herself, gone through the storm to the anchorage. That calm of hers defended her and diminished me. It could not go on. After all, I thought, she did not know how far things had gone between Eva and me, and there was no way of her ever finding out.

I said, 'I never meant that to happen. There was nothing in it.' For that one sentence alone I deserved everything I later got. There is no spectacle more disgusting than that of a man denying a woman he has said he loves in order to creep a little closer to the hearth.

All Naomi said was, 'But when your letter came about the holiday – I don't know. I don't know.' And she hung her head. 'It was the disappointment,' she said.

'Stay with me, Naomi,' I said later, as she tucked me into bed.

The cock crew for the second time. And for the third as I made love to her. And she clung to me and wept while I was manly. I confessed, explained, soothed and made vows and muffled a groan when I moved my leg. I believed what I said but underneath I knew that I was not acting from total candour or remorse, but saving my skin, surviving. The cunning of the husband in such situations can be very great and the cunning of the cripple is legendary. Against a crippled husband no wife can stand.

And yet, with all that, I do not want to make my feelings seem any less than they were. At that time I realized I did love Naomi and, helpless, I loved her more. She had borne my children and brought them up. She had made my home. We had a history, a shared life, which I needed. It was a combination of human affection and gratitude, of the animal's attachment to its feeder and helper. I did not now want a separation or divorce – the fortnight with Eva looked, at that point, like a dream. I wanted my wife, my children, my home.

So, for the next few weeks, as my leg mended, we were happy. Naomi went to a restaurant and held the customary conversation with Roderick, while I sat gloating at home, clutching my plaster cast and watching television. When my leg was better I went to meet Eva in Berlin, making sure, first, that Naomi and the children would be with a strict aunt in Scotland while I was away. I did not want Roderick swooping down in the Merc. during my absence. In Berlin there were scenes, tears and recriminations, just as much from my side as from Eva's. But I had made my decision. And I came back – with yet another jumper for Eva's brother in Bayswater – back to my recently saved marriage. Slowly the excitement vanished, leaving perhaps, a certain flatness behind and then – peace. A peace not broken at the Department where my work seemed to dwindle, fewer papers reached my desk, fewer summonses to meetings came until in the end I noticed that Julian, who was theoretically my equal but in fact had always been less useful than I was, attended meetings instead of me. I minded very little. With the reconstruction of my life my passionate interest in my work had somehow evaporated. I assumed, in fact, that my lack of enthusiasm, and the fact that I was no longer initiating ideas, explained my growing isolation. One day I found a set of figures which should have come to me, open on Julian's desk.

'What are these doing here?' I said, nettled because it was a project I had been pursuing and was hoping to get some answers from.

'Oh – ' he said. 'They must have been misdelivered. I'd like to have a chat about it – ' he began, concluding, 'Oh, all right,' in a discontented tone as I removed the folder and put it under my arm.

It was a rainy Wednesday afternoon and I went back to my office, sat down and gazed at the rain pouring down into the grey Thames, thinking that perhaps I should investigate what was happening. And at that moment my internal telephone rang and I was called in to see the Director, Crosby, straight away.

I put the phone back on my secretary's desk and said, 'I'm going to see Crosby, then.'

'All right,' she said.

I looked at her and decided to ask no questions, although I could see she knew there was something up. He might want to post me, promote me, transfer me – or perhaps my carryings-on had at last come to his attention, and he wanted to warn me for my own good.

I went up in the lift, curiously unworried.

As I walked across the carpet towards him my gaze hit his vast desk and stayed there, transfixed. He himself sat in an armchair by a long window looking down into the Thames. I moved my eyes from the desk with difficulty. He waved to me to sit down in the chair opposite him. Below a toy tug moved downstream.

'You saw the stuff on my desk,' he said easily.

Indeed I had. In a row on the long, empty desk, lay two letters in my own handwriting, letters from Eva, and a bunch of correspondence which I could tell, even at a distance, came from the Hungarian and British Embassies, and the Foreign Office. Worse than that, there was the brown wrapping paper, well smoothed out, in which the sweaters for Eva's brother in Bayswater had been packed.

'Yes,' I said. 'I saw it.' Below us a miniature pleasure-boat moved upstream. Two buses crossed the bridge. I said quickly, 'What is it, then? A revolutionary group?'

He looked at me, I thought, hopelessly, but seemingly with some affection. 'That's right.'

'The oldest trick in the book,' I said. 'I hope I've done no real damage.'

'At the moment it seems not,' he said. 'I've gone to a lot of trouble to protect you – to protect us all.'

'I thought my mail was being opened,' I said. 'But there seemed no reason – what's happened to her?'

'She got out,' Crosby said. 'She wants to go to Canada. I daresay you've saved her life, indirectly. If they'd gone ahead with their half-baked plans to oust the present government there's almost no doubt they would all have been killed, one way or another.'

There was a silence. 'There was a small group over here, sending money,' he said. 'When the moment came they were going to slip in and start the revolution, hoping for popular support – and no Russian tanks.'

'Some hopes,' I said. Then a thought struck me. I said, 'My God if they'd got hold of me with those parcels I could have done fifteen years in a Hungarian gaol.'

'You could have been shot, in a bad year,' he said.

Sitting in that quiet room above the river I was struck merely by how silly I had been. All the time I had thought I was jeopardizing that essentially dull thing, my marriage, I had been trafficking in revolution, in guns in the street, in death.

Finally I said, 'I've been stupid. I'm sorry to have been caught out like this. It must have made things very difficult for you. I'll let you have my resignation.'

'That may not be necessary,' he said. 'I've had discussions all round about your fate. I'm trying to persuade those involved that you're too useful to be lost because you stupidly allowed yourself to carry messages. Your resignation will help no one but the Hungarians – and they know perfectly well that you weren't engaged in espionage on our instructions. For my part I'm content to let it all blow over. There are others involved in the decision though.' He added, 'You would of course, have to be especially circumspect from now on.'

I could not respond to him. The deadly fatigue was coming

down, blotting out my thoughts, throwing a mist over the future.

'In the meanwhile I propose to put you on sick leave,' he said. 'We'll leave it at that until the final decision's made.'

'Thank you,' I said. Then, 'I don't feel competent to decide – perhaps I can talk to you about it later.'

'I think that would be best,' he told me. 'You'd better go home – you look as if you could do with it.'

I stood up to go. As I walked to the door, he said, from his chair, 'Coverdale.'

I turned. He was rolling a cigarette, tipping tobacco from a tin on to a paper on his knee. 'See your doctor,' he told me. 'Get a medical report – physical and mental.'

I nodded. I walked slowly into my office and left instructions for my secretary, returned the files I was holding, said, 'I'm going on leave. If there's anything you need to know, I'll be at home.' A grey haze hung between us. She tried to vanquish it, saying, 'I'm sorry, Joe. Is there anything wrong? Can I help?'

'I got caught out, Elizabeth,' I said. 'Carrying stuff from Germany for a Hungarian woman I got involved with. They used me as a nice safe courier – they were plotting to overthrow the régime. Silly, isn't it?'

She nodded. 'It was all bound to end in something like that,' she said. 'Will you be back?'

'That remains to be seen,' I told her.

'Keep in touch,' she said.

I left my briefcase behind and walked out of the building. In the entrance I bumped into Julian.

'Sorry,' he said, then, recognizing me, 'Going home?'

He knew of course.

'Perhaps permanently,' I said.

'I'm very sorry – ' he said insincerely, but his spite finished me and I pushed out through the swing doors with tears in my eyes.

I took a taxi home and arrived to find Katie Mulvaney and Naomi in the living-room. Naomi, who was sitting on the sofa, had been crying.

Katie stood up, saying to me, 'Julian rang me – I came to

see if I could help. But you hadn't rung up – she didn't know – I'm sorry. I'm sorry I had to be the one to tell her.'

After she left I raged at Naomi. 'Why did she come?'

'She thought you'd told me everything,' said Naomi. 'She only came about your suspension. When she found out how little I knew she wanted to leave – but I made her tell me – I can't cope with all this, Joe. You never told me all this. And there were so many things she wasn't telling me – things Julian must have told her. It must have been so much worse than I imagined. And telling the Hungarian you'd marry her – ' and she began to weep afresh, saying, 'I thought you'd been frank – a fresh start – I can't bear it. I can't bear it. It's unbearable.'

She threw up her head suddenly and said, 'How can I believe you now? Now – when there's been so much deceit and treachery?' Then she began to cry yet again. I went over and put my arm round her shoulders. She flung herself away from me. 'Don't touch me,' she cried. 'You've touched too many women.'

She sat at the end of the sofa, looking out at the leafy trees which tossed in a slight breeze.

'We'd started again,' I said.

'But you didn't tell me,' she said, 'how much of it there was. You let me believe it was an episode. Now I know you were planning to leave me. That was serious. If you hadn't broken your leg you would have gone. Only an accident kept you here. And you didn't tell me. And the children – '

'I loved you all the time, Naomi,' I said.

'You don't love the woman you leave,' she said. 'You love the one you leave her for.'

'You've been watching too much TV,' I said. 'Things are more complicated than that.'

'They are not complicated,' she said. 'You've lied to me. I don't need to know any more.'

'I didn't lie,' I said. 'I just didn't tell you the truth.'

'I don't want to hear any more,' she said. 'I can't live with you any more. I'll never trust you again.'

And so I talked round and round, while she sobbed, and sometimes I cried while she talked, and talked while she packed, ran from room to room, collecting wellington boots, pairs of jeans, and throwing them in disorder on the bedroom floor. Then I spilled out all her packing and ordered her to stay. I cried, 'Don't leave me,' and she sat down on the floor and put her head in her hands, saying, 'I don't know.'

But Edward Trent came next morning in his Bentley for Naomi and the children. In bright sunshine I helped them load the luggage in. The children waved cheerfully at me until they went round the corner. Naomi, sitting next to her father, did not look back. And I went back into the empty house with the dog, put my foot into the ashpit of depression and began the fast, scraping slide down its gritty, unstable sides, landing soon at the bottom.

As I have said, I did not really understand then what had happened between Naomi and me. I saw my despair, infidelities and betrayals as being essentially the fruits of an unsatisfactory marriage. And so they were, but there are other factors and actors in marriage beside the two people concerned. I had left out of the reckoning the fact that marriage is a social matter.

Looking back, I think I made, as we commonly do, the mistake of trying to work out my future in terms of the past, fighting, as you might say, the last war but one. Therefore I had gone over the top to leave the tenantry and join the landlords, ensconce myself in the heart of the middle class, with a good job, a good home and a good standard of living. Naomi was one of the tools I used to do this work. But when I got there, into the middle classes, I an outsider, could see all too clearly that I had raised myself to join a class the function of which, as administrators, defenders and exploiters of a vast empire, industrial as well as territorial, had largely disappeared, and which no longer deserved, or would get, the privileges it claimed. I was in a dream world – a denizen of Overdraft Manor, Stoneybroke Hall, treading the run-down chambers of a palace with crumbling foundations, where the owners proudly clutched about them the tattered rags of virtue and self-respect, defying the world to point out the rents in their clothing. I could listen to the lute and even join in the dance but all the time I could hear in the background the steady march of the approaching Roundheads.

It was a world neither good, nor safe, and I did not want to leave my children in it.

Smart work, Coverdale, I seem to hear someone say, with what spirited and sophistical arguments do you justify and give dignity to your own sloth, incompetence and constant self-gratification. Perhaps so, but I still maintain that lust often has a strange bedfellow, whether it is boredom, love, pity, rage, or revenge. In my case I was using my body to release that whole side of me which had been supressed in the interests of home, family and career, and, above all, that contained an unacknowledged rage about how I was living. I used myself like a bomb, to hurl through my own front window.

And it was because I knew what I had done, but did not understand why, that I was confused and helpless.

Elmira and I were walking round the garden under a leaden sky one Sunday afternoon in December when it began to snow.

'Oh,' Elmira exclaimed on a lingering note. 'Oh.'

She pulled her enormous fur coat round her as the air filled with big slow snowflakes. I wanted to lie under a tree and sleep, with the snow falling over me.

Skittering through the flakes came a big, bounding Afghan hound. Philip and the dog began to play, leaping, barking and mock-biting. In the distance I saw two tall, thin figures and some children. The dog went circling and jumping. I thought of drifting off to sleep under the broad, bare branches of the tree with my head against its thick, cold trunk.

'That must be Polly Kops and Abdul el Malik,' Elmira remarked. 'She just got back from living on a lonely Yorkshire moor. Her mother-in-law bought the house and gave it to her. That must be the son of the Senegalese who swindled her out of all her money. She said he was coming because his father died and he decided to give the money back to her. Life's very complicated.'

We approached the fur-coated woman with the red hair streaming down her back, the tall thin black man with her, and the skinny adolescent boy and the two little blonde girls chasing each other, the tottering baby in a wide fur coat and the two dogs, now running round them all. The group certainly seemed, especially after Elmira's scarcely comprehensible tale, to have a strange air. Then I observed a blonde girl pop out from behind a tree and begin photographing the group. My desolation was penetrated by a notion of terrifying activity and the randomness of events. It made me shudder.

The woman, Polly, turned and waved at Elmira.

'Coming in for a cup of tea?' she called through the snow.

'No thanks,' shouted Elmira. The party began to move back to the houses. I called Philip back from the group. He came leaping back to me. I stared after them as they went through the gate. Someone shouted. There was a laugh.

'Now there's a lucky woman,' Elmira said reflectively as we walked back to her house. 'She endured old-fashioned womanhood in its most violent form – financial dependence – not that there was any money anyway – fed-up husband, treacherous lover, four kids, two by each of them – got it all over with fast, because it was so terrible, retired from the scene and now she's all right again. It might have taken another woman twenty years.'

'Are you sure she's all right?' I asked.

'Can you ever be? Come on, Joe. I'll make you a cup of tea.'

We passed the Greenwood children, who were standing under a tree in their anoraks. Two pairs of large, pale-blue eyes stared at us – empty stares, blankness masking confusion.

'Wonder what's going on in *that* house,' said Elmira, the gossip. 'Can't you get into the house, kids?'

'We've come out to play,' said Faith.

'Oh – right,' Elmira said, remarking, as we passed them, 'I don't know what it's all about, I'm sure.'

We walked across the snowy paving-stones of Elmira's garden. In the semi-darkness of the basement I fell across an open coffin. Stuffed birds looked down at me from shelves. Behind me, Elmira shut the door, looked into a corner behind a tattered chaise-longue and said, 'Ha! I thought as much.'

'What?' I asked.

'Rats – there's a rat in here.'

'Rubbish,' I said, following her through into the kitchen. 'But if there are it's your fault.'

'I only realized the other day why that room was starting to look like the attic at Death Abbey,' she said, taking a fruit-cake out of a tin.

'Because it's your practice room,' I said.

'It's just my little attempt to swamp the classical, disciplined side of me in a tide of Gothic.'

'Hum,' I said. I was depressed and lethargic and had my eye on the fruit-cake.

I carried the tray upstairs to Elmira's long room, where a great uncurtained window showed the big blobs of snow still drifting down over the darkened park. Elmira threw her coat down on to the thick, ruddy-coloured carpet, and tossed two logs on to the fire in the huge fireplace. She had already been fined for air pollution earlier in the year. She threw herself down on some cushions in front of it. She wore a blue-and-green dress, embroidered and covered with little, jingling bells.

'Well, what does the doctor say about you?' she said.

'I think she's telling me to pull myself together – in psychiatric jargon, that is.'

'She must think you can.'

'I suppose so.'

'Ah,' she said, kicking off her shoes and holding out her arms to me.

I lay on top of her with my cheek on her hard, jangling breast. Then I moved up and kissed her.

'I can't, Elmira. You know that.'

'Oh – you're not trying.'

'That's what Dr Smith tells me.'

She gave me a warm embrace. We lay there in the firelight and I felt no humiliation. Two attempts to make love to Elmira in her huge brass bedstead had failed, leaving me stranded, impotent, across her strong body, feeling oddly like Gulliver with a Brobdingnagian queen. Of course it was not her strength, nor her massy good-nature which deterred me. I knew I was impotent and, after one or two attempts to prove I was not, I had resigned myself to it.

'I'm putting on weight,' she said.

'It's not that – ' I said.

'I know. I know,' she said. 'But I am.'

'You should go back.'

'I'm tired,' she said. 'I've had twenty years of dedication and discipline. I don't want any more. I wish I could give up the practice, though. I keep filling that room with more and more junk, and every morning I get up and go down there, and kick aside a couple of stuffed animals and a pile of old books and get started again. I can't stop. It's harder than leaving the Catholic Church.'

The phone rang and she got up and lolloped over to it. She pulled it over and lay down by the fire, talking and making faces at me.

'Not there,' she said. 'There's bombs all over the place. And how will I get a taxi in the middle of a transport strike – all right. Fine. I'll see you.'

Making another face she put the phone down and said, 'I wish you'd ring me up, take me out to dinner and then come back and make love to me. I'm so lonely.'

'I wish I could,' I said, with a gallantry I did not feel. I wanted no more of women. The idea of the coming Christmas visit to Stonebridge, where I would, or would not, be reconciled to Naomi and, would, or would not, get my children back and restore my family and my place in the world, only increased my inner determination to continue in my clinical depression and remain lifeless and impotent forever.

I walked across the garden recalling how, after my last night with Elmira, last summer, I had mooched back home to kill myself, only to hear the thud of Elmira scudding over the grass, barefoot and in her nightdress, behind me, to hear her shouting, like a malignant older sister, 'I know what you're planning, Joe Coverdale, and I'm here to stop you.' And as I remembered it I knew that Dr Smith was right. I was getting better but, like a dog which goes on limping after an accident, out of habit and fear, I would not relinquish my illness. Without it, I could get hurt. Without it, I would have to take action. I went home, took some more pills, lay down in my unironed pyjamas, in my tumbled bed, and drifted away into coma.

In the early morning I awoke and prowled my nightmare-ridden house, clinging hard to the nightmares and the ready tears which sprang into my eyes – I knew that if they had been natural at first, they were now produced solely by the drugs. Daze, terrors, numbness of the heart and brain are often the shields we produce, or get out of a bottle kindly supplied by the doctor, to ward off the sharp blows dealt by the facts. Insomnia, nightmares, paranoia and strange terrors, are often more bearable than the clear vision of ourselves and our situation. The headless horror stalking behind, which we dare not turn to face, is often standing mercifully between us and the unfaceable reality, whatever it is – bills, bereavements, neglected children and parents, corrupting work, betrayed friends.

I, at any rate, did not want to look at what I had done, confront my present state of affairs or contemplate future action. I had got to the stage of cheering on the strange knockings at the window, working hard on the notion of the Thing in the airing-cupboard, straining my ears desperately for the sound of the eerie sobbings from the attic. In the end I went to bed.

When I got up later I saw, from the bathroom window, that they were burning rubbish outside in the street. In the pile of mail in the hall was an unexpected invitation to a party at the Lombards, a note from the vicar, a letter from Eva, inviting me to meet her in Austria in the New Year before she set off for Canada, and a long love-letter from Diana Webber, with whom, I am sorry to say, I had had intercourse standing up in a broom cupboard at a party in Hampstead. There had, of course, been other meetings later. I sat holding the letter at my kitchen table, drinking Nescafé out of a mug, staring at my slippered feet and listening to advice on Social Security payments on the radio, wondering vaguely if I really had mysterious powers over women. There was a loud, heavy-vibrating bang in the distance. I had had little power over Naomi, I knew. Svengali had not been married to Trilby or we should have heard a different tale. There came another bang. I felt the table shake.

Probably my chief appeal was that I bore the sign EXIT so clearly about me and women, looking, as they still do, for a future through men, saw me as a good way to get out of whatever uncomfortable or downright intolerable situation they were in with husbands, children and jobs, and so in to a world of boundless romance, love and glamour, a world in which anything could happen. To myself I was Coverdale, a rather dull man with a head full of statistics and an aptitude for home improvements, while to them I was instantly a figure of myth – a Heathcliff come from the moors to carry them away, a Viking chief in a horned hat, a deliverer from the North. Sometimes the most intelligent of them still seemed to me to have their heads stuffed with the dreams of a twopenny romance. Perhaps without such banal dreams they could not have gone on believing in men like me at all. Perhaps they could not have gone on believing that there was any point in considering any man as part of their lives. Certainly, from their accounts, those lives had been more distorted and overturned by what society demanded of them in their sexual relationships – exams failed, careers blighted and unwanted children born – than mine for example ever could have been. No man, I concluded, would have put up with it. My attitude, although I was not proud of it, was the one which the privileged normally feel towards the downtrodden – a natural sympathy mixed with a slight secret disgust at their situation, a strong impatience with their seeming passivity, a suspicion that they could pull themselves together and do something positive, if they wanted to, and a sneaking feeling that perhaps some inherent weakness in them accounted for their miserable state.

At bottom I knew I was just a sympathetic Nazi, listening to the Jews' tales of their maltreatment and then going out at night and doing nothing about other Nazis throwing bricks through their windows – even chucking one myself from time to time. I felt a guilt so intense that my only defence became, in the end, to ignore it. I was only obeying orders, after all.

'Two small bombs went off outside a shop in Bayswater Road earlier today,' the radio announcer said into my dark and lifeless kitchen, where the stench of burning rubbish filtered through drawn blinds. I wandered upstairs and saw cars easing themselves round the smouldering mound of black plastic bags and spilled rubbish, and two women shoving their pushchairs rapidly round the nuisance.

I rang the Town Hall but a woman said, 'I'll just leave the key in the usual place so you can get in without disturbing him. If you do there'll be the hell of a row.'

When I tried again a man said, 'Look, I'm telling you informally here, I'm trying as hard as possible to get the parts but unless those buggers at the works get off their backsides for once I'm not sure we can make the delivery on Tuesday. Quite frankly, I'm doing my best – '

Then I spoke to the girl at the Town Hall who advised me to ring the fire service. Once the firemen had put the fire out they would collect the charred rubbish, but not soon. 'It's the same all over London, since the strike,' she said.

My phone rang and two men were making an assignation in French. Behind them I could hear Naomi saying, 'Hullo, hullo.' The line cleared and Naomi asked, 'Are you coming by car, Joe?'

'No. I'm not fit to drive,' I told her.

'Oh,' she said. Then, 'I was hoping you could bring one or two things with you.'

'I'll hire a car and a driver,' I said. 'Give me a list of what you want.'

'Look here, Joe. You'll be all right when you come, won't you?'

'I'll be perfect,' I said. 'I'm bringing old port and after-shave for your father and for Mum, a great big kiss. I hope it snows, to give me the opportunity to make a snowman in the garden – '

'You *are* better, Joe,' she said accusingly.

'I'll never be better,' I said, banging the phone down, knowing full well that my outburst only confirmed my recovery. I wanted some peace and quiet. She wanted me to be somebody I did not know. Not her father, Edward Trent. I knew him and he didn't come close to the being she desired me to be. Who was he – this *X*? The Henry Trent she had known when she was nine years old? The Henry Trent she had always longed for? The hero of her childish dreams?

The phone rang again, as I knew it would. 'Joe,' she said. 'Have you any news of Eva?'

'Is that Roderick still hanging around?' I asked her. This time she put the phone down.

Naomi was greedy, I thought. She wanted me in good working order, trying hard to reach the unachievable goal of *X*-ness while still holding on to Roderick, just in case – let us call Roderick *Y* – he is the dream, sitting expensively-suited behind a big desk during the week, saying 'I don't think, Sir Nigel, that I'm utterly convinced by their figures' – and at weekends, the hero with the riding-crop smacking against a jodhpured leg.

Then I heard another bomb go off. It shook my cup on the table. Later there were fire-engines and police-cars.

I came back from the cinema in the late afternoon, dropped the badminton set and the jars of delicacies from Fortnum and Mason in the hall, for wrapping later, and went to see the vicar.

'He's out, I'm afraid,' Laura Greenwood told me as she led me through a gloomy hall, papered with thin, rose-covered wallpaper, past a hatrack, a pile of yellowing newspapers, some cardboard boxes containing old clothes and shoes. 'He's hospital-visiting.'

The smell of cheap food, indifferently prepared – shepherd's pie, fatty lamb, greens – lingered as we went into the study, a small room with bookshelves all round it. She knelt down on the dusty carpet and turned on an electric fire.

'He won't be long,' she told me. 'He's gone to see one of the parishioners – a poor old man who got his leg blown off at lunch-time.' She spoke flatly, as if the story meant nothing and as she spoke she stared past me at the net curtains at the windows. 'I must take those down,' she said, as if to herself. Then, 'Would you like a cup of tea?'

'No, thank you.'

'I was just going to make one,' she said.

'I'll have one with you, then,' I said. She went wearily out of the room, her back sagging. She was wearing a green sweater and a pleated tweed skirt. She was a tall, strong woman, big-bosomed and big-hipped, sturdy-legged. Her blonde hair escaped down the back of her neck. You could see her stepping from a longboat with her skirt whipping in the wind and her baby held firmly against her in a shawl. You could see her building a fire on the shingle by the tossing grey sea. She had no place in this grimy city vicarage. I walked over to the desk which was heaped up with papers. In the middle was a yellow pad. I read:

Though I speak with the tongues of men and of angels, and have not charity, I am become as sounding brass, or a tinkling cymbal. And though I have the gift of prophecy and understand all mysteries, and all knowledge; and though I have all faith, so that I could remove mountains, and have not charity, I am nothing.
And though I bestow all my goods to feed the poor, and though I give my body to be burned, and have not charity, it profiteth me nothing. *1 Cor 13.*

Love will never come to an end *(New English Bible)*
Charity never faileth. *(King James)*

Let us examine what we mean –

The small, spikey writing then tailed off, leaving the rest of the page blank.

Laura brought in the tea and we sat, on either side of the

electric fire, I in the armchair, and she on the floor. She became calmer, perhaps because my presence made it impossible to do any of the fifteen things she must have had listed in her head for attention.

'He'll be back soon,' she murmured.

'His note just said he'd like to talk to me,' I volunteered. 'I thought that very kind.'

'I think he – wanted to help – ' she said. She raised her eyes to mine, seeming to grope for some understanding of my situation, and then looking away. 'He is a kind man,' she said. Two red blotches stood out on her fair, pale cheeks. It seemed to me that Roy Greenwood's help and advice might not be what I needed – he had problems closer to home which he had been unable to solve for himself. Not that I really hoped for help. I did not want to reject his kindness.

And to cover the confusion of this woman, whose instincts were telling her what was happening to her while her conscience and notions of life would not let her acknowledge the information, I said, 'He must be a good man. After all, I'm not really one of his parishioners – not an active one.'

'Roy,' she said, 'is a good man.'

This tribute, which comes so often, in my experience, frozen, from the lips of wives who have at last given up hope of happiness in marriage, dropped sadly into the dusty room, like Roy's obituary.

'Joe!' Roy Greenwood said heartily. 'Good to see you.' He sat down behind the desk and said, 'Would you like a glass of sherry?'

I did not much want one but I felt the glass of sherry might be part of the ritual, like communion wine. I said, 'Thank you.'

His wife gazing at him from large, pale eyes, went off to fetch the bottle. I regretted having accepted.

'How's the man who got bombed?' I asked.

'Mr Bennet? Well, he's got two broken legs, poor old chap, and they won't mend quickly at his age. But there's no other damage, fortunately. Shock, of course. He was lucky. He was standing very close when it went off. He's a street-cleaner.'

'A dangerous job these days.'

'I don't know where it will all end. And all done in the name of religion, too. Still, we must go on hoping – and praying of course.' He spoke rapidly and there was something strange and distant in his manner. It was not until Laura brought the tray with the bottle and glasses back into the room and I observed the glance she shot at him that I recognized the cause of his flurried and peculiar manner. I remembered my mother looking out of the window of the bus at the Rector of Thackness, who was walking unsteadily up the long, bleak, wind-racked main street of the village. She had turned to my father and said, 'Eh, dear me. The parson's drunk again,' and my father, no church-goer, sitting there with his big hard hands folded in his lap, had replied stoutly, 'So would I be, if I had his job.'

'Will you have some sherry with us, my dear?' Roy Greenwood asked and she said, 'No, thank you. I'm going up to see to the children.'

It was partly because of that scene recalled from my childhood and partly because it is easier to talk to someone else in a mess, that I leaned forward and said, 'Perhaps you can help me, vicar?' At any rate, I thought, I was doing him the kindness of consulting him as a professional, the way you might consult a doctor or a dentist.

'I'll try,' he said, sombrely. 'People, of course, are helped by God and themselves. Not by me. But what is worrying you?'

'Anomie,' I said.

He poured himself another glass of sherry and said, 'Come, come. Jargon won't help us. Is it your wife, your job, your health – '

So I told him my tale candidly, not interpreting but giving dates, details and times. As I went on speaking I began to see him droop. He was used to people trapped by circumstances. Even his own predicament – the job with impossible targets he could not reach, his sad and unsatisfied wife, his drinking – were the products of inertia, bafflement, inability to act. My situation, as I saw, was the fruit of action, however compulsive. His patients wriggled in the grip of fate. I had gone out and found mine. They had never had a chance. I had thrown mine away. In trying to understand, his charity stretched and almost broke. In the end his advice was, more or less, to go back and reconstruct my old life.

'But I can't go back to all that,' I protested.

He could not understand. 'Wait,' he told me. 'Soon you will see things differently. Do nothing until you feel – pray, if you can.'

Courtesies were exchanged. I had sought his professional advice and I told him I was sure his prescription would work.

As I left the house I saw Laura Greenwood standing at the end of the dark passageway, by the kitchen door, watching me. In former days I might easily have opened and shut the front door, crept back along the passageway, passing the cardboard boxes and the cellar door, might have thrust her back into the kitchen and, kicking the door shut behind me . . . But I had learned that these acts, compounded of a squalid desire for felony and a simple, kindly response to human need, did more harm than good in the long run, so I bade her a respectful goodnight and went out into the misty street resolving to go and pray in church instead.

I decided to knock on the Lombards' door as I passed. I was let in by Hugo.

Ah, the difference that money can make, I thought, as I stepped inside the wide hall with its cool, leafy, wallpaper, and well-kept pot plant. At that moment the children dashed past me and upstairs, pursued by the plump and spotty au pair. Jessica appeared in the living-room doorway, holding a pair of glasses and a newspaper, checked the scampering and shouts instantly, looked coldly at the au pair and greeted me with a humorous look directly inherited from a grandmother with an incompetent cook. I ignored this, knowing full well that the Lombard au pairs were hired to be spotty and ineffectual and have a hard time controlling the high-spirited and intelligent Lombard children, just as the children were encouraged to be high-spirited and intelligent with the au pairs. This procedure made Jessica seem even more clear-complexioned and effectual and gained her a certain amount of domestic help without interfering with her hegemony over husband and children.

The perfection of the long living-room can barely be described. It was clean and practical, as was necessary for a large family, but quite opulent and adorned, in two embrasures, with a pair of eighteenth-century paintings, portraits, no doubt, of ancestors. The Galt toys on the carpet might have been put there by a photographer from a Sunday colour supplement to add just the right touch of homely disorder and if the casserole on the table was too small to contain food for a large family, well, at least the design was attractive. Even the dinner-plates looked smaller than the normal kind, I thought suddenly, feeling the primitive fear of starvation.

The cairns yapped outside in the garden.

'I'll leave them outside so that we can talk in peace,' Jessica said, pouring me coffee. 'How are you, Joe?'

I knew I was better, or they would never have let me in. Had Hugo sensed malaise about me, I would have delivered my message from the step and departed.

Drinking my coffee I noticed Hugo Lombard's face, drawn all over with fine lines like an engraving on copper. Jessica was tight with controlled anger.

'I'm improving,' I told her. 'I threw all my pills down the lavatory this morning.'

'Are you sure that's wise?' she said. 'I'd be dead without the occasional sleeping-pill, myself.'

'They are like any pain-killer,' I said. 'They take away the pain but leave you, at best, muzzy and confused. They're only what the doctor gives you to shut you up when you keep crying in the surgery. They hide the symptoms and the disease as well. Then they hide the cure, if it comes.'

'An anaesthetic can be useful, though, at times,' said Hugo.

Jessica disliked this remark. Perhaps she felt that men should not confess to a need for opiates. The phone rang and Hugo went to answer it. As I finished my coffee I heard him in the next room saying, 'Yes,' 'No' and 'I see,' and sensed Jessica's attention in that direction.

'Thank you for the coffee. I really only came to say that I'd like to come to the party.'

'Oh good,' said Jessica. 'I'm glad you won't already have left for Stonebridge.'

'Are you all right?' I said.

She stared at me, with a hint of anger and said, 'Yes. Of course. Why not?'

I left her feeling angry with me because, as usual, I must have penetrated, with the tip of one finger, that impermeable force-field, that aura of all-rightness, which she never lost, holding it around herself and her world to ward off germs, hysterics and failure. But as I turned and waved at her she looked lonely, standing there in her lighted hallway, backed by the green and white jardiniere against the wall behind her.

I walked a mile through the misty streets, feeling like Jack the Ripper as I heard my own heels hitting the pavement. The church, standing there in the fog surrounded by dripping evergreens, was of course, locked. I had tried to follow the vicar's prescription too literally.

So I went home and ate pilchards on toast in front of the television and then, almost without thinking about it, sat down and typed out my resignation from the Department. I knew that I did not want to go back and more important, that if I did my career was blighted. I would probably never get promoted again, or get interesting work to do. I might sit at the same desk, bored to tears, for the next twenty-five years, the outcast of the islands, the man they never discussed in the mess. I came back from the pillarbox and nudged my depression back into place. Having sacked myself from my job I did not want to contemplate what I would do next, think how Naomi would take the news or, perhaps worse, try to work out how responsible I was for my own present state of affairs. Was it suicide or murder? Had I fallen or was I pushed? I found three old pills in a medicine bottle, lit the fire, washed the pills down in whisky, went into a daze and passed out staring into the garden.

While I slept whole cars, buildings and people exploded into the grey dawn, coming down in fragments. I woke, hearing the detonations, and slept again, dreaming of sirens, ambulances and police-cars, hearing, improbably, a woman sobbing outside my window.

'Delicious buns,' said Katie, biting one with her even-spaced and strong teeth. 'A delicious tea. Crumpets. I'll do the same for you, Joe. I'll make soda bread. We can have afternoon orgies.' From the carpet by the fire came the steady drone of Ajax, who, with a chocolate biscuit in each hand, was sharing a battle with his friend, Action Man, a doll dressed in Nazi uniform.

'What's his name?' I had asked him.

'Hitler,' Ajax had replied confidently.

'Come on Hitler, let's get them,' I heard him say to his trusty *oberleutnant*.

'It's funny – you having had him,' I said to Katie.

'I suppose he expresses my dark side,' she told me.

I looked at her as she stood in the hall, wearing her old fox-coloured fur coat and a long brown dress. Her hair fluffed out above the collar, her big blue eyes were mild and her cheeks rosy.

'Have you got a dark side?' I asked her.

'Surely we all have,' she said vaguely. Downstairs in the kitchen the kettle began to whistle.

We carried the tea, plates of iced buns and chocolate biscuits upstairs. We toasted crumpets in front of the fire as the early night of winter came down. Philip sprawled, ears outspread, next to Ajax and gazed worshippingly at the flames.

I poured her another cup of tea and said, 'And how are the visions?' And she said, 'Like a thread running through the days.'

'Golden thread?' I suggested.

'No. It isn't like that, Joe. It's only clarity, a heightening of vision. It doesn't conflict with the rest of life. Perhaps it makes it more joyful, but it isn't the difference between waking and dreaming. Father McGrath talks to me – thinking I'm stupid as well as mad – and one of his theories seems to be that the visions are a function of an unused imagination – that is, when he's not hinting about sex – and that I use the – they aren't really visions, you know – as a kind of waking dream to get me through the drabness of the days. But you see, I don't see my life as that awful. Of course I've known what it's like to be so bored or miserable that life seemed not worth living. But although it isn't perfect bliss, my life is not so bad. What have I got to complain of, after all? I have a good husband and three fine children, enough money – why should I feel so bad that I need a dream to help me through? No, no. It's not a dream at all, that's the point. Anyway, I think he's given me up. He sees that its harmless and he has to accept, if only intellectually, that I may be doing what I say I'm doing.'

'And what's that?'

'Communing with God,' she said. 'It's like a current flowing between us. Of course,' she said, and hesitated. 'Of course – the danger is that I might break through. That would be alarming.'

'Break through?' I said.

'Well that,' she said quite matter-of-factly, 'would, say, be like putting your hand on an exposed wire. The voltage would be too great. Say, at some point I saw God. It would be the greatest of joys, but would I, after that, be able to go on as I am? I doubt it. And the worst of it is, if I go on, that moment will come – '

She stared at the fire. Ajax's mumble continued. 'That's it, men. Come over here. Start shooting.' A dog barked in the dark gardens outside.

I could not imagine what she was talking about. In the end I said, 'It's difficult for me – because I don't believe in God and I've never had any religious experiences at all.'

'I know,' she said earnestly. 'But I don't mind talking about it to you – because at least you don't invent theories about it. Ah – what a miracle it is, though, and how lucky I am – but of course Father McGrath felt it his duty to talk to Julian and that was that. So now the Thought Police are ransacking the cupboards and ripping up the carpet, prising up the floorboards of my mind. Not that they'll find anything, mind, for there's nothing there, nothing there at all.' And she smiled at me as I groaned inwardly, imagining the bony fingers of Julian Mulvaney poking into the convoluted folds of his wife's brain, searching for the cyst which had turned his wife into a religious maniac, ready to pluck it out like a pea from a pod and bottle it in formaldehyde to keep on his study mantelpiece.

'I expect I'm boring you,' she said. 'Well, Polly says – '

And, at that moment, came a voice from the garden. 'Kate – Kate, are you there?'

'Oh, that's strange. There she is,' said Mrs Mulvaney. 'I wonder what she wants.' She put down her cup on the small table by the fire and went over to the window.

'Kate,' the woman shouted. 'I'm sorry to disturb you. The banks are shut and I need ten pounds.'

'Would you mind if she came up?' said Katie. I shook my head.

'Come up, Polly,' Katie cried down. 'I have it in my bag.'

Soon there was a clumping tread on the stairs, Philip came cringing to me and in came Polly Kops in a torn Afghan coat with a torn-looking Afghan dog, which Ajax jumped on.

'I'm really sorry,' said Polly. 'Believe it or not, but Alexander and Clancy are coming round to see the children and won't be put off. I haven't any drink, food or cigarettes in the house and neither of them seem to have any money, so I'm desperate.'

She was a tall, thin woman with a long face, rather lined. Her dry red hair, half caught in the ragged fur on the collar of her coat, fell about in tired abandon. She was like the woman who comes to the door of the hill-farm when she hears a car arrive and stands there, expectant, curious, unworldly in her cotton dress and wellingtons.

Katie said, opening her bag, 'I have fifteen, if you want it.'

'That would be safer. I'll pay you back tomorrow,' Polly said, taking the money. Ajax and the big dog were rolling on the floor.

'Cup of tea?' I said.

'I'd love one,' Polly said, sitting down. 'I won't stay. I've left the children alone and Tracy's baby is asleep, but she won't be for long. I'll drink out of your cup, Kate, that's OK. No – the girl I had in to look after the children left because of the baby. Tracy's gone off to a gig in Bolton with Toddy. Then this TV producer came to lunch and got drunk and I'd just cleared him out when Alexander rang – from Paris, of course – wanting to see the girls and Clancy said he had to come and see Max and Margaret because he was just off to the States. How could I refuse? They've been haunting me recently. I can't understand all this sudden passion for paternity.'

'Times have changed,' said Kate. 'They're being forced to wonder if, somehow, all that should have happened to you. It probably seemed natural enough at the time but these days – '

'Ah,' said Polly stoutly. 'I brought it all on myself, I maintain. But it's true they both look sad and lonely these days. Still give them a screaming baby and a tired woman standing at the sink and see how long their compunction would last.'

'It's the system,' I said, mournfully.

'I suppose so,' Polly said to me, trying to hold back what I thought at first was pain, until she suddenly burst into laughter. And Katie leaned back in her chair and laughed as well. At me. When women laugh in that way it is frightening. It is the dear old lady whose wrinkled face changes from bewildered benevolence to malice as she produces the carving-knife from behind her back. These alien creatures who have swelled, travailed, got up at night to feed the baby, nursed us in illness, nodded agreement, smiled their thanks and indulged us with their attention, spoiled and pampered us as if we were so many children ourselves, cannot, suddenly, contain their mirth at our antics any longer. Suddenly they are laughing at us and at themselves. But we cannot be sure what the joke is. And in this way Polly and Katie laughed and laughed, half stopping and then, like schoolgirls, reading each other's glances, bursting out again.

'Oh dear, oh dear,' Polly gasped at last, wiping her eyes. 'That's done me good. I almost feel I can face Alexander and Clancy now. Oh – what a life – I feel quite breathless. Oh, I'm sorry, Joe. I wasn't really laughing at you. But it's funny really, when you come to think of it. The system, I mean. And I must go. Thanks for the money, Katie. Thank you for the tea Joe – I'm sorry if I've been rude. Come on, Hester.'

And off she went, followed by the tall, loping dog, giving, as I imagine she always would, the impression that you might never see her again, that the stringy old hawk had left your glove for good and soared away into the blue sky.

Katie, still grinning, looked at me and said, 'Don't misjudge her – she's a good friend of mine.'

'I'm glad,' I said, though when I came to think of it I would not have liked raunchy Poll to be a good friend of my own wife's, of Naomi's.

'At least she's broadminded about my visions. She's been in the drug culture so long.'

Oh, God, I thought, this is all rubbish. God, drugs, whatever next? Was it all another version of the servant-girl's dreams of lords and pirate captains, tents in the desert and horses galloping over the mountains? Or was it the alternative to Naomi's pragmatism, self-protection and clinging to cash and the conventions?

And in the meanwhile Ajax, excited by his fight with Polly's dog, Hester, fell on Philip, who snapped at him. Ajax burst into tears and Kate took the boy away, bawling and clutching a last chocolate biscuit, leaving behind the empty room, fire burning low, the scattered tea-table and the crumbs on the floor.

Recovered I might have been; all this had still been too much for me and I still fell asleep.

That night, walking Philip round the dark garden in the cold air I saw the Lombard children making their Christmas cards round the big table in their living-room. These children, so Jessica had told me, carried the genes of the wicked lairds of

Cromarty and Ness, thieves, murderers and rebels to a man, who had decorated gibbet and dungeon generation after generation. And as I contemplated this, from the basement came the thrum of black music and the cries of the brown-skinned children whose blue-black ancestors had been shipped in their tens of thousands from Africa to the West Indies by the ancestors of Hugo Lombard, who, I had been told, came of an old and respected West Country mercantile family. On arrival, no doubt they had been employed in an agricultural capacity by descendants of the lairds of Cromarty and Ness, who had, leaving the Highlands, been granted lands in the West Indies by their monarch in the eighteenth century.

While in the Mulvaney home the Mulvaney children, descended on Julian's side, he maintained, from impoverished Irish aristocrats, and on Katie's, as Julian also maintained, from the starving, roofless, tubercular tenantry, were probably running about, wrapping up little presents in crumpled tissue paper.

Now was the time, I thought, when we all looked down at our roots, and other people's, contemplating the grim Scottish pair, Jessica Lombard's parents, sitting in their still, chilly house on the outskirts of Edinburgh, where solid, ancient furniture stood against the walls, on which were hung bad oil-paintings of ancestors in kilts and water-colours by spinster aunts. And on down to the doucer air of the West Country where Hugo's parents were having tots and nightcaps in front of the television, and the Spanish couple who looked after them sat in the big, warm modern kitchen beyond, she embroidering and he reading the paper. And on to Dublin, where Katie Mulvaney's mother took a taxi back through the rainy streets after Mass and went through the crumbling portals of the crumbling house, scanning the world for her seven children, making herself a strong cup of tea and settling down in front of a banked-up fire with the taste of the host washed from her mouth, to read the *Universe*. Up in Stonebridge the Trents organized their immaculate, irreproachable festivities – the handsome, well-wrapped presents, the turkey from the farmer down the road, the banks of wines and whiskies, the Scottish grouse, the nuts from Brazil and Spain, the donation to Oxfam, last year's mature Christmas pudding, the gift of money to Naomi's old nanny, the tree cut and hauled in as usual by the aged gardener

– very different, indeed, I reflected from the frozen turkey, mince-pies and half-bottle of rum which was now ready for the small Coverdale Christmas table, up in the cold hill-farm. Christmas at the Trents would demonstrate, not by design of course, for me, the outlander, loutish fellow from the North, what life could be like, should be like and, for friends and connections of the Trents, always would be like. It lay before me, a mouse-trap baited with Stilton, and I shuddered at the thought of it. Up there, they had my children chained to the Christmas tree up to their necks in heaps of presents. One more gaily wrapped badminton set, one extra game of Monopoly, one more pair of football boots and a doll, and the little hostages would disappear under the heaps of bulging wrapping paper, stifled and suffocated. And it would be my fault. I hoped I could find myself believing in the tree, the fire and the silver on the dinner-table. I hoped that seeing my children would convince me. I hoped I would fall in love with my wife again. I hoped, in short, that some magic might be worked on me, knowing this to be deplorable and unmanly. I was behaving like a woman – not deciding what I wanted and going to get it, but waiting for that magic moment, across a crowded room, when Mr Right is spotted and the rest of life decided. But for twenty years now I had carved out my own life, and when I saw what I had made, I disliked it. Right or wrong, I could decide nothing. I no longer knew what I wanted.

So I walked through the night, catching sight of Philip bounding through the darkness, disappearing and reappearing again.

Then Ajax Mulvaney, wearing wellingtons and pyjamas, came dawdling through the tree-trunks like one of the seven dwarfs mumbling something about finding Father Christmas. I took his hand and began to lead him home explaining that Father Christmas, like the Holy Spirit, could not be seen by little boys and girls. I met Siobhan, flying down the path in her nightdress. She grabbed his hand and hauled him back to his own gate.

Up in Polly Kops' large, lighted window the thin African in tribal robes moved to and fro gesticulating. The windows of the Greenwoods' house were all blacked out. I walked through the trees, home, as an ambulance or a police-car raced along, howling.

Jessica continued to load, with swift, sure movements, filled *vol-au-vents* on to the large plates on the tray on the kitchen counter. But her face was crumpled with disappointment, like a child's. 'Oh yes. We can keep going – but from now on it will be my money,' had been her last remark, delivered in a challenging tone. She had slightly emphasized the last two words, and that was when her face had started to go.

'How long?' I asked and, being an efficient person, picked up the tray and made ready to take it out to the guests. 'How long will the crisis last?'

'From three to seven years,' she said despondently. 'That is,' she added sharply, 'if things stay as bad as they are and don't collapse utterly.'

I think she still disliked me and always had, but she knew I was the right person to talk to. I would not be shocked, or over-sympathetic about her troubles. I would not be shocked by her. Meanwhile from the living-room came the sound of restrained music, a bit of *Sergeant Pepper*, and the muted rhubarb-rhubarb sound of the guests talking. We were alone under the strip-lighting in the kitchen. On the counter was a neat rubble of celery tops, cheese rinds and garlic skins. Snacks heated in the oven. A few glasses drained on the steel draining-board. Jessica, in a black, beaded dress stood with her hands on the counter, looking at the formica.

'Well – can you take those in, Joe, and come back for the sausages? Might as well do it properly this time. There won't be any more parties.'

I left her, to feed the guests, whom she obviously now saw as eating her seed-corn, wasting her substance like so many profligates invited in by the prodigal son.

In the long room a well-heeled crowd – mainly, I thought, business friends, old school-friends and the like – stood about under subdued lighting, holding glasses and talking. Beth Lombard, in a long dress, came up to me, took a morsel from the tray with a speedy and practised hand and popped it into her mouth. 'I'll circulate these,' she said smoothly, with a vulture's look in her eyes. 'I'm the only one allowed to stay up,' she said confidentially. 'I've been eating bits and pieces all day long.'

'Good for you,' I said, relieved that her skimpy frame had got, for once, the filling it needed. She took the tray and went, looking like a peg dolly, through the crowd, offering the contents to the guests and quickly refreshing herself as she went.

'Tom Propert,' said someone nearby, with assurance, 'has always been a complete fool.'

Over in a corner Roy Greenwood was nodding reassuringly at an anxious-looking young woman who was pouring words at him. Intermittently he put his glass to his lips and nodded at her again. I waved at him and went back to the kitchen.

'Sausages ready?' I asked Jessica.

'Here you are,' she said despondently.

'Beth's taking the other things round.'

'Stuffing herself with food, no doubt,' Jessica remarked. 'Oh well, that's all, except for these. Is the drink holding out?'

'I'll look.'

In the doorway I bumped into Hugo Lombard. He looked drawn and his hair trailed on to his collar, seeming darker and lanker. He had lost weight. His big strong body sagged inside his suit. His eyes flinched past Jessica, straight as a stem in her black, bead dress, as she assembled a few dirty dishes standing on the counter and turned to put them on the draining-board.

He said to me, not pleasantly, 'Helping out in the kitchen, Joe?'

'Jessica wants to know if the drink's holding out,' I explained, as if excusing myself. 'I was just coming in to have a look.'

'I'll do it,' he said. 'Here. Give me those.'

His eye, as I went back into the kitchen, followed me. The mistrust he had always felt for the seedy fellow I had proved to be, had become more open perhaps in order to counter his suspicion that he, through no fault of his own, might be now, or might come to be in future, one of my own down-at-heel, no-hoping, corner-skulking party.

Now Jessica was leaning against the cleaned-off counter, a bottle and a glass in front of her.

'I've poured you a whisky,' she said.

I took it and sat down at the table opposite her. She poured herself a drink.

'I don't want to pry,' I said, 'but what is the real situation?'

'Simply that Hugo, by buying as if there were no depression, has run into so much trouble that unless we can live without taking any income from the firm for some years, it will fold. It might even mean a bankruptcy.'

'And can you do that?'

She hesitated, then said, 'Hugo has no capital to speak of as long as his father is alive. I have an income of slightly over £4,000 a year. But that won't be worth much in three years' time with inflation at its present level. Even now I'm worth less than the average car-worker.'

'£4,000 before tax?' I asked.

'After, actually,' she said.

My first response was surprise at the size of Jessica's income. A capital sum like hers – some £60–80,000, I supposed – indicated that when the lairds of Cromarty came down to the Lowlands from their fastnesses they had started up some very profitable satanic mills and sailed away to create some really lucrative diabolical plantations. After that bit of information I had to conquer the feeling that Jessica's financial problems were not problems at all. But a drop in income is, I told myself, always a disaster, whether it involves moving from the Ritz to the Cumberland Hotel, or from a shed into a haystack. Jessica's predicament might seem ludicrous, or contemptible, to someone on social security, but in turn, their payments would spell untold wealth and freedom from care to half of the people in the world. One side of my mind considered Jessica and Hugo, crying over their swollen bank balances, to be a pair of great big babies. I could, I thought, go broke tomorrow myself, with no such cushion to fall on. I tried to consider the problem seriously, saying, 'It seems to come down to selling the cottage and making real economies all round, or else breaking into the capital.'

She took another drink and said, 'I know. And either way you know where the hardship will strike. It's good-bye capital, or else I bear the brunt of the domestic economies. Who loses their car? I do. Who loses the au pair and the daily? I do. Who tells Beth she can't have new skating-boots? I do. Who sweats out the school summer holidays in London? All right, perhaps I should take it all in good part but the problem still falls more heavily on my shoulders, and frankly I resent it.'

'You're shocked at the moment. You'll get used to it,' I said.

'I can't sleep,' she announced fiercely. Then she finished her drink and said, 'I'd better go in.'

'I'll give you this, Jessica,' I said as we went through the door. 'You're an outstandingly bad loser.' I spoke in perfect sincerity, admiring her toughness if not her generosity. She had plenty of fight in her. She chose, probably deliberately, to take this amiss and said, 'Thanks, Joe. You're a real comfort in trouble.' Nevertheless, it was me she came to.

As we went through the door her face lifted and she cried, 'Monica! I didn't know you'd arrived.'

I went in and talked for a while but Jessica's parties always had too many of the kind of men who laughed on a deep, bass ho-ho-ho and too many women who laughed, in turn, on a high, trilling note and, flexible, compromising and two-faced as I am, I still found that too much to bear.

Roy Greenwood said, 'I do choose to wear my clerical collar, rather than masquerade as a layman, but I find the men won't talk to me. The women do, though.'

I said, 'It's a pity you can't take advantage of your calling.'

He said, 'I often wonder if they may be inviting me to.'

I said, 'I have found that sympathy and sound advice are the seducer's best weapons. That's why women fall in love with their doctors.' He nodded. 'Women need a lot of sympathy,' I said.

'Men are certainly trained to ask for less,' Greenwood said. As we talked he began to seem drunker. It was as if he had been holding his tipsiness in check while he talked to the anxious woman, like a doctor suddenly called out of a pub to attend a traffic accident. In the end I got him to eat something, although at that stage I wondered if it might not make matters worse. We stood over by the buffet, looking around at the guests, overhearing snatches of conversation about plane strikes at Rimini and cases of terminal sunburn, of staggering bits of good fortune – coups on the Stock Exchange and wins on the horses – of adroit avoidance of misfortune – sales made before the shares dropped, the radiator fell out or the roof fell in – of collapses – businesses bankrupted, boys forced to leave public schools and wives having nervous breakdowns. In the end I had to say to Roy, 'Sorry – I think I'll go home and leave you to face out the world.'

'It's my calling, after all,' he told me.

As I walked back I felt that the cessation of Jessica's parties would not rob the world in the same way that the cessation of Louis XIV's, or Sardanapalus's must have done but, I supposed, the loss would be great to Jessica. It is useless to point out to those complaining about a piece of broken Spode or the shortage of restaurant carriages on British trains that their griefs are small compared with the problems of the homeless of Calcutta. It's all according to what you're used to. And Hugo, too, had had his morale as breadwinner and defender of his family broken.

As I opened my front door I reflected that although I had emotionally committed myself to these people, had married into them, in fact, being now an unemployed adulterer separated from wife and family with nothing in the world but an unpaid-for house, £300 in the bank, and, probably, something to come back from the pensions scheme once my resignation was accepted, I was no longer in the club. I need masquerade no more. I could abandon them to their unholy, stylized laughter, their talk, which hinged always on money and what you got for it. I need never again see the air of tired fortitude, masking a real rage, which they assumed in the face of the army of comprehensive school-teachers, strikers, overpaid workers, lower-class holiday-makers and insolent chars and garage-hands, all of whom threatened them so deeply. Yes, I was free of them, I thought, but underlying the thought came the deep, aching sadness which told me that I might, like a defector, have to leave my wife and children behind when I left. Naomi would never come through the wire with me. Or, perhaps, she might.

And . . . 'I had to talk to somebody,' Jessica said, standing on my freezing step at 2 o'clock that night. She was a bit drunk and, obviously had left the house in a hurry, not bothering to put her arms into the sleeves of the fur coat which she clutched round her. But I also saw – for the long-standing womanizer's observation never deserts him, even shivering in an open doorway on an early morning in December – that before leaving the house she had combed her hair and put on fresh scent and make-up. I saw her drifting upstairs to freshen up, unconscious of what her next move was to be, carefully, but with some sense of underlying excitement, repairing herself at the mirror and then, suddenly, admitting the impulse, letting the thought surge; *what about some fresh air, why don't I pop round and have a chat with Joe, I'd like to talk things over with somebody.*

'Well,' I said, 'I was – '

'Oh, I'm awfully sorry, Joe,' she said, speaking perhaps a little fast. 'I know I'm trading on your good-nature but the house is still full of people and I did want to get away. Probably I'm a bit drunk – ' And as she spoke she had come in, like a commercial traveller.

'I'll make some coffee,' I said, starting for the kitchen.

'A glass of whisky would be better,' she said.

'I think some coffee would be better, Jessica,' I said.

'I don't,' she said.

Faced with the saucy *vivandière*, the woman-of-the-world on the Orient Express, and suddenly realizing the implications of the black bead dress, I said, 'Come on, Jessica. If you want to talk, clear your head first,' whereupon she outflanked me and told me, 'I'm sick of being clear-headed. Let's go upstairs and have a drink.' It was not the dashing statement which got me. It was the tears in her eyes.

I did make coffee and took it and the whisky upstairs, where I lit the fire and, knowing full well that I was sitting in my pyjamas pouring whisky for my neighbour's wife at 2 in the morning, said, 'How was the party after I left?'

'Hugo's drunk,' she said, 'and being very silly.' She paused and muttered at the floor. 'He's got no guts.'

'What,' I said, 'do women expect of men?'

'He's acting like a five-year-old,' she said. 'Whining and wanting me to make it right.'

'He'll pull himself together,' I told her. 'Don't forget he's worn out with the strain of trying to make it come right himself. For goodness' sake, Jessica, be patient and start trying to deal with it yourself. It's probably a blessing in disguise.'

'What a stupid thing to say,' she said.

'You've been proud, Jessica,' I told her, 'proud of your children and their achievements, proud of your connections, proud to be Mrs Lombard. Keeping all that pride going must have taken it out of you and you haven't ever been able to be proud of your own things, only things connected with you. Now you can start again – get yourself a job, for example.'

'What job?' she asked me. 'I've no qualifications and no experience. I left the Slade to marry Hugo and had Beth a year later.'

Her bitterness went deeper than a mere resentment of the failed husband and the possible inroads to be made into her capital. She had gambled on marriage and children, expecting a success, and lost. She had done the natural and expected thing for a woman of her time – and probably she had not been a very brilliant, or a very dedicated student – and, so far as she was concerned, the manoeuvre had not paid off.

'You say I've been proud,' she said fiercely. 'Well, let me tell you, pride was all I had. Is there any more whisky?' and she held out her glass.

'Jessica,' I said firmly, 'we both know where all this is – '

And then, sitting on my sofa, she began to cry. I knew a set-up when I saw one and the voice inside my head said, 'Here we go again,' but I am an affectionate and warm-hearted man brought up to respect human emotion and little sisters, so I crossed the carpet to where she sat, bent like a bough and crying her eyes out on my sofa, reflecting that from the moment when you totter independently across the room for the first time and fall into mother's arms, nearly everything that happens to you depends on five paces across a carpet, somewhere. So as if I had not thought anything of the kind, I sat down beside her, put my arms around her and said, 'Never mind.'

'I'm so lonely,' she wept. And it was true. The conventions of her life and her own pride had made her lonely.

You cannot let people cry alone, so I said, 'Never mind. I'm here.'

'Oh – Joe,' she said leaning against me and turning up a tear-stained face. I kissed her gently, as you might a child, and she was in my arms in a second, as, of course, she had always planned to be.

Anyone would say I should have been firmer. Naturally I should have prevented it. But I did not.

She lay on my bed, with her arms wrapped close about me, saying, 'If only it could have been like this before.'

'Hasn't it been?' I asked.

'Hardly ever,' she replied.

No man of decent feeling will ever challenge this statement from a woman by asking for chapter and verse, and good, hard evidence about the sexual failings of his predecessor. I suspect this conspiracy of silence is generally encouraged by men. If the actress told all, what bishop could meet the eye of another in the Athenaeum? Nevertheless, I seldom take these whole-hearted repudiations of previous lovers – or more usually, husbands – to be literally true. The failings, I believe are in the hearts, lives, minds of the men, or the women, or both. The faults are not always genital, but it is often simpler to believe that they are. 'We have no sex-life,' is an easier statement to make than 'He hates me, I bore him, he traps me, we dislike each other.'

I turned my head to look at Jessica, lovely, soft, pliant, and at that moment realized what a cleverer man might have thought of earlier. She had me, her best friend's husband, lined up as Hugo's successor. I went rigid and forced myself to relax. I was to be her next husband. I now suspected the slow growth of that idea, through all those months of hatred and contempt, through all those sympathetic conversations with the exiled Naomi, which, after all, must have produced much valuable information about my advantages and disadvantages, and so on and on until, quite without realizing it, Jessica had struck. Why should she not have? I was a handsome and well set-up man, and when in my right mind I was a good earner and fond of children. I was even fond of hers. What a convenient, practical and eminently respectable solution. All she had needed to know was that I suited her in bed – then she could fall in love with me. Jessica's unconscious had planned the matter meticulously. It had to be now, before I went to Stonebridge and was reconciled with Naomi. What tactics – what a betrayal. There she was, a desperate woman, a trapped woman, a woman who, through her very nature, wanted and could not help wanting the best, who had been deprived of it and could not reconcile herself to the loss. There she was, a woman whose first instinct was to plan and work for what she wanted, who knew her own worth, and mine, that of her best friend's estranged husband, and had decided that this was the deal she wanted to strike. And there I lay there with her head on my shoulder, feeling the greatest affection for her, and regretting that I would not be able to sign the contract. As a bargain, it was a good one, but I wanted no more bargains. I was resolved to conduct my life in accordance with my feelings and not my calculations. And if feeling refused to come, then I would do nothing. Here, I felt, just like the emotional Lutheran I was, I would stand. I could go no further. Meanwhile we went on talking.

'I hate him now,' she said of Hugo. 'I wish he'd die. He only thinks about himself.'

'Everybody does,' I said.

'You don't,' she told me fiercely. 'I don't know how I can get through another Christmas.'

Hugo, it seemed was not interested in anything – not his work, nor his wife, nor his children. He collected figurines which Jessica, she claimed, wished to smash. I had seen Hugo's collection once. He kept it in a locked boxroom. Inside, in poor light from a small window which looked out on to the street, against plain, slightly discoloured white walls, his collection lay on shelves along three sides of the room. There were Meissen, and Chinese figurines, Roman and Etruscan pottery figures. I, who know nothing about such things, found some of them very beautiful and was touched by Hugo's shyness and evident love for them. It was plain, too, that his interest in them was entirely uncommercial. He stood there, well over six feet and a bit overweight, blond, large and far from graceful, looking at, but not touching, the little figures which he had been collecting from boyhood. Perhaps it was not startling that he and Jessica were ill-matched. Hugo, said Jessica, was bored, passive, uncommunicative, unloving and ungenerous. Hugo had died, said Jessica, a year after they got married. She had been living with a stone for twelve years. He did not know her, did not recognize her. How could she describe living intimately with a stranger? How could she say what she felt when Hugo locked himself, as she described it, into the room with the figurines, as if he were shutting himself in with a prostitute? I sympathized quite genuinely, but now it was time to tell the truth.

'All you find in me,' I told her, 'is just a little sympathy and the want of hypocrisy. I am not a better man than Hugo. I am probably a worse one. I am probably much more selfish. You are lonely, Jessica, and you think no one loves you – although of course Hugo does. He is just too afraid to express it. The trouble is that like most women you have been trained to put too much reliance on the emotions and on some kind of ideal condition of life which probably you can't have, and which if you got it, you'd hate. But would that quiet, loving life with a reliable husband and affectionate children – the life you see Hugo as having deprived you of – really satisfy you? No, of course it wouldn't. It's the life you've been told ought to satisfy you but in reality, if you had it, you'd still want talented and successful children, still want more prestige and a different husband. What you should want, Jessica, is something of your own. You're not, and never have been, a woman who should spend her life looking into her own back yard expecting that if she concentrates hard enough it will turn into a forest. Nor should you be egging other people on to achieve, when all they probably want is to be left alone. You've frightened Hugo to the point where he daren't come near you. Fancy coming home and finding Henry Ford in an apron basting the joint and arranging the flowers. You should be out in the world. The best thing you could do is to go into Lombards now as a help-meet, and learn the business. Within five years you'd probably be running the place.'

'I'm a woman, Joe,' she cried, and clung to me.

'Is anyone going to deny it? Using your talents – your energy, your clear-headedness, your organizing ability – that can't alter your sex.'

Perhaps it was blackguardly to tell a loving woman who was offering me her life to go into the City and become a tycoon, particularly as it implied, none too subtly, a rejection of her as a partner. Nor was my description of her virtues very lover-like.

'I want to be happy,' she told me and I kissed her and said, 'Of course you will be.'

At dawn we had breakfast in bed. Putting on her tights Jessica turned to me and said, 'What did you mean about Hugo being afraid of me?'

'You're too good for him,' I said. 'It wasn't that he got tired of you. It was just that he noticed you had a better head than he had. It's frightening when you observe, suddenly, that the woman with your baby at her breast is likely to be able to do your job better than you. It makes you feel useless. If you're no gentleman you hit her and if you are a gentleman you have to find another way of cutting her out, protecting yourself, hurting her. Hugo, being a perfect gent, withdrew himself and pretended you didn't exist.'

Jessica was not listening. I got up, and went into the living-room to fetch her coat. She looked dazed. I had done her a cruelty in depriving her of a wonderful affair, in carrying on, in my reasonable way, telling her truths she was not ready to hear. Having started, I should have allowed her the dream which would, one way and another, have enabled her to sail through, on a tide she would have felt she could not resist, to a new life which would probably have been much like the one I was recommending.

She bent down, painfully, and picked up her coat.

'When shall I see you again?' she asked.

'Soon,' I said. 'Of course. Whenever you want to.'

And, as she traipsed off down the path in the rain, to cook the children's breakfasts, drive Beth to a dancing lesson and make whatever explanations she was going to contrive I went, ashamed and foolish, back to bed. I should not have done it, I thought. And now Jessica, the lovely and passionate Jessica, the planner, searcher for definitions and commitment, was going to declare that she loved me and wanted to marry me. And I was afraid I might start to want what she wanted. And I was due in Stonebridge soon. I had to get out of bed.

Down in the hall the pile of Christmas cards addressed to that amiable couple, Mr and Mrs J. E. Coverdale, was still growing on the hall table – the Suttons, the Nimmos, the MacDonalds, the Pattens and even the Lombards, I noticed, sent us Christmas greetings from themselves and their children. As Philip and I stood in the hall, I opening the cards, and he wagging his feathery tail wildly, thinking we might be going out, I saw how my world had somehow been taken over by couples, had become filled, like a surrealist landscape, with home freezers, Cortinas and Rovers, Mothercare pushchairs, and cocktail shakers. I could not fathom my rage at this thought. Why did I hate and fear the Suttons, the Nimmos, the MacDonalds and the Pattens, nice people all, maintaining their cars, their hedges, their health and their bank balances in good order? Perhaps because I knew the power of divorce, drink, nationalization, and trades unions to be so strong, because I did not know how ruthless these people might become in order to protect themselves from such anarchies. And I was now part of the anarchy – I had left their world, marked *Private* at every turn – private road, private school, private medicine, private mooring, private fishing and private parking.

Among the cards there was a letter from Crosby at the Ministry, asking me to reconsider my resignation. He would like, he said, to discuss the matter with me. And he wished me a Happy Christmas.

I had not even managed to resign. I still had a good job and, waiting for me in the country, my pretty, capable wife and two handsome children. Nothing, I told myself, in spite of everything, had happened.

I walked into the room beside the hall where I kept my books and began to unpack the cardboard boxes in which I had brought back the books I had bought at a sale six months before. I recorded them, put them on the shelves, and stood looking around.

There were 8,000 books on the shelves. The room was the only one which had not been done out with smart wallpaper and freshly upholstered furniture. I stared at the string and bits of packaging on the dull, buff carpet and, suddenly there was another crash, another vibration, as a bomb went off, miles away, to pay for the death by starvation of Patrick Flynn in his hospital bed in prison.

Further down Knightsbridge the bomb squad worked while I walked through the empty hall of Harrods and pulled from a decorated plastic Christmas tree a green and gold shirt, with a matching turban, in what I thought was my mother-in-law's size, wrote my cheque on the empty counter, and left it on the till.

I walked through Hyde Park, already gloomy and dank with December chill, eating a hamburger and throwing bits to the racing dog. I stopped and broke pieces off to feed the greedy geese which Philip alternately attacked and fled from. I heard a child call out behind me and was suddenly happy, believing that my children were with me there, as they had been so often before. And so I turned, seeing, of course, another blond boy, not Paul, in a blue anorak, being pulled from the statue of Peter Pan by another cross mother, not Naomi. So I turned back to the geese and ducks padding round me, with the sparrows hopping among them like tugs among liners. The boy in the anorak was led away. The bread was all gone, the birds had retreated. Philip by leaping up all over my coat, was urging me to go home. The bare branches of the trees seemed burdened with the weight of cold, heavy air. And I knew, too,

I had to go home and get ready for Stonebridge. And ring Jessica.

I had started to take the path back when a short young man, in an old but stout tweed overcoat and heavy round-toed shoes, came towards me. He said, 'Could you please direct me to Notting Hill Gate?' He spoke very clearly, with a slight Irish accent.

'This way,' I said, pointing in the direction I was going. 'Or if you like I'll come with you. I'm going that way myself.'

'Thank you,' he said, and we fell in beside each other. Neither of us spoke as we walked beside the pond and on to the water gardens, where the Italianate white marble statues and fountains stood out strangely in the misty air. There was an uninterrupted roar of traffic from the Bayswater Road.

'It's very beautiful,' he said, staring at the garden with his large blue eyes.

'Like a piece of another world, put down here, in the park,' I said. 'We go up here.' On the edge of one of the fountains two sparrows fought in the spray.

We walked up to the gate which led us out into the Bayswater Road. I turned and caught sight of Philip, trotting behind, uncharacteristically subdued, miming the behaviour of a good dog.

He said, 'Is that your dog?'

'Yes,' I said. 'His name is Philip.'

'Nice dog,' he said, with the same air of a despondent boy he had shown when he praised the fountains, as though fountains and dogs were things forbidden to him. Yet with all that he was young, healthy, and well-knit. His complexion was fresh and ruddy and his longish light-brown hair, which seemed to conflict with his down-at-heel look, had been well cut and combed. And he walked with a light step. There was no hint of a labourer's shamble, of the gait of men who have grown up hard-worked, badly nourished and used to heavy loads from childhood.

We passed the playground, where, through the mist, swings went to and fro and the cries of children could be heard. I said, 'Here we are. What do you want – the tube station?'

'No – no thank you,' he said. 'I can find my way from here.'

'Good-bye then.'

'Thank you,' he said.

I crossed the road with the dog, relieved not to be with the boy any more. I told myself that if I did not lead such a lonely and unoccupied life a chance encounter with a stranger would not disturb me so much. Then I looked sideways, across the street, and there he walked on the opposite pavement, slowly under the trees which overhung the road. Then I turned my attention away for the exuberant dog had cannoned into an old lady and her wheeled shopper. I put him on the lead.

'Joe,' she said with that profound, welcoming pleasure which, to my shame, I knew to be typical. 'How nice.' Behind her I could hear children playing.

'Are you very tired?' I asked.

'No. Not at all. Hugo's at work. May I pop over for a little while?'

So I put the kettle on. She arrived, trembling, bruised under the eyes and smiled at me like a girl smiling at her father. That open joy and defencelessness of course is one of the real things women out in the world cover up for their own protection.

We had tea and biscuits, in the kitchen. 'Oh, Joe,' she said, looking at me. 'Oh, Joe. I am happy.'

Being an educated person I chose to let my body betray me and not my tongue. I walked round the table and kissed her. She said, 'I must go at 5 o'clock.'

'You're a right bastard, aren't you, Joe Coverdale?' said the voice in my head as we went upstairs to the bedroom. He was developing a strong Yorkshire accent. Now he sounded like my father, when justly angry with me. For that reason I ignored him.

As I lay cuddled up with Jessica on that murky December afternoon, with curls of mist coming out of the darkness through the window-frames, I could so clearly see, behind my eyeballs, the figure of the young man I met in the park, walking in the rain up a scrubby field covered with rocks. He had a dog at his heels. I watched him – it was like a film – to see what he would do. Then he turned and shook his fist at someone lower down the slope. I heard Jessica's voice.

'Katie told me Julian said you'd resigned from the Department – '

'I did,' I said, 'but they want me to reconsider.' (Shake your fist if you like lad, I told the figure in my dream. You'll know better when you're older.)

'Will you?' (He had gone now. Then the field went, too.)

I said. 'I don't enjoy the job any more and they'll never promote me again. I'll just sit there mouldering in the same job until I'm old enough to draw my pension. I don't think they realize that exactly themselves.'

She was silent for a while. 'What will you do then?'

'I don't know,' I said. 'I'm able – I can do anything. But I don't fancy anything at the moment.'

It was a disappointing answer from Jessica's point of view but better than my first considered answer – that I was thinking of becoming a mercenary soldier. Oddly enough, in spite of my cowardice, the idea often appealed to me. Nevertheless I knew that Jessica, like Naomi, like nearly all of them, while liking me for my kindness, nevertheless needed a man of steel, a strong man in a crisis, a man who would always know what to do next. I said to her, frankly, 'I've been in a bad way Jessica. And I don't know if I should, or want to, go back to Naomi and the children. If I do, I need this large expensive house and a good job to pay for it. If I don't I'm at liberty to do what I like with my life, just as long as I give money to Naomi. But after all, she has her own income, rich parents and a wealthy second husband in mind, so I don't think I'll need to give her a fortune.'

'You really haven't made up your mind?'

'No,' I said, feeling a fool. 'It all depends on what happens at Christmas.'

'I must go,' she said. 'Hugo's coming back early to help put up the Christmas decorations.'

She got out of bed and I, always the gentleman, rose to dress with her.

'I feel as if I'm on a tightrope,' she said as I did up the back of her dress.

'We all are,' I said and in the doorway, 'Good-bye, love, I'll see you soon.'

I watched her going down the path so sad, so sweet, so loving and, ultimately, so threatening. My wistful mood was quickly interrupted by Patrick Mulvaney, shambling past my garden gate with a packet of tea in his hand.

'You never came round to tea today,' he remarked gloomily

in the demotic accent of the London schoolchild. 'We were expecting you. Stop it, Ajax,' he said and I saw that Ajax, earlier concealed by my hedge, had turned up and, bent on coming in, had started wrestling with the catch on my gate. Suddenly he was kneeling on the pavement, trying to get his head through the bars.

The warning came just too late. The lad was stuck. As I ran down the path he, with his head trapped between the bars of the gate and his knees on the pavement outside, set up a great howl. Patrick took hold of his shoulders and tried to tug him out.

'Leave him, Patrick,' I cried, pushing a hole in the hedge and climbing my low garden wall. I upended Ajax and, holding him by the waist and shoulders, gave a cruel heave and pulled his head back through the bars. As I put him on his feet again and bent to examine his ears for damage he realized what had happened and began to howl with pain and fright.

'All over now, Ajax,' I said. 'No harm done.'

'Serves you right, Ajax,' said Patrick.

'There, there, Ajax,' I said. 'You're out, now.'

Patrick looked at me appreciatively and said, 'Very neat. I'd better get him home now. Shut up, Ajax. It's all your own fault. You're lucky we didn't have to call the fire brigade to get you out.'

Ajax stopped crying and looked at the railings.

'And it's very *painful* when they come and get you out.' Patrick said speedily. 'Don't want him going and doing it again, do we?' he said to me. 'Well, we'd better be off.'

He took Ajax by the hand and began to lead him away. Then he turned and said, 'Was that Mrs Lombard I saw going out of your house?'

'That's right,' I said.

'Cor,' he said in the style of workmen on building sites when they see a pretty girl go by. He grinned, winked and gave a leer, unsuitable on the face of a nine-year-old.

'What – ' I began threateningly, advancing on him.

'Better take Ajax home, I suppose,' he remarked and, towing his brother, walked on. Finally he turned and said reassuringly, throught the mist, 'Not a word, mate. You're all right with me.'

'Go home, Patrick, you filthy boy,' I cried. All I got back was a disgusting laugh.

I thought, as I went up the steps, that you had to hand it to the Mulvaney children. Even with pettifogging, jealous Julian for a father and Katie, their mother, seemingly always in a trance, they managed somehow to maintain their cheerful attitude about the small catastrophes of life – to which they so often contributed – and the disorders and randomness of events, in a way which could only inspire confidence in the human spirit.

My reconciled attitude drained away, however, when I found that, while I had been getting Ajax out from between the bars, my front door had shut behind me. I was locked out. So I went to Elmira's house to see if I could get the spare door-key I always left there.

But the tall figure coming at me bizarrely on platform heels through the mist was Elmira. She stopped on the pavement, looked at me closely and said, 'Joe! Thank God. I was on my way round to see if you had my spare door – oh, I see. Well, let's go round to Jessica's and ask her to let us through into the garden. One of us can get on to my balcony and push up the sitting-room window. It's not locked.'

'Let's go through the Treadgolds,' I said. 'It's closer.'

'No it's not.'

'Well, it is,' I said.

'Oh well, let's go through Polly Kops'. At least I know she's in.'

We were let into the hall by a tall boy, who took us downstairs to the long kitchen so that we could go out through the back door and then across the square to Elmira's house. We were only too glad to get out after the Hogarthian scene in the kitchen, where the two blonde girls, twins perhaps, were cooking spaghetti on the stove while, round a long table overlooked by paintings and on which stood some typing and a typewriter, an iron and some ironing and an ignored black-and-white cat enjoying the last of a leg of lamb, a tall red-headed man sat with a red-headed toddler on his knee. He was talking earnestly to an elderly crippled lady in a wheelchair, who was knitting a striped sock. Next to her a man was sketching Polly, who sat with her arm consolingly round a woman in tears. The dog, Hester, lay on a collapsing sofa in the corner. As we walked through, unnoticed, the telephone was ringing and the dog suddenly leapt up, galvanized, and chased the cat upstairs, nearly tripping up a girl who was at that very moment coming down with a crying baby in her arms.

I was shocked but Elmira burst out laughing just as we got outside and, as we crossed the garden, said, 'And did you see that black-and-white rabbit in the corner, quietly gnawing through the telephone wires?'

'Oh – it's ridiculous,' I said.

'A visit to Polly's certainly makes anyone else's life look simple and uncomplicated,' she said. 'It'll be a treat only to have to climb through a first-floor window and get home. After five minutes in that place anywhere else feels like a two-week holiday – every day a dress rehearsal for the greatest show on earth, but never a performance, that's Polly's motto.'

'How can anyone get even the simplest thing done in an atmosphere like that?' I asked crossly.

'Who gets anything done?' said Elmira. 'Don't be so morbid, Joe. I suppose you've been sleeping with Jessica Lombard again?'

'Again?' I said.

'Caught you,' she said gleefully. 'Fancy falling for an old one like that. God, Joe. You're pathetic. Can't you control yourself at all?'

'I didn't rape her,' I whined. 'She came round with – '

'Faugh!' exclaimed Elmira. 'Sometimes you really disgust me.' We had reached her garden gate and she regarded me with animosity. 'Well, you'd better get up there and let me in,' she said, just to punish me. So I had to get on to the balcony from the water-butt and climb in through the sitting-room window.

I let her in and she opened a drawer in the kitchen and handed me my key. She poured me a drink and said, 'Come upstairs. I've got to go out at 8.'

So I followed her upstairs like a bad child and, once by the fire, said, 'It was only that Jessica – '

'Don't tell me anything,' she said, tough as Ned Kelly's mother. 'I don't want to know – and you've got the nerve to sneer at Polly.' She paused and then said, with an attempt at being casual, 'I've got my old job back.'

'No?' I said. 'That's magnificent.'

'Royal Ballet,' she said. 'I start rehearsing on Monday. In

Giselle. I've got to start a rung or two down for throwing up my job.'

'What made up your mind?' I asked.

'I was bored,' she said. 'I've spent the best years of my life working hard with some aim in view. The idea of stopping was marvellous but in the end it got tedious. That job's harder to give up than debauchery. I'll get you some tickets. But see here, Joe,' she said, 'I'm not sorry I'm angry with you about Jessica. To start with, at the moment you're no use to her, or anybody at all. You're wandering around in your own desert, doing fuck all, and the least you can do is keep yourself to yourself. Even that wouldn't be so bad,' she said, 'if anybody couldn't tell you were getting better. You haven't got an excuse any more.'

'She wants to marry me,' I said.

'You don't surprise me,' said Elmira. 'But you don't want to marry her, so you can't do her any good. Not that I like Jessica – I don't – but I wouldn't wish you on my worst enemy. You're selfish, and self-regarding and irresponsible and worse than that, you're stupid. At least she's got the sense and guts to make up her mind what she wants and go and get it. It's a shame that with Jessica that always means somebody else has to do what she says, like those poor bloody kids of hers, but it'll serve you right, Joe, if you don't manage to jump out of the way in time. I'll come to the wedding and laugh my head off.'

'I'm going,' I said, getting up and putting down my glass.

'You'd better get up to Stonebridge as soon as possible and get all that sorted out,' was Elmira's parting remark.

It was all true, I thought, as I moved back across the garden, feeling like a dead man animated by some scientist, kept going by its appetites, by a cunningly revived system of flesh, bone, nerve and muscle. I felt another descent into the grey, sensationless, tasteless, odourless pit of depression, where all I would feel was grit on my skin and grit in my mouth. I stood in the damp mist, in the dark, trying to hear the traffic, disconnected again, questing for something where there was nothing. I was miserable as sin.

As I stood there I thought I saw the figure of the young man I had met in the park. He maundered alone through the trunks of the trees, under the bare branches, seeming quite lost and aimless. Was it the same man? And could I really see him?

The telephone was ringing as I went in. It was Naomi, making some requests and checking generally on my condition.

'We're getting very excited here,' she said, with a genuine lift of the voice. Poor Naomi, I thought. She must never know that her best friend had betrayed her, that the jolly fiction of sixth form she and Jessica had maintained had collapsed the minute Jessica no longer found it useful.

After that Jessica rang to say she'd like to come that night. Then Joy Cross invited me out for a Christmas drink. Then, as I was weakly getting out a suitcase, knowing that in Stonebridge, a hundred and fifty miles away, I was wanted and looked-forward-to in a tranquil atmosphere with my children, meals on the dot and no worries, the doorbell rang. There stood the Greenwood children, in their old coats, their faces pale in the darkness, singing:

Star of wonder,
Star of light,
Star with royal
Beauty bright,
Westward leading,
Still proceeding,
Guide us to thy perfect light.

It was a message I wondered if they could understand, for all joy must have been doused in them when they were two or three years old, when it is most easily extinguished. What had they learned then, as they watched their parents drifting helplessly on tides of anxiety and moral doubt, took in the boxes of discarded clothing in the hall, received the chipped second-hand tricycle, found that the world never contained a good laugh, a bright thread of clothing or a freshly painted toy, that God's chosen servants only got piles of old clothes and junk, rooms made dark by low-watt electric bulbs and chilly by one-bar electric fires, that good intentions were easily confounded, hopes were dashed, and that they never got what they wanted and had to pretend that they did? So I paid the children for their carols in some despair, knowing that every halfpenny would go to a good cause, and would not be diminished by so much as one 10p stop at the bright lights of the chip shop.

As I shut the door the phone rang again. It was Katie Mulvaney. 'I'm sorry, Joe,' she said. 'I'm afraid I'll have to cancel tea tomorrow.'

'Never mind,' I said. 'It's a pity. But it gives me the excuse I needed for going to Stonebridge a bit earlier than I said. I was half-thinking of going tomorrow anyway. Now, I've got the impetus to start early in the morning.'

'I'm glad of that,' she said. 'I hope things go well there.' After a pause she said, a little awkwardly, 'I wouldn't cancel it, really, but it's difficult just now.' She paused again and then said, 'I have visitors.'

Still thinking nothing of the exchange I said, 'Well, never mind. Let's do it after Christmas, when there's less going on.'

'All right, Joe,' she said. 'I'll look forward to it.'

'There isn't anything wrong, is there?' I asked, struck by the flatness of her voice.

'No, no,' she said. 'There's nothing wrong.'

'Do you mind if I bring a few presents round for the children,' I said, 'before I go?'

'Well, no,' she said. 'When will you be coming? No – I'll send Siobhan.'

'No need,' I said.

'Oh – ' she said.

'I'm on my way,' I told her, putting down the phone.

I fancied the walk, and for all I knew Katie had gone mad or been excommunicated. The house looked the same as usual. Siobhan let me in, wearing the detached look which often in children means anxiety. As we went upstairs she asked me, 'Do you know Uncle Sean?'

'No,' I said and I sensed that she was checking on Sean, trying to get other people's reactions to him.

Kate was sitting stiffly near the window in an armchair, under the lamp. On the green sofa sat the young man I had met in the park, and thought I had glimpsed among the trees in the garden.

I put the presents on the television and Katie stood up. She was wearing a black rollneck sweater and baggy green trousers. 'Thank you very much, Joe. It was kind of you to think of the children. This is my brother Sean – Joe Coverdale.'

'We met before. In the park. I was lost and he told me the way,' said the young man. He had stood up and he now said, 'I'll be going now, Katie dear.'

'You'll spend the night here, Sean,' she told him.

Perhaps it was being the tallest person in the room, or the oldest, or that both Sean and Katie were round-faced and vulnerable-looking, but I intervened and said, 'If you're in search of a bed – '

'There's plenty of room here,' Katie said.

'I'm going to my friends,' Sean announced.

Katie stood still as he walked out of the room. Then she ran out and called down the stairs, 'Come back, Sean! Come back!' And I heard a voice say, 'I'll phone up, Kate,' and the sound of the front door shutting.

She obviously stood there, looking over the banisters for a moment and then came back, saying, as she came through the door, 'Dear God,' under her breath. Then she turned and said, 'Do you want a drink, Joe? I'm having one,' and, without a word from me, poured two glasses of whisky from a bottle standing on the hatch.

'I'd better be on my way, Katie,' I said.

'Stay and have a Christmas drink, at least,' she said. Then she paused and said, 'I'd like your company for a little while. I must just make a phone call, though.'

As she spoke into the phone by the window in a low, rapid voice I looked about me, finding an air of unusual neatness and order in the room. The Christmas tree, trimmed and covered in presents, stood in the corner by the hatch. There were two armchairs in front of the television near it, and a small table with a pot of chrysanthemums on it. She made another phone call and then crossed the room rapidly, going to the door, calling, 'Siobhan! Patrick! It's plan A.'

There was the usual thudding on the stairs and Siobhan and and Patrick appeared in anoraks, with holdalls in their hands. Patrick carried a large teddy-bear wearing football colours. 'Now – out through the back with you and straight over to Mrs Kops,' Katie said. 'And behave yourselves now. Help all you can, but for God's sake don't try to help if you think you'll be in the way.'

'All right, mum,' said Siobhan. They looked a hardy and resolute pair, ready for anything as they stood in the doorway.

'Tell me what I said about coming back.'

'Don't come back without phoning first.'

'Remember that – it's very important.'

'I still think you should tell us what's happening,' said Siobhan.

'Later, I shall,' said Katie. 'Off you go now. Just a second – I'll come down with you and lock the back door behind you.'

She came up later and listened to their voices as they crossed the garden. Finally I said, 'Where's Ajax?'

'Staying with my sister and her family in Maidenhead,' said Katie. 'Oh, there it goes again.'

And she answered the telephone saying, 'I did what I had to – they're at the neighbours now. I might send them to you in the morning. I'll stay here and be damned to them – let's watch and see. Don't worry now. – Yes, that'll be all we need to make a happy Christmas, Old Mother Ireland coming over from Dublin in person.' Then she poured herself another glass of whisky saying, 'I shouldn't be doing this.'

'Where's Julian?' I asked.

'In Brussels,' she told me.

'Are you sure you should be staying here alone?' I asked.

'Well, I'm not,' she said. 'But I've decided I will.'

I did not really understand but all the clues pointed to trouble.

Now we both sat by the window and she said, 'All I wanted to do was wish you a merry Christmas at Stonebridge. And it was kind of you to think of the children.'

'It's only a few paints and things,' I told her. 'You're spending Christmas here, then?'

'Oh yes – I expect so,' she said.

'You're in some kind of trouble, Katie,' I said. 'Your brother, if you don't mind me saying so, carries a very easily-felt air of desperation and sadness with him. Now – I don't understand – '

'Don't pry, Joe,' she told me. 'And I'd better not offer you another drink – '

'Rubbish,' I said. 'I can feel nonsense starting up all around me. What's your horrible secret? Why have you sent the children away from the house? Why are you staying here alone? Why are you trying to get rid of me?'

'I'm expecting a man friend,' she said.

'Rubbish,' I said.

'You think I couldn't?' she said, nettled.

'Of course you could,' I told her. 'But I'm too old a hand to believe that. Come on, Kate. I'm sure you want to tell me, really. And think how I'd feel tomorrow if I heard something terrible had happened to you and I'd walked out of here without even making an effort to find out. Anyway, my guess is that you'll be up all night, unable to sleep, and by 2 in the morning you'll be very sorry there isn't someone here to play cards with.'

'I can't allow you to stay.'

'You can't force me to go. Anyway, my guess is that you're expecting the house to be bombed or attacked in some way. I'll go on believing that until you tell me otherwise, and I'll stay, too, unless you can prove to me there's no danger here.'

'Well, do you mind watching the last episode of *Dombey and Son?*'

'I'd hate to miss it.'

So we sat by the television, eating Katie's doorstep cheese-sandwiches and drinking coffee, until *Dombey and Son* ended. I felt confident that no one would attack a house at 8 in the evening, with the streets still full of people. That gave me some two hours, at the very least, to persuade Katie to get out of the house.

'It's funny,' she remarked as the credits came up, 'I feel more peaceful than I have for ages. I don't really think I've got much of a taste for the quiet life. And yet,' she added, 'I used to think of joining the contemplatives.'

'There's complete stillness at the centre of the typhoon,' I said.

The room seemed isolated, becalmed, as if the rest of the world outside, even the rest of the house, did not exist. The mist hung outside the windows, muffling all sounds. It seemed that the peace could never be broken and at the same time it did not seem at all implausible that at any moment there might be the expected knock on the door, and the expected storm of violence.

'Why didn't you become a nun?' I asked.

'It was a notion I had as a girl. I was very religious and I expect, without realizing it, I was affected by the sight of the lives of the women I saw around me. It didn't seem very enviable to be an ordinary woman in Ireland during my girlhood.' She paused.

'And then?' I said.

'I became less religious and found I was clever – or the other way about. I don't know. At any rate, I was busy passing examinations, and that led me to university, where I lost my terrible fear of being an Irish wife – '

She caught my glance, and smiled. 'Julian doesn't drink, and he doesn't raise his hand in anger to me or the children. And I don't have to lead my life in Ireland, where the fences around a woman are hard to climb. When Ajax is older I can get a job. I can't say any of these things about two out of my three sisters. And the third one's married to an Englishman and lives in Maidenhead – to you it might all seem a negative view of marriage.'

'I've given up having views on marriage,' I said sourly.

'Poor Joe,' she said. 'You must feel nervous about going to Stonebridge tomorrow.'

'I do,' I said. 'I don't know what I'm going to do when I get there.'

'God will help you,' she said in a sensible voice.

I tried to imagine a God who would help and found I could, if I stretched my imagination a bit. But the bubble of contemplation was burst, as in so many hagiological tales, by the claims of the world. I suddenly realized that Jessica would be on my step in half an hour, ringing the bell and expecting me. I could not leave Katie and, I did not want to abandon Jessica, nor could I really bring the two events together, being a lover on the one hand and a sturdy friend on the other, a kind of trouserless Tonto. And all the time, as I sat there, Elmira's jibes rang in my ears. It was all true. Why had I done it? Through idleness and that kindness which gives the wrong thing to the person who insists loudly enough, like cramming a crying toddler's mouth with sweets, loading the gun and handing it to the suicide – and because it was easy, because if it did not answer a desire, at least it filled a vacuum and because this time, perhaps, it would supply me with some feeling of meaning, some core to a pulpy life. And, I thought, from vanity. What a dirty bugger.

I said, 'Is there a phone downstairs?' I was too ashamed to let Katie hear me.

'In Julian's study,' she said. She was knitting a small green sweater with purple stripes. The two balls of wool bounced on the floor at her feet as she knitted. 'Keep to the back of the house,' she added.

Back of the house, I thought, going downstairs and along the passageway to Julian's study. It was not 9 o'clock. There must be at least an hour, and probably more, before it happened, if it did. So I sat at Julian's desk with my feet in the thick pile of his carpet, admiring his tapestry curtains, his orderly bookshelves, which ran all round the room, his stereo, his neat desk with *The Times* on one corner and a few papers neatly docketed in the other. I did not hold it absolutely against him that, in this disorderly household, he had a private place to retreat and to keep his things safe from damage, nor even that more money seemed to have been spent on his comfort than on the rest of the house, for if the Mulvaney children had been given a palace they would soon have wrecked it. But I could not help thinking that if he had taken a more constructive attitude to his wife and family he might not have needed to bolt himself in. And, no matter what the provocation he should certainly have replaced the dangerously shredded stair-carpet, which must have come with the house, before he put down Axminster in his own study. However good the reasons for the arrangement, that study still made Julian Mulvaney look a mean sod. And all the meaner because of the way he invited you to see him as a man of intelligence and culture, half-crucified in his sensibilities by the boors and peasants he was obliged to live with.

Then I observed, quite suddenly, that in many respects he had here created for himself the office of a civil servant of much higher rank than his own. If this, I thought, was the fantasy he was playing out at home, what a dull, unimaginative, solipsistic and limited one it was. It would have been less depressing if he'd come home, torn off his jacket and got into an Alaric the Goth set, making Katie dress up as the prioress of a looted abbey. But, I reflected, Julian had not half-lied to, seduced, betrayed, let down as many people as I had, so who was I to criticize?

Rejecting Jessica's long, white, smooth arms, soft breasts and sweet gasping cry, I said, 'I'm sorry, Jessica. A friend in trouble. I'd like to tell you, but I can't.'

In reply she said, 'I think Hugo suspects.'

There was no reason why Hugo should suspect anything, unless Jessica went out of her way to make him suspicious. So I said, 'Good heavens.'

'Oh, why can't you be there, Joe?' she implored.

'You'll have to believe me,' I told her. 'I really can't help it. Do you want me to come and talk to Hugo?'

Pulling her queen back suddenly to a position of safety she said, 'No. I'll handle it.'

'I'll come round tomorrow morning,' I said, 'if I may.'

She'd have me in check and a bishop waiting, I thought gloomily as I walked carefully back along the passage and up the stairs. I could not even work out the strategy, but I knew I was being manoeuvred. Tomorrow I should have to tell her that I could not go on seeing her. There would be no point in talking, for she could probably reason me into a stay of execution. I should have to deliver my blow, and depart. I was not going to like myself whatever happened and she was not in the end going to like me. The only thing I could do was get it over with quickly.

'There's something to be said for the prospect of danger,' I said to Katie as I sat down. 'It clears the head wonderfully. One little glimpse of yourself with only one leg gives you a lot of perspective.'

'I've noticed that,' said Katie, getting on with her knitting. 'My first thought was, how can a maimed woman look after her children, and then I thought Julian might leave me. Then I found myself thinking, God will still love me, but would any mortal man love a woman with no legs? What do you think?'

'That I'd go back to Naomi. She'd look after me for a bit, anyway, until I'd adjusted. Then she'd get someone else.'

'Well, it probably won't happen,' said Katie.

'Not to us,' I said. 'Because we're both leaving in half an hour, or less.'

'You're leaving,' she told me. 'I'm staying.'

'Oh no I'm not,' I said. 'Not without you. In my book there's only one reason for staying and that's to lure them into a trap and capture them. I don't believe you're doing that. I think you're staying because you think you ought to be punished by them. The name for that is masochism.'

'And obstinacy,' she said.

'And probably foolish pride. I believe that any woman with children to rear who endangers herself for no good reason is irresponsible.'

'That's what they all say. Don't do this, don't do that, and you must look after yourself – you've children to bring up. Keep your body and mind within four walls – even your thoughts can affect a child, you know – because you've got a family. Half the time it's an excuse to keep you in slavery.'

'It probably is the easiest weapon to use against a woman,' I said. 'This time it's to keep you in one piece.'

'Oh dear,' she said crossly. 'I wish you'd go away. I wish you'd never come here at all.'

'It's a better way for me to spend the evening than the one I had in mind. I've been foolish, Katie,' I said. There was no point in further argument. I would have, in half an hour, to grab her and get her out by force. She was plump, but not tall and I thought I could do it, if I surprised her and got it over with before she had time to start struggling.

'I suppose you shouldn't have done it,' she said vaguely. 'I couldn't be the judge of that. Julian's told me all about it – the women and that business with the Hungarians and I do feel sorry for Naomi. I always considered you such a happy couple, Joe,' she said sadly. 'So handsome and with such nice children. You seemed to have everything. I wondered what led you to imperil all that.'

'I suppose I thought I could get away with it,' I said. 'Men often do. But I must have known it was a risk – and I didn't mind taking it.'

'Was it boredom?' she asked.

'Disgust,' I said. 'There were all those nice friends, and nice holidays, and all that smoothing over of anything disquieting. All the things you couldn't ignore got called "problems" – a drinking problem, a sleeping problem, a marriage problem, the problems of the third world – it fell just short of describing India as a place with a starvation problem. It was another form of Victorian whitewash. These days you're allowed to mention things but they have to be labelled as problems to make sure they have nothing to do with you, and that there are always solutions – nice, clean homes with good staff for difficult relatives, sick pets humanely put down, jumble sales for the third world and cheques dispatched at Christmas to good causes. It may be necessary self-defence, but in the end, it gave me, in myself, a feeling of unreality.

'I was living in a nice home with a good wife, good children and everything was nice. Naomi saw to all that – anything not nice was dismissed in a phrase, rushed into the hall, out of the front door and into the street. Nothing not nice came into my home, I can tell you. But eventually it did – and it was me.'

The phone rang. Katie went to it. Even from where I sat I could hear the high, foreign cadences of the old lady.

'Of course I told the police, Mother,' Katie was saying in a level voice. 'Do you want your son caught and given a life sentence? Do you want to die knowing he's in Winston gaol and will be for another five, ten, fifteen years? – I blame you for nothing – Sean is my brother and I have a right – I've warned him. If they raid the house he won't be there. None of them will if they've any sense. If he is there, he'll have done nothing. – Of course they will, of course they will. – If they're fools enough to be standing there with sticks of dynamite in their hands . . . – Because he'll be innocent and that will mean a shorter sentence. – You never have thought anything of me, Mother, and you never will. Now it seems you think nothing of Sean either. – Then where did he get the fare to England? He had no money . . . – Yes, yes, to buy a suit. Well I know, and you both knew what use he would make of it. To come over here and try to take innocent lives. – I've heard all that before. But I'm too old for it now. Uncle Paul may have been an Irish martyr but that's different from sending an eighteen-year-old boy over here to blow the hands and feet off a lot of Italian waiters and, for all you know, your sister's child Theresa, who's working on the make-up counter in a big store in the West End. – You may never have the chance, mother. Your patriots have threatened me, you know. They'd always rather kill an Irish traitor than an English. – That's what I thought you'd say and I'm not surprised at all. – Yes, all right, mother, of course. – Of course, I forgive you, mother. We all say things we don't mean. – And blessings on you, too.'

She came from the telephone, smiling weakly in self-defence and saying, 'There's a fine specimen of Fair Rosaleen for you. Did you catch that story about the suit? When Sean said how he wanted to come to England she said nothing and gave him £50 in cash from the drawer to go out and get a suit. And she's laid a mother's curse on me – that woman's curse would be a blessing to anyone in their right mind. There's pure Irish womanhood for you. Ah –' she said, sitting down in the chair, 'pour me a drink, Joe, and have one yourself. I feel weak. It's just as well Julian's not here. He couldn't bear it at all.'

'You've given the police the address where Sean and his friends are to be found so as to prevent a bombing?'

'Yes,' she said. 'It was to be tomorrow, in the West End, in the afternoon. You can imagine what that means at Christmas time. I couldn't let it go on, even if it means my brother, who heard the song of Kevin Barry in his cradle, gets a year or two in goal. Perhaps it'll teach him to stay out of trouble in future.'

'And you really think they'll come for you.'

'Sean told me they'd said they would. That may mean nothing. Called me a traitor, so they did,' she said mockingly.

'It's disgusting,' I said, scornful of these melodramatics.

'I daresay,' she said. 'But you didn't grow up in Ireland under two laws, the Irish and the IRA's. I did. And I grew up as an Irish patriot, which I still am. And I have the Irish tolerance of ambiguities and that means I can love and detest my country at the same time and love my religion and hate my Church and see the IRA as deeply patriotic murdering hooligans, hate the British in Ireland and for what they've made of us over the ages. We're your Indians, you know, the drunken lazy Cherokee you can laugh at and feel superior to – but when you beat people up again and again, so that in every generation they lose the most intelligent to the Church, for civil power isn't open to them, and the most ambitious to the rest of the world, because there's nowhere in Ireland they can get what they want – then what do you expect?'

Instead of answering I walked out of the room and along the landing. Through the mist I could just see a car coming down the road on the left. I saw the indicator go on and it slowed down as it neared the house.

I ran back into the room, pulled Katie to her feet and lifted her over my shoulder.

'Wha–' she said.

'I've had enough,' I gasped, walking over, bent-kneed, to the window, wondering how I was going to get her down if she decided to struggle. 'I'm not staying here to be murdered.' I reckoned it was only ten feet to the grass below, possibly less. I might have to push her. I got her on to the sill with her legs dangling over the edge. The car probably contained Julian, I was thinking. He'd come upstairs and find me trying to shove his wife out of the window.

'I'll go down the drainpipe,' she said, suddenly co-operating and wriggled along the sill, grasped the pipe, turned, with some agility and was on her way down, gasping, 'It's tugging away – ' when, with a great roar the front door blew in and seconds later, another explosion hit the sitting-room door. As I leapt from the sill, which shook violently under me, I felt stone and plaster coming down heavily behind me and the whole room filled with a sudden fire.

I landed badly, on my back in the wet grass with all the wind knocked out of me. Looking up, as I scrambled to my feet, wondering if I would be able to stand, I saw the upper window full of flames. Inside the room something exploded. The window-sill came down in chunks around us. Mist still hung round the windows above. The air in front of the burning window was clear.

'Are you all right?' came Katie's voice.

'I think so. Are you?'

Windows began to go up and lights go on all round the square.

'Was that a bomb?' said someone from a nearby window.

'Will you call the fire brigade to my house? It's Katie Mulvaney?'

'My wife's doing it,' said someone else. 'Is anyone inside?'

'Oh – the cat,' said Katie.

'I saw him streak out of your basement when the first bang came,' said a man, who had come up the garden path behind us.

There was Elmira. 'Kate! Did they do it? Are the children out?'

'Even the cat,' said Kate, looking up at her burning window. From inside the room there came a series of pops.

'The fire-brigade – ' Elmira began when the clanging of bells on the engines came from the distance. 'They're coming,' she said. I felt dizzy and fed-up. 'Joe,' she said turning to me, 'Were you there?'

I went on rubbing my sore head and said, 'No. I always leap out of windows in the middle of the night.'

'I know that,' said Elmira quickly. 'Only this time you've got your trousers on.'

I heard a startled laugh from above. I could have killed Elmira.

Katie said, 'If it hadn't been for Joe I'd still be in there,' and Elmira, suddenly looking up at the house said, 'Jesus Christ.'

The man above said, 'Come on, Claire. Let's go round and see what's happening. Katie – would you like to come inside?'

'Can you just unbolt your back door and let us through?' called Katie.

We went out of the dark and mist and under the strip-lighting of someone's well-appointed kitchen, ran through the hall and into the street. It was lurid with flames. One or two people – a man in dungarees carrying a tool-bag, a couple of sixteen-year-old boys, one leaning on his motor-bike, a man and woman from further up the street – stood on the opposite pavement. The front door was open, flames flickered on the stair-carpet and the paint on the banisters was alight. From the top of the stairs came the crackle of fire.

'I've attached this to the tap in my basement,' said a competent fellow in a plaid dressing-gown. 'Turn on, Mimi.'

He began to play the hosepipe through the shattered windows on the ground floor next to the hall. Inside the house, the telephone began to ring.

'Dear God,' moaned Katie. 'He'll just ruin the carpet in there – there's hardly any fire.'

'Hold everything, Jake,' cried Elmira. 'Here are the engines at last.'

A fire-engine, and then two more, came round the corner.

'Good show,' said Jake, retreating. 'Can I do anything?'

'Would you ring Polly Kops and say I'm safe?' said Katie.

'Will do,' he said, and went indoors.

Elmira, Kate and I stood on the other side of the road watching the firemen.

'Don't worry, Kate,' Elmira said. 'They'll soon have it out.'

'I'm enjoying it,' said Kate instantly.

Even Elmira looked surprised.

Like a bonfire on Guy Fawkes Night, which has cast its great flickering flames over house and garden, lighting the sky and dominating the darkness for hours, once out, the great fire at 2, Blenheim Crescent had done comparatively little damage. There were the blackened hall, the charred edges of the first few stairs, the skeleton banisters and the long streak of burnt and sodden carpet. Only the top floor still had its windows intact. We climbed the damaged stairs. The sitting-room was black, the furniture had caught fire and the carpet was half-burnt away. It did not seem much of an effect after the drama of the explosions, the leaping flames and the jumping from the window.

We stood on the reeking carpet and Katie said, 'Good. I've been paying insurance for years. Now I'll claim and have a real turn-out.'

There was something in her tone which indicated the turn-out would be as much mental as physical. Then she said, 'Supposing I'd been in here,' turned to me and said, 'Joe, – you saved my life.'

Her eyes were full. I muttered ungraciously, 'If I'd had any sense I'd have rung the police. None of this need have happened.'

'Come on,' said Elmira. 'Before the fireman catch us in here. You'd better come back with me, Kate. You're bound to collapse sooner or later.'

'Not time yet,' murmured Katie, and as if to confirm this a voice cried up from the foot of the stairs, 'Mrs Mulvaney – if you're up there – the police would like a word with you.'

'This'll be the worst of it,' she said.

She walked stolidly across the road with Elmira and me following like anxious parents. Near the edge of the road her step faltered. Then she said to the man sitting between two policemen in the back of the car, 'Hullo, Dermot. I might have guessed I'd be seeing you.'

'And this isn't the end of it, Kate Green,' he said.

'Do you identify this man,' said one of the policemen.

'I know him,' said Katie.

'You're Mrs Katherine Mulvaney?'

'I am,' said Katie.

A second police-car drew up and a policeman jumped out.

'Mrs Mulvaney has identified this man,' the man in the first car told him.

'Is that true?' he said to Kate in a bullying voice.

'I've known him since I was four,' said Katie.

'And this man,' he said, pointing to a second man, sitting next to the driver.

'I don't know him.'

'We'll see about that,' said the policeman. 'And who are these others? I'd be grateful if you two would go about your business.'

'I am a victim of an attack, not a criminal, I'd like to say,' Katie said. 'And these people are my friends, who've been helping me.'

'I'm talking to this lady,' he told me. 'Will you go over there – is that your house?' he asked, turning sharply to Katie.

'It is,' she said.

'Do you own it?'

'Well,' she said uncertainly, 'my husband – '

'Is this him?' he said turning to me.

'No – '

'Was he with you?'

'Yes – ' she said.

'Look,' I said, 'you can't conduct bullying interviews on the pavement with someone who's just seen her house on fire. You'd better ask her to come to the police station and give her the chance to call her solicitor.'

'And she needs protection now,' Elmira said.

The policeman looked at Elmira, who was taller and in better condition than him. She was clutching a scarlet satin kimono round her. Then another car drew up and he went to it, saying, 'Don't go away.'

'Have you got a solicitor, Kate?' asked Elmira.

'Only for conveyancing and so forth. I don't even know his telephone number. He'd be hopeless.'

'I'll get my cousin,' said Elmira. 'He'll love it.'

'No,' said Katie suddenly. 'Innocent people don't get lawyers in for things like this.'

'Well, good evening, Mrs Mulvaney,' said an elderly police officer appearing at Katie's shoulder. 'What a dreadful shock for you all this must have been. Now – it seems one of my officers has been abrupt but I'm sure you understand how important it is for us to get information as soon as possible after a crime's been committed. From what we can gather there's at least one other man still at large. One of the neighbours saw three men in the car which drew up outside your house. So we'd be grateful if you could talk to us tonight. Speed's essential in these matters, you know.'

Katie said, 'Elmira – perhaps we can go and sit down in your house.'

Elmira, heels slapping and kimono flapping, and I, covered on one side with mud from the garden, with Katie between us walked up the road, closely followed by the police.

'I'm just going to stagger about a bit,' said Kate in a low voice. 'Hold me up when I do. I have to establish dizzy spells for when I can't think what to say – ' and she stumbled. We supported her, pulled her upright. She passed a hand over her brow and said audibly, 'It's all right – I just feel a little confused.'

'I think I'll call the doctor, Joe,' said Elmira.

'I think you'd better,' I said.

But, spotting Dr Fraser's lights were on opposite, I asked him to come straightaway. This gave Katie fifteen minutes lying down in Elmira's room before she had to face the police.

The story she told, finally, lying on the sofa with a blanket over her in Elmira's sitting-room, was almost the truth. Her brother Sean, she said, had come over from Ireland to spend Christmas with the family. He had innocently looked up an old friend of the family from Ireland, a kind of honorary uncle, Dermot Walsh, who had been the man in the police-car. In the pub they had let it out that he and some others were planning a bomb raid. Sean had come to her, Katie, with the tale. She had told him to go back and tell them that if they went on with plans for the raid, she would inform the police. Her brother had come back and, she said, pleaded with her not to interfere, because Dermot had threatened to kill her or injure her children if she betrayed them. She insisted on making the anonymous phone call saying where the group was to be found. Sean, she said, was staying with a girl friend whose address she had written on a piece of paper, and put under the pot of chrysanthemums in the burnt-out room. The police shot names at her, one after the other, and Katie denied them all, weakly but clearheadedly. I still do not know how much she knew and I suspected from her too-calm manner, that all the names, the dates, the places, were not unfamiliar to her. Elmira said afterwards that her manner was that of the women of Calabria faced with strangers, asking questions – there was a thickness of secrets about them which made them look at you as if you were a child. Katie, she said, gave her the impression that she had grown up not talking about a network of people and activities and which everyone knew about and no one mentioned, while the rest of life went quietly on.

It was obvious when they left that the elderly policeman was not satisfied. He made Katie promise she would get in touch with them if Sean appeared. He said, 'We'll be in touch again.'

I went out with them, in order to nail some planks across Katie's open door, but a policeman watching me from a car parked across the road gave me the impression that Katie's house would never be safer from burglars. There were many more footmarks, too, on the sodden carpet than there had been when we came out. There was a smell of wet smoke and I was glad to bang in the last nail. I walked, very tired, back up the street, holding the hammer. It was 1 in the morning. Katie was sitting up in Elmira's brass-knobbed bedstead, drinking a cup of tea while Elmira sat in the hearth toasting crumpets. A green lamp burned by the bed.

I poured myself a cup of tea, sat down and stretched out my legs. It all felt very comfortable.

'What a night,' remarked Elmira.

'Oh, Joe,' said Katie. 'And you're going to Stonebridge tomorrow.'

'Never mind,' I said. 'How do you feel?'

'All right, just as long as I don't start thinking what Julian's going to say. Or about my mother.'

'The family always finishes you off,' Elmira said. 'You can stand the condemned cell until your mother comes and tells you how she always knew you'd live to be hung.'

'I can't face ringing that murdering old woman,' Katie declared. 'After she sent Sean over here to blow up innocent people and get thirty years for it. And nearly got me killed into the bargain. I ask you – what duty do I owe her?'

'I'd ring her,' said Elmira, 'and gladly. But she can sweat it out – it's a pity she can't sacrifice herself for Ireland, instead of her children.'

'Men's affairs,' muttered Katie, adding, 'She's a terrible woman. It's my opinion she put paid to my father.'

'Something like that happened in my family,' said I. 'If the truth came out we'd find there was no family without its assassin, one way and another.'

'What happened ?' asked Elmira.

'Well – the night Father fell in the Liffey – ' began Katie sleepily, and laughed, 'I know, I know,' and she yawned.

'I hope it's a short one, Kate,' said Elmira. 'I have to get up early these days. No, no. You stay here. There's a beautiful little attic room. Yes, well, the night Pa fell in the Liffey – ?'

'He was a respectable Dublin solicitor, mind,' Katie said, 'but in the habit of taking a drop too much from time to time – do I sound like an O'Casey play ?'

'Not at all, not at all,' Elmira told her.

'So one night,' she went on tiredly, 'coming home he fell in the river and was rescued by two men who brought him back.' Her eyes shut and she opened them again. Elmira winked at me. Katie said, 'Oh dear. So he was put to bed with all ceremony and hot-water bottles and hot toddy and apparently fell asleep, just as you'd expect.' There was a long pause and she started up again. 'But in the morning there he lay when I took him up a cup of tea, not a stitch of bedclothes over him and the room as cold as ice. "Dear God," said Mother, coming in after me at a fast trot in her nightdress, and I thought later she looked shocked to see me there. "He must have thrown off the blankets during the night. And the window's blown open, too." ' She fell asleep and mumbled, 'That was how my father came to catch pneumonia and Mother became a wealthy widow – '

Elmira said crossly. 'Well, I don't think that's much of a murder story.'

'Ah, well,' Katie said with her eyes shut. 'It was the way the bedclothes lay – pulled back, not tossed. After the funeral do you know, one of us had to sleep with her every blessed night for a year or she'd roam the house at night moaning and wringing her hands – it was so frightening – we used to hide and watch – hold my hand, Joe.'

Elmira and I sat there in silence for a while until Elmira muttered, 'Thank God I'm not Irish. All I have to do is keep my ego under control – oh, God, Joe. I must go to bed. I know it's selfish but can you hold on till Katie's fast asleep. Stay here tonight. I'll put an electric fire on in the bedroom next door.'

'Right,' I said. 'Good night, Elmira.'

'Night, Joe,' she said, and was gone. Then she came back and said from the doorway, 'What were you doing there, anyway?' I stared at her. 'I was taking round some presents for the children – that's all.'

'Just wondering,' said Elmira. She looked at Katie, lying asleep and said, 'She takes it all for granted.'

'Takes everything for granted,' I said.

'She was sitting there, waiting to be blown up, that's what I can't understand.'

'I think at the back of her mind she sees herself as a betrayer. She betrayed, she thought, her brother into the hands of the police and good old Uncle Dermot, the mad bomber, and Ireland itself. She didn't want to be involved but her whole background involved her. I suppose she thought she had to face it out.'

Elmira's face, transformed with rage, seemed to loom at me. 'There's a woman who built herself a cage, got inside, locked it and threw away the key. If it's not that whingeing Julian, it's those hooligans of kids, and now she wants to be a martyr for old Ireland – it all makes me sick. I'm going to bed.'

'Right. Right, Elmira,' I said pacifically. 'You do that.'

I tried to make myself comfortable in the chair but every time I tried to slip my hand out of Katie's her grip tightened and I hadn't the heart to tear it away abruptly. And there she lay, obedient to Julian, God and even owing an unwilling and detesting loyalty to Dermot Walsh, sleeping peacefully, with a round, plump face like a child's. It was impossible to imagine the new day ever coming to disturb her with more lies to be told and a mass of burnt scraps of carpet and charred wood to be cleaned up. Once more I tried to release my hand but she moaned and moved towards me in her sleep. At 3, very tired, I took off my shoes, lay down beside her on top of the blankets, took her hand again and fell, instantly, into a deep, dreamless sleep.

I shall not easily forget the horror of that moment, at 10 o'clock next morning, when Jessica Lombard, wearing an olive-green trouser suit, stormed in and began to shriek at me. For half a minute I could not hear her. I just lay under the still-burning lamp, seeing, in the doorway, that arrow-sharp figure, the tension of her limbs and face, the movements of her mouth. Then I recognized her.

I said, 'Jessica – wh – ?'

Then I began to hear what she was saying, 'So this is all I mean to you – I came close to breaking up my marriage for you –' She must have made up her mind earlier, perhaps overnight, that either she would not, or could not, break up her marriage for me. And the voice went on – 'What sort of a monster are you, anyway – sorry for Naomi, sorry for any woman who – and now poor Katie –' And then Katie, perhaps hearing her name, struggled up in bed, looked at me, still with my head on the pillow and my face turned towards the door and said, 'Jessica?' and then, reconstructing the events of the day before said, 'My house –' and Jessica went on, 'and all the time I believed in you. Believed in you. You're not like other people. You're so selfish you must be insane, psychotic – it makes me sick to think about it – sick –' and suddenly weeping she ran out.

I jumped up and ran after her. 'Jessica!' I cried, 'come back!' but the front door slammed and I was looking down into the empty hall.

Elmira appeared in a leotard and old, footless woollen tights. She stared at the door and then up at me and said, 'She said she'd like to see Katie – ask if there was anything she could do. I said Katie should be left to sleep. She must have gone up anyway. Were you up there?'

Katie, in Elmira's nightdress said, 'Wouldn't it be better if you caught up with her and explained –'

'I haven't got any shoes on,' I said doltishly.

'Ring up after you've had breakfast,' Elmira said. 'I'll be ready in half an hour.' She went back to the practice room, some music started and her thumps began. I went into the kitchen and put some coffee on. I felt ashamed of myself. At one time, in the days of female chastity and unavoidable pregnancies, the fornicator had had a bit of dignity, being a sinner, a defiler of purity and scot-free fatherer of nameless children. His status now had dwindled to that of a public nuisance, a buffoon, someone who got into stupid, farce-like situations he could not control. The sin had dwindled to a shady bit of business, like pocketing more change than you were entitled to in a shop, the effect was like that of dropping litter in the street, untidy and aggravating, but not much to make a fuss about. I made some toast. Katie came in, dressed. She took the coffee I held out to her. I felt unable to speak. She said, 'Oh, Joe. How could you?'

'I don't know,' I said. 'I'm disgusting. I'm just going to drink this and be off.'

Elmira came in in a dressing-gown saying, 'I took the liberty of ringing some fellows while you were asleep, Kate. They'll be round at 11 to start clearing up. I said you might want them to start repairs.'

'If they're reliable,' said Katie. 'Julian's coming back this evening. I don't know what he'll say.'

' "Thank God you're still alive," I hope,' said Elmira briskly. 'And as for you, Joe, it's just as well you saved Katie's life last night because your overdraft is running so high now that the great Bank Manager in the sky must have been pressing for a bit on account for some time.'

'I'm leaving,' I said. 'Kate – by the way – if you want to move into my house while I'm away, Elmira's got the spare key. Don't hesitate to do it if you want.'

'Thanks, Joe,' she said. 'But supposing they try again.'

'The police will watch out for you,' I said, hoping it was true.

'Perhaps I'd better wait for Julian to come back and then take the children away,' she said.

I could not stay now. I was afraid. I had to go to Stonebridge and sort something out. I said, 'I'm leaving at lunchtime – if you want me before then I'll be in. I'll go straight round to Jessica's and save your good name.'

'Yours too,' said Kate.

'I don't think it's salvageable,' I said.

'Well, you don't want people to think that you don't take your socks off,' she said.

'That's true,' I said, in deep depression. 'It might be bad for business.'

The shabby grey houses in the wintry street, the boy wheeling a bicycle, and the old lady with her shopping, seemed quiet and neutral. I walked past Katie's blackened front door and round the corner. I knocked on Jessica's brass angel door-knocker and was let in by the au pair. As I stepped in I was very conscious of my stubble, dirty shirt, and the mud left on my suit after the fall into the garden.

Beth popped out of the kitchen door, wearing a long blue-striped pinafore and holding a chop.

'She's ill,' she told me. 'So I'm starting the lunch. Monique's leaving too, but she doesn't know yet.'

'Where is she – your mother, I mean.'

'Lying down in the little sitting-room upstairs. Dad's there. How did your suit get so muddy?'

'There was a fire at Mrs Mulvaney's last night and we both had to jump out of the window. I fell in the mud,' I said. I felt even more gloomy as I spoke the last sentence. It seemed to contain a general truth about me. I went upstairs, knocked at the door and walked in. It was a small, pretty room, overlooking the garden. It had flowered wallpaper, cane furniture, a china cabinet and a chaise-longue, on which Jessica was lying when I arrived. Hugo was reading the paper. He looked up when I came in, but said nothing. I did not know what he knew or what he felt.

I said, 'I only came past to wish you a merry Christmas – I'm leaving for Stonebridge today. And to ask if you could get in touch with Katie Mulvaney and see if there's anything she needs. She's had a fire.'

Meanwhile Jessica stared hard at me. That stare, the stare of a woman whose hopes have not been fulfilled, so reminiscent of mothers, makes me either break down, child-like, and offer everything or, conversely, go for broke, prove that her worst suspicions are more than true by kicking the starer, smiting the starer, doing anything at all to establish that not now, or ever, can any decency be expected of me again. Here, I merely gave a brief nod and said, 'Merry Christmas, all.' I could think of no way of telling Jessica the truth while Hugo was there.

'Guess what?' Jessica said in a high voice. 'Hugo's taking me into the firm. It's all arranged.'

Not with Monique, I thought. She was going to leave.

But I said, 'Good. What a good idea.'

Hugo looked at me. There was contempt, envy and tolerance in his gaze. So the good and patient heavy-laden mule looks at the horse which overtakes him on the rocky path. Jessica must have told him her tale – perhaps how I had taken advantage of her while she was drunk and upset – and Hugo, knowing her, had interpreted what had happened and made his judgement. Hugo had failed her, he knew, as a husband and as a provider. She had tried to bring me up to scratch and abandoning that plan, was seeking solace in him and using me as a stick to beat him.

Making a gallant attempt to show there were no hard feelings, he said, 'How is Katie this morning?'

'Not too bad,' I said.

'Lucky the children weren't at home,' he said. 'Have they found out what caused it?'

'It was a bomb attack,' I said.

Jessica said, 'What?'

'I don't think anyone else needs to worry,' I said. 'As you know Katie's from Dublin. It was a private bomb in a way.'

'Good Lord,' said Jessica, giving an impression of disgust. 'I can hardly believe – well I'm relieved we're leaving for Scotland tomorrow. Have the police caught those responsible yet?'

'Two, I think. At least, they've got two suspects.'

'Poor Katie,' said Jessica in a half-blaming tone. 'Fancy being subjected to a bomb attack. Poor Julian, having his house half-destroyed. How is he, by the way?'

'In Belgium. Katie doesn't know the name of the hotel.'

'Oh,' said Jessica.

'Can happen easily enough,' said Hugo. 'You don't think, when you go away for a couple of days, that your house is going to get bombed. It does seem alarmingly typical of the kind of thing that happens to Katie, though. Not that one dislikes her of course. Quite the reverse. Nevertheless – '

'Well, yes,' I said. 'Ah well, must go. I'd rather drive up to Stonebridge in daylight. Merry Christmas.'

'Give our love to Naomi,' said Jessica.

And, 'I will,' said I.

I left them in the pretty sitting-room, Jessica on the chaise-longue and Hugo on the chair, jewellery in the safe and money in the bank. I felt every inch the penniless scrounger, civilly treated to his face but behind whose back the front door is finally shut with wordless relief. 'Time to turn in, I think, my dear,' he says and 'Would you like a nightcap first, darling?' says she. And, with a little pitch around the seams, the good ship *Matrimony* is off the shoals and afloat again.

The air hit me as hard as I walked home. As I turned the corner a voice called 'Mr Coverdale' and when I looked up a flashbulb went off. I answered a few questions from the reporter on the step, let myself in and firmly shut the door. The air inside was cold and stale. I stepped over yet another pile of Christmas cards and drank coffee in the kitchen, hearing feet on my steps and feeling, for the first time since Naomi had left, positively lonely, remembering the flames, the drop out of the window into the misty garden, Katie asleep under the green lamp. Had we once dined with so many interesting, youngish couples in their thirties, I thought, opening the cards, had they dined with us, taking back snippets of us to their friends, as we took snippets of them – tales of house prices in our area, schooling, the names of good dentists, prospective legislation on car hire, prospects for the builders of wood houses, recipes, cures for thrush, for worms in children, tips about the exchange rate, the price of fatstock, news from New York and Brussels? It all amazed me. There was a card, a stencilled Christmas tree on rough, red school paper, from Olivia, the black girl, and a picture from my son, Paul, showing a shark and signed HAPPY CHRISTMAS. There was a small religious card signed, in a round schoolgirl's hand, Laura Greenwood. On impulse I tore the cards from two of the handsomest presents I had bought my own children, a pretty gilt clock with enamelled flowers for Harriet and a Mickey Mouse watch for Paul, and relabelled them for the Greenwood children, determining that they should have a sample of the worldly, temporal Christmas of other children, as a reward for usually having to carry the spiritual side for all the others. Then I wrote to my mother, rang Naomi to say I was on my way, and finally spoke to Elmira, who told me that Sean had turned up. 'He never went back to Dermot's place at all after the row with Kate,' Elmira reported. 'And do you know where he spent the night? The YMCA.'

'Have the others said anything about him?' I asked.

'No,' she told me.

That was that then, I thought, I've finished with it. I posted the letter to my mother, delivered the presents at the Greenwoods and went home to load the car. As I did so the same reporter turned up again and then another. I drove away up the grey motorway under sullen skies out of London to Stonebridge. I was, by now, very tired and there was an idea bouncing in my brain like a pingpong ball on a fairground rifle-range, but I could not work out what it was, and was in the end overtaken by a merciful amnesia until I drove up country lanes, then up the long drive to the house, and was, finally, emptied of the last six months, freed of the past.

So I came in, through the Trent beeches, under a sky as grey and sunken as my cheeks, to where my children were. As I drew up beside Henry Trent's white Mercedes they came running out shouting, 'Daddy! Daddy! You're here!' and skittered over the gravel to me. They were taller, and rosier and strangely, more solid. Behind them standing on the steps I saw Naomi and then Henry and Irene Trent. They watched as I swung the children round and answered their questions about the journey. The dog barked and jumped up and down. I glanced at them as they stood there in their tweeds, and saw them waving me off to war. At any rate I got the impression I was being given a farewell, perhaps because I had not been given a greeting. So, with the children hanging on either hand and the dog bouncing round me I went up the steps, kissed Naomi and Irene firmly on the cheek and detached Paul's hand so that I could shake Henry's.

'Glad to see you, Joe,' he said, and with the children bumping and jostling me we all went in. I hoped I would not cry. I hoped I would not find Roderick there, as he, the old friend of the family, easily might be. Then I would have to choose between despair and starting a row with him, and it would be the latter.

In through the double doors to the sitting-room, where the dreaded tree stood by the dreaded log-fire and the windows looked out across the drive and down a long sweep of lawn. I tripped over a skate just inside the door and was glad to hear Naomi laugh as she always had laughed when I got out of bed and planted my foot on a stray toy car. I was glad to hear Henry say, 'Harriet – are you trying to kill your father before he's even in the door?'

Irene and Naomi brought in the tea. The children showed me the little nativity figures which they had made out of clay, and painted and put on straw under the Christmas tree.

I told them about Ajax getting his head stuck in the gate. They were polite and did not take more than one chocolate biscuit apiece. Like dogs they understood more than they knew, and were wary, as an animal will be wary, of an unfamiliar atmosphere. Throughout tea Philip lay at my feet, looking at me and rolling his eyes round the room distractedly. At one point Naomi said, 'Nice to see old Phil again,' and Philip shrank from her hand as she bent down to touch him. Naomi said, 'He's not used to me any more.'

'He remembers us,' cried Harriet.

'I expect that's because you used to take him for walks,' Irene said, covering up the dog's blunder quickly. Is it only in England that dogs so habitually act out their owner's parts for them while, like a play conducted in masks, the real actor is in hiding? Or sometimes have the parts assigned to them? 'I don't think Rover has taken to you at all,' cries the owner, who wants to bite you himself, or 'Fifi seems to have fallen in love with you,' says the owner who is about to try to do the same. At that moment I felt the situation might have been expressed faster and more clearly if the Trents had turned out Prince Arthur of Godhawk, their uncontrollable bull-terrier who was normally kept chained near the backdoor in the kitchen and spent his days alternately choking himself with wild straining to get away or lying on the floor in a state of malignant apathy. Or, perhaps, if Roderick had swept up and released the Alsatian over which he had such absolute mastery that it only got out of control when faced with class or other enemies, and let the brute rush in and savage silly Philip.

After dinner I broke away from the table and went up to see the children in bed, in the room which had been specially decorated for their visits.

'When are we going back to London?' Harriet asked me.

'I don't know,' I said.

'I think Granny wants us to stay here,' Paul observed.

'I don't want to,' said Harriet.

'Nor me,' said Paul.

'I have the idea,' said Harriet, 'that nobody ever tells you what's going on.'

I certainly shan't, I told myself. But I won't have you brought up by smarmy Roderick. He'd have you packed off to boarding school in five minutes, detaching you, in the classical manner, from your mother's apron strings, so that he could cling to them more easily himself.

When I got downstairs again, in a grim mood, Naomi and Irene had disappeared.

'Washing up,' said Henry Trent, who was seated in front of the fire with a brandy. 'They don't like to leave it for Mrs Edwards in the morning – it slows her down. Help yourself to a drink.'

'Just between the two of us,' I said, sitting down, 'is that Roderick still hanging about?'

He had heard too much about what a bad husband I was. He said, in no friendly tone, 'Better ask Naomi. Her mother and I are trying not to interfere. These things are best worked out by the couple concerned.'

'I've got my doubts about that,' I said, 'as a theory.'

'Outsiders generally make matters worse,' he said, 'in my experience. However,' he added, in order to show no positive ill will, 'in answer to your question – yes.'

Poor Henry, who had wanted a son anyway, had got a daughter instead, was now faced with a prospective son-in-law he privately considered to be a stuck-up nuisance, and me, whom he knew to have treated his daughter badly.

I said, 'How's business?'

'Not bad,' he said, 'considering everything. I haven't had to lay a man off yet. We've benefited a lot from the threat of continual gas and electricity strikes. A lot of people who might have given up solid-fuel ranges and so forth have replaced them with new ones when the moment came, instead of throwing them out, and a good few people are having them installed as an extra precaution. It's an ill wind that blows nobody any good, as they say. I'm beginning to think it might be safe to expand – I must say it looks safe enough but the general atmosphere's got so bad you almost hold back from doing something you'd have gone ahead with in all good faith a few years ago.'

So until Naomi and her mother came back into the room we talked about the future of Henry's company.

'Still going on about the TUC and NCB,' Irene said. 'Well, Joe. How are your mother and father?'

'I don't know,' I said. 'I haven't been there for over a year. They seldom write and they aren't on the phone. Dad sends me the local paper every week, though. He's had to get rid of some of the sheep – the cost of winter feed's too high.'

'Lovely air up there,' murmured Irene, not keen on my humble parents. 'Like wine.'

Naomi, sitting on a stool by the fire, passed her hand over her brow. She looked well but the past few months must have taken their toll. While I, the author of the trouble, had wallowed in the ashpit moaning, she had been obliged to play her part in Stonebridge, presumably keeping quiet about what was going on in front of her mother's friends, maintaining some kind of equilibrium for the sake of the children and having the situation neutralized for her by her mother's platitudes. She bore the marks, or rather lack of them, of someone who had had scarcely a moment alone to confront the situation in her own terms. She had no doubt visited the neighbours, and told them I was abroad, talked to her mother and told her I had gone too far, dined at country restaurants with Roderick and described me as a young girl's mistake. Now, her smooth numbed face made her unapproachable. I sat there, extremely tired by now, thinking of my children upstairs in bed. I said, 'I think I'll stroll down the drive and then go to bed.' And then I told them, briefly, how I had been delivering presents at Katie's house when the bomb went off.

Irene Trent said, 'I heard on the news at lunch-time that a house in London had been bombed and that two people had escaped. Fancy it being you, Joe.'

Naomi said, 'But why Katie's house? Is she mixed up in something?'

'Not directly,' I said. 'It's a long story.'

Henry Trent said, 'It sounds as if it would be.'

'What do you mean not *directly* mixed up in it?' Naomi insisted.

So I told her the story Kate had told the police – that her brother had heard of the planned bombing and that Katie had told the police and had been threatened with reprisals from the IRA.

'Do you mean she waited in the house to be bombed?' Naomi said. 'Why didn't she ask for police protection?'

'I think it's because of the atmosphere she was brought up in,' I said. 'It might have looked like – a betrayal.'

'Well – ' Naomi said incredulously. 'And you stayed with her? Joe – I can't believe it.'

'I only stayed with a view to getting her to leave,' I said. 'When the bomb went off I was trying to shove her out of the window.'

Here, in that quiet room, with the three Trents all manifesting concealed disbelief and distaste of one kind or another, I could hardly credit it all myself. I dared not tell Naomi I had offered our house to Katie as a refuge. Her fear of what damage the bombers might do to the house would be only slightly greater than her fear of the destructive Mulvaney children. I knew she would be very angry about it so I saved the information for another day.

Irene looked at Naomi and said, 'Well, Joe. You do seem to get mixed up in some funny situations.' And Naomi said nothing at all until she said, 'Was much damage done to the house?'

I was suddenly angry but, not knowing quite why, I said, 'Not too much. She's looking forward to doing it all up again.'

'Knowing Katie's taste, I don't suppose it'll look much different,' said Naomi with a smile.

Mist hung round the poplars as we walked down the drive, our feet crunching on the gravel and the breath coming in steam from our mouths. Naomi wanted to talk about the explosion. Instead I said, 'How's it been?'

'How do you think? It's the obvious place to come, but just thank God you're a man and not a runaway wife with two children in her parents' home. Still, I suppose it's been a strain on them, too.'

'And the children?' I asked.

'All right. A bit subdued.'

There was a silence.

'Am I coming back?' she asked, suddenly.

I turned off the drive. We paced across the lawn away from the lighted windows of the house.

'If you want to,' I said.

'You don't sound very enthusiastic,' she said. 'I'd hoped – '

'We probably both hoped we'd look into each other's eyes and it'd be all right. But it hasn't been like that, on your side either. Let's give it time. My only feeling is that I don't want to go back to the same old life.'

'What life?' she said. 'What was wrong with it? And what do you want anyway? It was orderly, comfortable – what's wrong with that? I worked for that, Joe. It didn't fall into my lap. And now you tell me you don't want it. Tell me what you do want. Sixteen children in a slum? Blenheim Palace? Or would you rather live like the Watsons, with a potter's wheel in the kitchen and drunken scenes every night? You can say what you like, Joe, but you couldn't take the children going to school in plimsolls because they had no shoes, or having their teeth out because I hadn't taken them to the dentist. Or bad cooking, come to that, or draughts and dirty sheets. It's a wonderful idea – that we're rich, comfortable and over-protected. Try it the other way, sending your children to a primary school where they didn't learn to read – do you think you'd like that? Just let me know what you do want – I suspect that it's to have your cake and eat it too. It's pretty nice isn't it – you can lead your life according to principles, but you're always going to know that your children, your flesh and blood are being well taken care of. Just as you were, Joe, just as you were.' She paused, saying, in a less angry tone, 'I'm entitled to know what it is that you want. Not in broad outline, not a dream. But clearly and specifically, what you want.'

We were walking, now, across the lawn, back to the house.

'Don't you see, Naomi,' I said. 'I was tired. Tired of the effort we both had to make to go on with that kind of life. I haven't missed any of it, living alone. Not the Pattens coming to dinner, or the clean towels in the bathroom – '

'That's because you're living alone,' she said. 'Bring children into that and the situation would soon deteriorate.'

'It was an unnecessarily complicated way of life,' I said. 'And it wore us both out leading it. And it all hinged on money – '

'There's a lot you're leaving out, Joe,' she said, lowering her voice as we approached the house.

'You too,' I told her.

'Perhaps.'

We were back in the hall. 'Where am I sleeping?' I asked.

'You have a choice,' she said steadily. 'The usual room, where I am, or the little green room at the end of the corridor. Both,' she said drily, 'have been prepared for your coming.'

'Well,' I said. 'I might as well come in with you.'

'You might as well,' she said.

It was obvious that Naomi had been sleeping with sly Roderick, but that she had also been very lonely. She lay in my arms and said, 'Joe – I've missed you too.' It was true in a way. I had missed her – her and the children, as a unit. But never, for a moment, had I missed our life together or felt the slightest impulse to ring up Naomi, or go to see her, for the sheer pleasure of talking and being together. I had known that within two minutes I would be feeling the same pressures on me to declare my feelings and make a statement of my intentions and within three we would be accepting invitations to Christmas drinks and discussing with intensity which Christmas turkey would offer the best quality for the least money and whether Beth Lombard's reading-age was as high as her mother claimed. Poor Naomi and poor me. I could no longer see her as a friend. I had been lonely, but not for her. Perhaps I could not afford to be; if I had been I would have lost the other things I was beginning, slowly, to learn and feel, like a small child who begins to walk, run and touch things, fall down on the grass, startle up a butterfly and embrace a tree-trunk. Naomi meant death to all this. Naomi was a wall-to-wall carpeted cell with hot and cold running water and the key in her apron pocket. Naomi was neatly-docketed bills, French farmhouse cooking, wines bought in bulk and patterned sheets. What Naomi touched was disinfected and became an easy-clean surface; where she moved became an ornamental garden with palings round it and flower-beds where ranks of tulips spelled out MARRIAGE, FATHERHOOD and HOME. Her candid gaze killed the spirit and turned the limbs to lead. She did not want much to make her happy, but whatever it was would have to have a fence round it and a proper map reference, or she would not feel safe.

She fell contentedly asleep, now, but I could not sleep. I had to face the fact that where I had hoped to feel a sudden surging of the spirit when I saw her again, all that had happened was that I had realized I could not go back, not if anything more was required of me than the mere act of going back, which after all would be easy enough. But there would be no point if I went back to sulk and fume, nag and rage. That would be fair on nobody. Or else I could learn to tolerate my situation, as people so often had to. That was a possibility, though not one I welcomed. And as I lay there in the over-warm air of the double-glazed, centrally heated bedroom, the faces of Harriet and Paul circled round me. In the end I got up and made tea and ate half a packet of digestive biscuits from the kitchen cupboard. I could cleave to Naomi, whom I did not love, or not in the way I was supposed to, and lead the life I found unbearable, for the sake of keeping my children, whom I did love; or I could abandon them, guiltily and miserably, in the name of some illusory personal freedom whose shape, in terms of action, I could not define. And even all that was conditional – I could go back and one or other of us could change, we could be happy again. One or other of us could renege and again wreck everything.

And I didn't even know what to do about a job.

I thought all this, and more, over and over again, until it seemed there was no point in thinking. I washed up carefully, so that no one would know I had been unable to sleep, hid the biscuits at the back of a kitchen cupboard, hoping the housekeeper or the children would not get the blame, went back to bed, lay down beside Naomi, and went to sleep.

In the morning Irene brought us tea, surveying us like an old beldame, and I thought that perhaps without her, we might stand a chance. After breakfast we went for a walk down the lane and into the copse and played hide-and-seek through the trees. Naomi wore a red woollen cap. Her eyes sparkled. Her face was soft and pretty. After lunch – good beef, apple pie and thick local cream – Irene suggested I might like to take a nap. There had been a picture of me in the morning papers. I had been mentioned on the BBC and the implication that I had done a dashing and heroic thing seemed to have removed the stigma of having been mixed up in some IRA hooliganism. I fell asleep peacefully. There were three days now, until Christmas.

I awoke when the front door banged and the sound of children's voices came up from the hall. When I came down I saw riding hats on the table and boots on the floor. In the sitting-room the children and Naomi were having tea in jeans and socks. 'Roderick fell off his horse,' Harriet laughed, spitting out crumbs. I caught Irene's quick and careful glance.

Naomi looked at her teacup.

'Was he hurt?' I asked.

'No – he just got up again,' she told me.

'What a shame,' I remarked sympathetically.

Irene made the slightest sound, 'Hmph' down her nostrils, rather like a horse blowing. Henry said 'Have some walnut cake, Joe.'

Naomi said, 'We arranged the ride when we thought you weren't coming until the day before Christmas.'

'No business of mine,' I said.

'That's right,' said Irene, declaring herself as quite a strong supporter of Roderick. You could see why she was rooting for the loyal, fond-of-the-children, faithful fellow, six-foot-two in his stockinged feet, good at business and handy with rod and gun. He was exactly what she had had in mind for a son-in-law since Naomi was born. He might have his little problems, I thought, but they would not emerge on the surface. Naomi could easily bear him a child, a half-brother for Paul, and Harriet. He would totter round this very room while they had tea and Harriet and Paul were standing on some wind-swept playing-field two hundred miles away, looking forward to the holidays, feeling, but not quite understanding, that they were a bit less part of the family than mummy and daddy and their new brother.

After dinner I went to the pub with Henry. It was carpeted and softly lit. There was muzak in the background. We sat in a corner, watching the local businessmen and their wives. Henry smoked a cigar, drank whisky and said little. We talked about local farming. Warmed by the whisky he said, 'Of course all that on that side' – and he gestured, 'belongs to the Glennisters. They don't farm it all themselves, of course. Most of it's let to tenant farmers.'

I nodded.

He said, 'At least you've got some go in you, Joe.'

'Not much at present,' I said.

'Perhaps,' he said, 'but you started at the bottom and made something of yourself. That's something, as I see it.' He paused and stubbed out his cigar. I lit a cigarette. 'Give us one of those?' he asked.

I lit it for him and he said, 'I won't say I like all this. And frankly, when you get to my age you get selfish – you don't want what peace and quiet you can get disturbed. It's for you and Naomi to sort it out between you in any case. But speaking for myself I'd be glad if you could make a go of it. For one thing I don't like the Glennisters. They're a shallow, snobbish lot. I tell Irene to keep out of it but she won't. I suppose it's natural in a mother.' He sighed and said, 'She should never have sent Naomi to that school.'

'Funny,' I said. 'I think that school had a big effect on Naomi.'

'Not just the school,' said Henry, 'it was everything it stood for. But there you are. It's all in the past and can't be undone now. Are you going back to your job?'

'I don't think my prospects are good there now,' I told him.

'I can see that,' he said. 'Look, Joe – I'll take you on at the firm if you like. I know you don't know anything about it, but you can learn quickly enough. I need help – someone I can trust – if I'm going to expand. I'm not a young man any more. And I know you may not fancy working for your father-in-law. It was hard enough working for my father, I remember that. But I think we could manage.'

I said 'My round,' and went for more drinks. I was touched by his suggestion that he seemed to have some faith in me.

I took the drinks back. 'It's a generous offer, Henry,' I said, 'and thank you for making it. But I don't think I can accept. I don't honestly think it's what I want and there's no point in coming in with you on that basis.'

'I'm disappointed,' he said, 'but not surprised. I had the idea you'd say that. Do you know what you do want?'

'No,' I said.

'You'll find out,' he told me. 'I daresay you do know really – something's stopping you from finding out. But you can't keep my daughter dangling on forever. She won't stand for it. Neither will I.'

I drank my whisky. He stood up and said, 'We'd better be getting back.'

As we drove through the dark country lanes he said, 'I'm like most men. I thought of leaving once – there was another woman. I stayed, for Naomi's sake, or so I told myself. It was easier in those days – harder to go, I mean. And there was the business. My father would never have forgiven me. He'd have gone and I needed him. It was simpler in the end to stay and knuckle down to it. I wouldn't like your choices, I know that.'

As soon as we got back Irene hurried him off to bed. I could picture him sitting there, propped up in his striped pyjamas, returning inadequate answers to her questions. 'Did you tell him he's got to speak out?' she would say. 'Yes.' 'And what did he say?' 'I don't remember him saying anything.' 'Oh Henry. You're hopeless. Haven't you any thought for your daughter – I'll have to speak to him myself, make him see he can't get away with it – '

Meanwhile, back in the firelight, slightly drunk and having another, I sat opposite Naomi with, as so often, nothing whatever to say, or everything to say again – stock words, attitudes and responses flowing between us and then washing away, with nothing changed.

I said, finally, 'Your dad had a word to say to me.'

'What?'

'Not much. There isn't much to say. He offered me a job.'

'Did he?' she said, amazed. 'He didn't say anything about that.'

'I think he needs extra help if he's going to expand.'

'Is that all he said – about offering you a job?'

'Henry doesn't want to interfere in our marriage. He did the sensible thing – offered me a job, which I need, because he needs me, too. He takes the old line that the women deal with the relationships and the men deal with the outside world.'

'Are you having another whisky?'

'Seem to be.'

'He never mentioned this job idea, even to Mother.'

'Said he'd once decided to leave your mother. He stayed because of you and because your grandfather might have left the firm.'

'No – ' she said. 'Not Father – it must have been Auntie Phyllis.'

'I shouldn't mention it to your mother.'

'Do you think I'm mad? She ran the local riding-stables. I just called her Auntie Phyllis. She and father's sister had been at school together.'

There was a familiar, muffled tone to her voice. I knew the school must have been the local secondary school in the town where Albert Trent had begun his scrap business. There had always been these elisions and vaguenesses in Naomi's stories, where bits of poverty and working-class background had to be covered up. She never told lies but she knew how to convey a false impression. I had been surprised when I heard her tell Jessica, 'Joe's family farms in Yorkshire.' I saw an ideal picture of my father as a thickset, betweeded figure driving over half the county in a Range Rover with the estate manager at his side. It was not the real man – tired and ageing, coming downhill in a flapping coat with a puny lamb under his arm.

'What happened to her?'

'She sold up. Perhaps that was why. I never knew that. Just as well he didn't do it.'

I yawned and said, 'Poor Henry. He was probably looking forward to a quiet Christmas – '

'It is quiet, isn't it?' Naomi demanded. 'No one's rowing.'

'Let's go to bed,' I said.

'I think we should try to confront things, Joe.'

'Confront them and work them through,' I said. 'That reminds me. I'd better ring Elmira.'

'What reminds you of that? Why have you got to ring her?'

'Find out how things are.'

'Isn't it rather late?'

'Not 11 yet – she's knocked off for Christmas.'

'What?'

'Practice. She's gone back to ballet-dancing.'

'Hm,' she said.

How I hated Naomi's constant questions which often seemed like a way of gathering information against people. How I hated the way she tried to stop me from doing things, like making phone calls and going to places. How I hated her efforts to try and lead my life with me, all the time. How I hated her hatred of other women, often women superficially at any rate, worse off than she was. How I hated, above all, the insecurity all this must mean. I was drunk. I was letting things fall apart. I did not want to be a petty hater. I must try to get on with Naomi. She must try to get on with me.

'I'll have to ring Elmira to find out how things are,' I said.

And I went into the small room Henry sometimes used as a study and rang Elmira. There was no reply. Then I tried my own, to see if Katie was there.

'You just rang our number,' said Naomi from the doorway.

'Katie,' I explained. 'I gave her the key just in case she needed somewhere until the house was repaired.'

'You did what?' said Naomi. 'Our house could be in ruins by now. How could you, Joe? How could you?'

'There's no danger,' I said. 'She probably won't go there, anyway. Look, Naomi, she's just been blown up – '

'They've tried it once. They'll try it again,' said Naomi. 'That's what I'm talking about. They'll try it again. How could you endanger our house? Not to mention those wrecking children – '

'I'm going to bed,' I said. I walked past her.

'You ring the police, first, and make sure the place is being watched,' said Naomi.

'You do it,' I said. 'I don't suppose she's there anyway.'

'This is intolerable,' said Naomi.

'Look,' I said, 'if she's there, do you think the police will leave her there without watching the house? That house has never been safer. Two of the men are in gaol – '

'It's that brother I don't trust,' Naomi said, at the phone. 'There's something fishy there if you – oh, thank you, Well, whoever's in charge will do – in connection with the bombing of the house in Blenheim Crescent – thank you.' She turned to me and said, 'If I find Katie's in that house I'm going to phone up and ask her to leave.'

'I defy you to do it,' I said.

Furiously she turned back to the phone and, as I left the room I heard her, in an altered tone, say, 'I'm the owner of a house – I've reason to believe – ' Back in the sitting-room I poured myself another large whisky and carried it upstairs to bed. I was in bed, drinking the whisky and smoking a cigarette when Naomi came in, took one look at me sitting up bare-chested in bed with a glass in my hand, said, 'Oh, my God,' and started getting undressed. 'Kate's not there anyway, it turns out,' she said. 'And they assured me a constant watch was being kept all round just in case. It all sounded fairly convincing.'

'Good,' I said.

She got into bed, saying 'There's something I don't understand about all this.'

'There isn't anything,' I said. 'For God's sake relax, Naomi. We can't get anywhere if you go on like this,' and I tried to kiss her, as men often do in an attempt to stop women from getting more and more nervous about hoovering the curtains before mother comes, going bankrupt, sorting out a pile of jumble to be ready in five minutes, worrying about a child they've had to leave in hospital. Men like woman tranquil. But their method never works.

'Get away, Joe,' Naomi said. 'You're drunk.'

I just said, 'Wrrr,' and rolled over on my side, with my back to her, but before I passed out I remember thinking that there was something I had not told Naomi but I could not recall what it was.

I heard the clock downstairs strike 12. Two days until Christmas. I was up at 3 with a headache, prowling the kitchen for more tea and digestive biscuits. The anguish was physical. I drank the tea in the sitting-room, staring at the ashes in the cooling grate and decided it was not worth it. Not worth the drinking, the quarrelling, the hurt feelings. I would get Naomi and the children back to London and make a fresh start. The only condition I would impose was that the MacDonalds, the Pattens, and all the rest of them would never set foot in the house again.

I would start a business.

I went back to bed. Next day we were all to drive to Stonebridge to lay in the rest of the Christmas food. At breakfast I told Henry to go to work if he wanted to. I would fetch and carry in his stead. He was grateful, and he went.

Before we left, Naomi and I walked over the flat fields, empty now of cattle, under a dull sky.

'Mother says you're not sleeping,' she said. 'She says she hears you moving about at night.'

I was horrified by the notion of Irene's ears, awake all night while she slept, twitching at footfalls, groans of passion, branches falling from the trees, people going to the lavatory. I said, 'Ugh. I'm worried, that's all.'

'You can't sleep peacefully beside me,' she said, hurt.

'I've been feeling guilty,' I said. 'I feel I'm ruining your life.'

'It would take more than you, Joseph Coverdale, to do that for me,' she said stoutly.

'I wish,' I said as a lonely ragged crow flew over us towards a clump of elms, 'that I could be what you like.' I looked, but I could not see past the hedge in front of us into the next field. I opened the gate and we went through. At the bottom of the fields ran the turgid river Slean. We walked towards it.

'But I'll try,' I said.

She said, 'Give up the job, if you want to. Sell the house. We'll live in a caravan, on a houseboat. Whatever you want, I'll try it.'

She was, suddenly, being more generous than I. Women often are.

I said, 'Naomi – '

Henry Trent's daughter was speaking. 'What difference does it make? Things couldn't be worse between us. And I'll always have this to fall back on. You tell me what you want and I'll go along with it. Mind you, I think you're behaving like King Lear, or God or somebody, asking for perfect faith and trust.'

'I don't want so much,' I said. 'I've been thinking. I'll have to leave that job. For one thing I'd be bored from now on. But I – '

By the time she had interrupted me I was conscious that while she had been talking to me, she had been using the word *you*, while so far I had said nothing but *I*. Before I could go any further she said, 'I do love you, Joe. So far that word hasn't been mentioned between us.'

I said nothing. 'Do you love me?' she asked. 'Otherwise the whole thing's pointless.'

That word *love*, applied to so many different emotions, directed towards so many different objects, given as an explanation for the best and worst of human conduct, has always frightened me. It seems meaningless. It is often a piece of fairy gold, a false coin used to purchase many things. When the seller opens his hand again, there lies the coin, changed into a dry leaf.

'I do love you,' I said. And of course it was true. All the same, I was lying to her, for I didn't love her as a woman, passionately, exclusively, romantically as a man is supposed to. I think I had, until after the birth of Paul, when Naomi got more and more busy, and the routine for both of us more demanding. Then we had accepted the pattern of a successful married couple and stopped taking any notice of each other. Perhaps I had no need to feel bad – I did not feel a mad, intolerable passion for her, but then I supposed she did not feel one for me, either. We would both, automatically, have gone to the stake in each other's stead, but our hearts did not beat as one. Nobody, I imagined, would have been more horrified and uncomfortable than Naomi if that had been the case. She did not really want passion. She wanted it simulated, to soothe and comfort her.

She said, 'You don't sound very convincing.'

'I'm standing in the middle of a field, freezing,' I said. 'I love you. And we'll go back to London and live happily together. I don't want to live on a houseboat, or to be a beachcomber or a horse-trader. All I ask is that you don't fill my house with foolish lefties from the local Labour party who'll start the revolution as soon as the *cassoulet* has been cooked for a week, and that you don't invite the Pattens, MacDonalds and their ilk to dinner ever again and that you stop the debate about moving Harriet to St Paul's. Send her or don't send her, but don't ask me what my principles say. I'm sick of dinner-parties, nice couples, scruples of conscience about the working classes and the third world and talking about holidays on the Rhône and whether to get a Simca or not. I don't want to make any more efforts for any more crappy people. In return I'll be a good and faithful husband. I'll even do up the spare-room.'

'Is that what it's all about?' she asked. 'Just holidays on the Rhône and St Paul's – well,' she said quickly, 'if that's what you want, let's do it.'

'All right.'

She gave me a kiss in the middle of the field.

'There's a confession I have to make – '

'Don't want to hear it,' she said cheerfully.

'No. You'll have to know.'

'Later, then,' she said decidedly as suddenly the children came swooping over the darkening field, wearing woolly hats and gloves and anoraks.

'Let's go home now,' I said.

'London?'

'Yes,' I said. 'Let's make our minds up now, tell Irene, help to get the shopping in, get our own Christmas grub and leave before lunch.'

'Oh, Joe,' Naomi said. 'The children are expecting to have Christmas here, now there's nothing in London – no decorations, anything. And Mother's gone to so much trouble. She'll be so disappointed.'

'If she's got any sense she'll be only too delighted to see us all set off hand in hand and settle down to a quiet Christmas.'

'Mother doesn't think like that about Christmas. She likes the family round her – you know that.'

'Naomi – I want to go. I want, if you like, a gesture to show something's happening. Let's just go and not worry too much about your mother's ideas about Christmas.'

But the old conditioning about forward-planning – the sheets, the Christmas pudding, the dog's breakfast – and about Mother's feelings was strong. Naomi stopped dead in the middle of the field hesitated, and said, 'I can't do it.'

'Oh, fuck it,' I cried. 'Fuck it all, Naomi.' I drew a deep breath, told myself to be reasonable and said, 'OK then. We'll stay. But we're leaving first thing on Boxing Day morning.' And we all went back to the house and got in the car to go and shop in Stonebridge. The sky lowered over streets that were almost dark. Standing beside Irene in the brightly-lit grocer's as she picked up crystallized gingers and pots of pressed duck, I felt happy that it was over, my children safe, my wife content. But I was uneasy. I wanted to be on the road to London. I knew we should have been going home. I had to get my final revelation, about my affair with Jessica, over. I was restless, and impatient.

On the way back we stopped at the farm for the turkey. I stood in the entrance to the farm, waiting while the children whooped and swung on the farm gate. Further down, beside the farmhouse, Irene and the farmer's wife exchanged civilities, Irene in her suit and smart shoes, the farmer's wife in her wellington boots and overall. I walked down and took the heavy bird from the woman and walked up to the car, willing Christmas to come fast and be over soon.

'Look after yourself, Mrs Wootton,' called Irene.

'Thank you. Good-bye,' called the other. We drove off, leaving her standing there in the semi-darkness. One light burned in the farmhouse window.

'Poor woman. She lost her husband at Easter,' said Irene. 'She's thinking of selling up and going to live with her married daughter at Brigstock. She'll be there all alone over Christmas.'

'What a shame,' said Naomi.

We ate a roast chicken for lunch, with creamed spinach and carrots and had raspberries and strawberries from the freezer. The telephone rang and Naomi went to answer it. I leaned back in my chair, finished my wine and, with a sudden feeling of friendliness for Irene, my wife's mother, said, 'Irene – you've done us proud.'

My enemy, as she always would be, was saying, cordially, 'It's a pleasure to have you all here,' when Naomi opened the door. She said, 'Joe!' I swung round, knowing the voice she used in emergencies. Her face was grey.

'What is it?' I said, standing up.

'Come into the study,' she said.

As she walked in front of me I realized that it was only partly shock she was feeling – the set of her back and the way her feet hit the parquet floor meant anger. And Naomi rarely lost her temper.

In Henry's study the phone lay, off the hook, on the desk. I heard its voice saying, 'Hullo – hullo. Naomi – are you there?' From the windows I saw heavy clouds hanging over the lawn, dark mist over the trees beyond. The voice, I realized, was Jessica's.

'How could you?' Naomi was saying. 'Joe – how could you?'

There were tears in her eyes. I said, 'I tried to tell you.'

The phone went on talking, 'Naomi – are you there? Naomi, I'll have to ring off in a second.'

I reached over and picked up the phone. 'I'll do it for you, Jessica,' I said, and put it back on its rest.

Naomi was shaking. I went to her. She said, 'Don't come near me.'

'Naomi,' I said, 'I know I was stupid but there wasn't anything in it – '

'It's not that – it's the lies. About having to ring Elmira and giving her the doorkey out of kindness. I knew there was something wrong all the time. It's just being deceived yet again, by you. How can I trust you again? It's not fair.'

'What doorkey? I gave the doorkey to Katie,' I said, bewildered.

'Are you all right, Naomi?' said Irene putting her head round the door. Naomi wiped the back of her arm over her eyes and said, 'Yes, Mother.' Irene flashed a furious glance at me and went away again. She like Naomi, must have felt betrayed. My midnight rambles, the secret discussions between Naomi and me had been tolerable, since they led to reconciliation, but this new affair must have made her wonder why I had come to disturb them.

'I really can't understand,' I said. Then, realizing what Jessica had told Naomi I said, 'Oh, my God. She told you she found me in bed with Katie Mulvaney.' I stood and looked at Naomi.

'Of course that's what she told me,' cried Naomi. She sat down suddenly, behind the desk and laid her head on it. 'I thought it was going to be all right,' she mumbled, like a child.

I stood there by the door, facing her, with the desk between us.

'I'll tell you the truth,' I said. And I did not want to. At that moment I thought it might almost be better to let her believe what Jessica had told her. But eventually I would be found out and in the meanwhile I would only create another lie between us. So I said, 'Jessica certainly found me in bed with Katie – at least, I was on top of it. Just because after the bombing she fell asleep holding my hand and every time I tried to get it away she moaned and tossed about. Don't forget she'd had to get her children out of the house and then barely escaped being burned to death. All I did was kick off my shoes and lie down on the bed to get some sleep, as you do with children. It was 3 o'clock in the morning by that time. Then Jessica burst in, raving mad and took it for granted I'd been sleeping with Katie – well, making love to her. She must know perfectly well I wasn't – I mean, I ask you – we'd been up all night jumping out of windows, Kate's house had gone up in flames, I was lying there fully dressed on the bed.'

'Who let her in?' said Naomi.

'Elmira. We were in Elmira's house. Elmira turned up having heard the explosion, then there were fire-engines, the police – ' Naomi had raised her head from the desk. 'But,' I said, 'that isn't everything, of course. In fact Jessica was like that because I'd slept with her – ' Naomi's face went blank and then, when she understood she said, 'Joe – ' and I went on. 'I'm sorry, Naomi. But she did it because she wanted to. Hugo's gone bust and they've never got on anyway. I think she had it in mind to replace him with me.'

'That's a wicked thing to say,' Naomi burst out. 'You might at least have the decency – '

'I'm telling you the truth, whether you like it or not. If you stop to think about it, it all fits. There's no point in going on about it now. I wish I hadn't done it, that's all.'

'My best friend,' said Naomi.

'If you believe that you'll believe anything,' I said. 'I know you feel you can't trust me now, Naomi. But look at the people you have trusted – your mother, all too ready to throw you into the arms of that prick Roderick, and make you lady of the manor and herself the lord of the manor's mother-in-law. Naomi,' I said, 'whatever happens, don't marry Roderick. And you've trusted Jessica who patronized you without your knowing it and was, in the end quite prepared to scoop me up and marry me, knowing full well I was coming up here to try and sort things out. You might try trusting me – or why not try trusting no one? Nobody in the world can be utterly reliable and sound in every way. We're all weak, we all let each other down sometimes.'

She was crying again. I went to her and said, 'Naomi – please try to think all that is over. Can't we forget it as much as we can?'

'I hate you,' she said.

I stood looking at the top of her head and said, 'I'm a bit tired of finding I'm dealing with a child all the time. I've hurt you, Jessica's hurt you, everybody's hurt you. But you're not immune from hurting people – you're hurting me now but I feel I can't say so, not to you, because I'm supposed to believe you're only four and you haven't done anything. If you don't come back and if you marry Roderick it'll kill me – but I'm not allowed to say so, because of course you haven't done anything and we're all supposed to know you're only a tiny tot and, what's more, we stole your teddy. And the longer you stay here, with your mother, the more you'll come to believe you're just a pre-school child, with no responsibility for anything. In all our discussions you've taken the passive part – I had to say what I was going to do with you – you had to agree to have it done. It's never even occurred to you to go out and get a job, for example. Every time, every bloody time, Naomi, you've laid it all on me. Now – you tell me what you want.'

'I don't know,' she said.

'Are you coming back?' I said.

'I can't – after this.'

I knew there was no point in going on with the scene. Naomi was shocked and frightened. But I was too angry and desperate, now, to control myself. I had to have an assurance from her, she had to say what I wanted her to say. So I went on at her in the angry, unstoppable, lecturing voice which always benumbed her. 'I'm beginning to wonder,' I said, 'whether you were ever really coming back. It all seems too glib. This morning – the grand statement about starting all over again. This afternoon – the rejection of all that. I wish I could believe in my heart of hearts that this wasn't the way it was meant to go all along. I knew we should have gone back to London. I wonder if you weren't playing a game all along without understanding what it was. You've kept old Roderick dangling on, just in case. You haven't told the children we're all going back to London after Christmas, just in case.' I could hear my own voice bullying and demanding. I knew she was blotting it out because she could not bear to listen to it. 'I think you suffered and waited for me but all the time you had a contingency plan. Then if I turned up and went down on one knee and offered you a bunch of red roses and told you I'd been elected MP for Stonebridge and that the MacDonalds were coming to live at the bottom of our garden, you'd agree. You gave me a chance, but it was a very little one.'

'I told you,' she said, 'I'd agree to anything.'

'That's what you *said*,' I told her. 'But you wouldn't even come back to London when I asked you to. And now there's this. You're all right when it comes to broad general statements. Now we're down to specifics it's not so easy, is it? Naomi,' I said bending over her. 'Naomi, for once, be grown up. Just say it's all right. Say you're coming home with me.'

She did not look up. She repeated, over and over again, 'I'm sorry, Joe. I'm sorry. I'm sorry.'

I said, 'Don't keep on saying you're sorry. Can't we forget it all? Can't we just go back to where we were this morning –'

'I can't,' she said. 'I can't now.'

I could not understand. I said, 'You're not to blame. But what is it? I know I slept with Jessica. It's rotten but it's not the end of the world. She came to me and started crying – oh, well, I don't know why I did it. It can't matter that much.'

And Naomi turned up a tear-stained face and said, 'It's just meant that when I thought everything was straight between us, and I'd started to trust you again, that there was still a lie. Now I think there always will be.'

'I tried to tell you in that field. First you didn't want to hear. Then the children turned up. I've been waiting for an opportunity. Why, why must you always think I'm worse than I am? Why can't you give me a chance?'

Irene said, from behind me, 'I hope everything's all right, Joe.' To Naomi she said, 'Your father's back.'

'Irene,' I said. 'It's not all right and you know it's not. And common as I am, even I would have knocked on that door before I came in.'

'There's no need to take that tone with me,' she said. 'This is my home and it's my daughter you've reduced to tears. Not for the first time if I may say so.'

'Well, cheer up, Irene,' I said. 'I'm leaving.'

'Now, Joe,' she said in a placatory tone. 'I'm sorry if I interrupted –'

'It doesn't matter,' I said. 'I'm sick of all this. I'm sick of breaking my heart trying to make amends and get approval. Trying to get through your hard, tight defences. I'll go up to my mother and father's for Christmas. You'll both feel better when I'm gone and you can go back to talking about what a wretch I am. I'll come back after Christmas to see the children. I've done for now.' As I left the room I said, 'I'll ask you then if you've changed your mind, Naomi.' It was more like a threat. I went into the living-room and told the children that Granny and Grandad wanted to see me. I would have to go there and come and see them on the way back.

'But you won't be here for Christmas,' said Harriet.

'Why don't we come with you to Granny and Grandad's?' said Paul.

'I'll give them your love.'

'We'd better go and get your presents so that you can open them on Christmas Day,' said Harriet.

I packed my things as they ran about, pulling things out of hiding-places.

'You'll give my regards to your parents, Joe,' Irene Trent said, standing in the bedroom, stiff as a ramrod, eyes like gimlets, as I fumbled with my things, trying not to start crying. How pathetic I must have seemed and how unmanly. How could I bear to leave my children like this?

'What is the trouble, Joe?' she asked.

'Naomi's decided not to come back to me.'

'But I thought – ' she said.

'She'll tell you,' I said. 'I was to blame.'

For a moment I think she found herself ignoring my own acknowledgement of responsibility and felt a flash of sheer terror at the background of fear and dislike she had created for Naomi, in the name of aiding her daughter against the hideous power and strength of men. I was after all, a sorry sight, dropping one of a pair of socks, stuffing things into a bag higgledy-piggledy. She rallied fast, though, shed all guilt and said, 'Such a terrible thing to happen at Christmas.'

I looked, once, at this stupid woman, drawing her own flesh and blood together for the only remaining celebration of her own former status and usefulness. She was glad to get me, like a splinter or a germ, out of the body of the family. Men must collude with these monstrous women who create domestic security for them. Then I got on with my packing.

'I've tried to do my best, mostly by keeping out of it,' she said.

'Yes, yes, all right,' I said, quickly, not wanting to argue with that figure, standing there puffed up with self-righteousness, greed and self-satisfaction. If I said one word too many, fifty years of hysteria, sexual, matrimonial and maternal, would come bursting out. She wanted the release of a row with me.

'I don't know what you mean, Joe,' she said. If I would not argue she wanted my approval, my acknowledgement that she had done right.

I said, 'You've won. I'm going. That's all,' and walked past her with my bag.

In the hall Harriet said, 'We sent Granny and Grandad's by post. But this is from me – and this – oh, I wish I could see you open them. Daddy please don't go.'

'I must, Harriet,' I told her.

'Here's yours, Joe,' Henry said, handing me a package. 'Pity you won't be here to open it.'

'Thanks, Henry,' I said.

'I hope everything's all right when you get there,' he said. He had obviously been told a tale about a sudden emergency.

I was making my way sickly to the door, clutching a pile of gaily wrapped Christmas parcels to my chest and carrying my bag in the other hand, when Paul cried, 'Oh – I forgot your secret present.'

So I stopped again. 'But it's not wrapped yet,' said Harriet in alarm.

'Keep it for me,' I said, but they looked disappointed and I could not help thinking what a sad token of absence that handkerchief, ashtray or bottle of after-shave would be, so I said, 'No, that would be a pity on Christmas Day. Perhaps you could just wrap it roughly and I promise not to look at it.' And away they ran, Harriet calling, 'Mum! Mum! have you any wrapping-paper?'

Behind me, on the stairs, Irene hissed, 'I don't know what you meant by "winning" Joe. I assure you I've done my best to keep out of this and be fair.'

I said, 'I'm sure you have, Irene. I spoke in anger,' as Naomi appeared with some wrapping-paper. Her eyes red with weeping, she knelt on the floor with her back to me and did up the secret present so that I would not see what it was. Paul handed it to me. Irene, seeing her daughter's face, looked shaken. Henry pursed his lips. With the children standing by I went through the rituals of parting, hugged them, kissed Irene, remembering, as my lips touched her powdered cheek, the poisoned half of the apple offered to Snow White. I shook Henry's hand. I said, fairly low, 'Sorry to leave all this behind me.'

'Can't be helped,' he said, forgiving, but not liking me for it.

And I drove north up the motorway with the dog in the back of the car, crying most of the time. It was a miracle I didn't have an accident.

I wound up narrow pitch-black roads. On either side were dry stone walls and the moors stretching beyond. What a fine Christmas present I was for my parents, I thought – the derelict son arriving empty-handed after a year's silence, coming back alone without wife or children.

I drove into the yard and got out into a biting, howling wind. The dog barked at me.

I put my hand on the latch and I heard my Uncle Joe call out, 'Elizabeth ? Is that you ?'

He sat alone by the kitchen fire. He was watching television. He looked at me as I stood in the doorway and said, 'Joe! How did you get here so soon ?'

'So soon ?' I said, bewildered. I shut the door behind me.

He looked older. His big face was lined. Beside him on the table, by the chair where he always sat, was a bit of wood he had been carving, some library books, and a half-finished glass of lemonade.

'How are you, Uncle Joe,' I said, going over to him. 'Sorry to come without warning.' I seemed to feel the gap where my mother should have been, like a draught from behind, as if the door was open. I suppose I expected her to come in from the yard. The fire was half out, so I knelt down, from long habit, and began riddling it out at the bottom, closing the doors in front to produce a draught.

He said, 'Elizabeth only left here an hour ago. She was going to telephone you on her way – ' Then he stopped and said, 'You didn't know.'

Perhaps I had known.

Finally I looked up from where I was kneeling and said, 'Is father dead then ?'

I stood up as he nodded.

'Dead.' I repeated. It was not a question, but he nodded again.

'It was very sudden,' he said. Automatically I went to fill the kettle from the tap, walked back and put it on the hob. 'He was taken ill after dinner,' Joe said. 'Your mother went with him to the hospital. They said it was a heart attack and sent her home. She'd no sooner arrived than the neighbours came up here to tell her the hospital had rung up. They told us he was dead.'

Just as I had been leaving the Trents, I thought. I seemed

to have lost the beginning and the end of my life at the same time. I had no tears left but my whole body was heavy with loss. I could not really understand the fact. All I felt was that another grievous thing had happened, that I had been punched again, was dazed now, too dazed to feel. I would begin to feel the pain later. I just made the tea, avoiding probing the gap my father left in me, trying not to think.

I took the tea over to my uncle and said, 'I came here on impulse. I must have been nearly here when mother phoned Stonebridge.'

'That's strange,' my uncle said. 'Have you eaten?' I shook my head. 'You should try to eat something, lad,' he said. 'You'll be needing your strength to help your mother.'

'Have you eaten?'

'Your mother put my tea out before she left. Joe,' he said. 'Will you help me to the lavatory?'

He did not want to ask me. That had always been my mother's, or father's job. I put my arms out to him and he grasped them, pulled himself up on to his weak legs. I helped him to the lavatory. My father had put a door inside so that he no longer needed to go through the back door and out into the yard to get there.

As he sat there on the lavatory seat with his trousers round his wasted legs I did not know whether to turn my back or not. In the end I stood, half turned, and said, 'Uncle Joe. My wife's left me. She may not come back and if she doesn't I've lost the children. Don't tell Mother.'

'Eh – dear,' he said. 'Joe.' Then he said, 'Help us up then – you pick some funny spots to break bad news.' As I helped him up and back into the room, into his chair, he said, 'Poor Joe. All the blows on the same day, eh? She may come back, though?'

'She may,' I said. 'How's Mother?'

'She's a strong woman. But she loved your father. She won't get over it easily.'

'And you?'

'I'm sorry I can't be more of help to her,' he said, and that was all. He had always had the courage not to talk about being useless, or a burden, knowing that saying so was self-indulgence and only made things worse for the people who loved him.

'You can comfort Mother,' I said, and we both knew it was true.

'Mary's coming,' he said. 'She can't start until the morning because of the children. And your mother sent Sue a telegram.' My sister Susan lived in Canada. 'You might get down to the bus stop to meet your mother,' he said. 'It'll save her the walk.'

'I'll do that,' I said. I put on my coat and stood with my hand on the latch. 'What happened?'

'He was just crossing the yard, going back out after his dinner,' said my uncle. 'First we heard the dog barking and then Elizabeth looked out. He was at the back end, lying on the ground. She managed to drag him in and laid him down in front of the fire, on the floor. He could hardly breathe and his lips were all blue. I got out of the chair and we both started chafing his hands – he couldn't speak, he was gasping for breath – and we soon saw it was something out of the ordinary. Elizabeth ran down to Whittakers to phone for the doctor and an ambulance. The doctor come up immediately and gave him an injection. That eased it a bit. He stayed until the ambulance arrived. But I think your mother knew what it was and that it was nearly all up with him. She went off with him in the ambulance, but the pity was that they sent her home. They must have known. But it seems they said he never recovered consciousness so I suppose it wouldn't have mattered to him if she was there or not.' He paused, then said, 'It mattered to her though.'

I said, 'Yes. It would,' thinking bitterly that as I had been eating my handsome dinner in Stonebridge, my father had been lying in the wind of the yard, feeling the life being choked out of him; and remembering that as I had gone through my argument with Naomi, up here they had been waiting for the ambulance to wind its way from the hospital in the next dale. If my father had dropped down in my house in London, I thought, where there were two telephones, not one half a mile down the hill, where there was a hospital ten minutes, not forty miles, from home, we might not now be talking about a dead man.

'I can't believe,' said my uncle, 'that I'll not see him again. I can't properly believe that.'

'Nor can I,' I said.

He nodded. He had lived, mostly in this room now, for thirty years or more. To him my father was a fixed point, his movements so familiar they might have been his own. To him my father's absence would be like living without one of the walls of the room. That perpetual space would never be filled.

I walked up to my mother at the bus stop. The bus rolled away between the walls, down the dark road. She cried, 'Joe! Oh, Joe! I didn't think you'd be here tonight.' The wind was pushing us about as I led her to the car. I tried to take the plastic bag she was carrying from her and put it in the back. She clutched it to her, with her handbag.

'It's his things,' she said and began to cry. I helped her into the car and started up.

'It was very quick,' she said. 'They told me that. And he felt nothing, they said. But I wish they hadn't sent me away. Surely they knew – they must have known he hadn't long. I wanted to be there . . . thirty-seven years. It seems wrong not to be there at the end.' Her voice trailed off and she said, in a different tone, 'How are you, Joe?'

'Very well,' I said.

'And Naomi and the children? We got their presents. It was sweet of them –' Her voice changed again and she said, 'I'll have to open his for him. Oh, Joe. He looked so shrunken. To think he was alive this morning and now, tonight, he's gone. I can't believe it. I can't believe I'll never see him again.' She stopped talking but it was as if the voice went on inside her. We had nearly arrived when she said quite naturally, 'I wish they hadn't sent me away. They must have known he hadn't long to go.'

The car's lights swept the walls and then we dipped down the moors beyond. There was a long, unfenced stretch of rising heath, then more walls. She said then, 'Stop the car.' She must have seen the Whittakers, the neighbours down the hill, come out when they heard the car coming. I walked to the gate leading up to their neat stone house and heard her saying, her voice taken by the wind, 'They gave me his things in a bag. They said "Haven't you a case?" but of course I'd not thought to bring one. Look,' she said opening it, 'it's his overalls, shirt and boots and things. We couldn't change him when he went. He went in his ordinary working-clothes. He was too bad, you see, to change.' Doris Whittaker who was nodding and saying 'Yes, yes,' saw me and said 'Hullo, Joe. It's good you're here now when you're needed.' Sam Whittaker said, 'He was a grand man, your dad. I shall miss him, I know that.'

My mother said, 'I'm to take his suit tomorrow – ' and I took her by the arm and said, 'Come on, Mother. It's getting late. We'd better go home.'

She pulled against me a little but let me lead her back to the car. Once home, she came into the room like a stranger, sank down into her chair, then turned and said to me, 'Oh, Joe, Joe, how am I to get your uncle to bed now? I could never manage on my own.'

'We can turn the parlour into a bedroom,' I said, for that was one of the surface thoughts which had come into my head while I was talking to my uncle. 'Don't worry. You wouldn't mind that, would you uncle?'

'I've always wanted it,' he said. 'So if it suits you, Elizabeth, I'd like that. That way I can get myself to bed when I please and hardly bother you. You'll miss the parlour, though. Anyroad, I'll sleep here tonight.'

'Oh – you can't sleep in the chair,' my mother cried.

'I'll sleep where I choose,' he said. 'So unless you can give me a good reason, this is where I'll be. Why don't you go up and get my pyjamas and slippers.'

After she left the room he said, 'It's a bad do. The doctor gave her some pills but she'll not take them.'

'I'll persuade her to take one tonight,' I said.

He shook his head. 'I don't know what'll become of us with your father gone,' he said.

'We'll have to talk about it later,' I said.

'Aye – after the funeral,' he said.

So they would bury my father, I thought, as my mother came back into the room.

We all talked for the best part of the night. My mother's voice went on and on. We comforted her as best we could. I doubt if she could hear us but at least we were together. 'There's Harriet and little Paul, now,' she would say, 'and Mary's Beth and Debbie,' as if to assure herself that my father was not really dead, so long as his grandchildren lived. 'And Paul will even bear his name.' My uncle looked at me and said, 'That's right, Elizabeth, that's right.' In the end my uncle fell asleep in his chair and my mother said, quite suddenly, in a normal voice, 'I'll try to keep the farm going. We can probably afford some part-time help.'

'If that's what you want,' I said with some relief. Honestly, I could not see Mary, with two young children and a small house, taking in my mother and uncle. It would mean sending my uncle to a home, and that was an idea I could never bear. Susan, in Canada, could not help. Naomi, if she came back to me, would not contemplate looking after my old mother and crippled uncle in our gentrified London home. And if she did not, I had no idea what I would do. The obvious thing was to take over here, in place of my father, but I had grown too far away to take up farming. I had always resented it anyway – resented the work, the demands it made on the people who did it, the hardships and the deprivations they took for granted. Nothing but duty would call me back to a harsh life in these hills, and duty, in the end, would not be enough to keep me there.

My mother was speaking again, 'I wish I could be thirty again, with you all growing up and your father a young man. It goes so quickly – you don't notice the time passing until it's too late.'

In the end we went to bed and as I fell asleep I heard my mother saying, 'There's still Harriet and little Paul.' The wind howling round the house and the cold air whistling through the window-frames could not come near the bleakness I felt. I was like a man looking down at the smoking ruins of his own city. I had almost lost any sense of my own existence. I was numb. I could not spare the time to think of my father, who was walking round the yard to see that all was well before he went to bed. There was a lot to be done. I must not grieve, or think of him, although I knew he was out there because I heard the dog bark and then stop barking, silenced by an intangible pat and soothed by inaudible words.

We buried my father the day after Christmas in the windswept cemetery that had so frightened me as a small boy. The tall grass among the tombstones was stiff, drooping with frost. It was bitterly cold. As they lowered my father's coffin into the icy ground I felt like crying out, 'You can't leave him here.' It seemed too bleak, too cold, too desolate, too lonely. It was like a betrayal to leave him there all on his own, abandon him and go back together to a warm house for food. I had not seen him get weaker or lie in bed ill for a long time or die. Now I almost believed he was there, alive in the coffin. It was only when we turned and left the churchyard and I turned round and looked for him that I began to part with him. As we were going through the gates of the churchyard, he was not there, standing among the gravestones. And I still wondered, at the back of my mind, where he was, and I still half-expected to find him crossing the yard when we got home, he, knowing that we were going to come, and us, knowing that he would be there waiting. Even when we pulled up the latch and went inside I still thought he must be somewhere in the house. He had always been there before.

On New Year's Day, ten days after the bomb explosion, a week after my wife had rejected me and taken the children, and four days after my father's funeral, I was on the road back to London. I had scarcely had time to mourn but I had wept. Now I was miserable, but purged, as if the poisoned ducts in my head had been drained and the first trickles of clear water were beginning to flow through those still-swollen and infected channels.

I had not liked leaving my mother and uncle behind at the farm. To them, of course, it seemed natural to stay, but an instinct, and I think it was a sound one, would have had them in the car, with their luggage and on the way home with me that day. I knew that my mother could keep the farm going and live there with Joe for a long time, but that after the grief for my father would come a slowly increasing misery and loneliness. Sooner or later they would have to leave.

I had already sent Naomi a telegram to say that my father was dead. Now I felt I must stop at Stonebridge to tell the children – they had been fond of my father and the mere notification of a fact means little to children. Someone had to talk to them. I hoped, too, that Naomi would come back to London with me but pain, as it sometimes will, had cleared my head. She might come later, although it was unlikely. She would not come now. When I arrived she was not there – she had gone out for a walk.

'Don't cry. Grandad's gone to Heaven,' Irene Trent had told the children. She had been present throughout my interview with them as if suspecting that unless she watched me I might use breaking the news of their grandfather's death as an excuse to get them on my side, or turn them against her on the sly. She looked with dislike at my own tears and urged the children to be brave. I did not argue with her about the proposition that Grandad was with the angels, although I could see the bewilderment on their faces at this vague and incredible tale, unsupported by any accurate detail, or even a feeling of conviction in the teller. If they were to be Trents, I thought, then they would have to begin to make the best of the Trent handling of pain and grief – in other words, learn to turn off fast on to a B road where the view was prettier and deny that there had been an accident on the A road they had originally been using. Fortunately they asked me for details about the death and burial, which I gave as fully as possible, to Irene's obvious discomfiture. At one point she said, 'Do you really think its wise to dwell on all this, Joe?' and I said I thought it was better for the children to know exactly what had happened. Then when they thought about it they would be able to imagine what had really taken place. Irene asked if I did not think this might frighten them. I said it might, but it would scare them less than the ghosts and bogey-men they might create for themselves if the actual events were not described. In truth I was frightening her. The children might be scared of ghosts, but Irene was frightened of a heart attack.

Naomi came in, wearing a sheepskin jacket and walking shoes. And I knew she had been out seeing Roderick.

I got her outside the room and she said, 'I'm sorry about your father, Joe.'

I said, 'I said I'd ask you if you were coming back to London. Will you?'

She shook her head. It was not fair. I needed her.

I said, 'All right. I'll wait. You've waited for me. Now I'll wait for you.'

And I got into my car, empty except for the dog, and drove away down the long, blank motorway to London.

I entered the house thinking, somehow, that I was going back into my own tomb. It smelt less shut up than I had expected. I worked out what had happened. The Christmas cards had been cleared away. There was a pot plant with red leaves on the table and the carpet was cleaner.

Upstairs, the fallen curtain had been put back at the window, and propped up against a vase of roses was a note reading, 'We came back to London after Christmas at my sister's to find the staircase still not done, so I took advantage of your invitation for a couple of days. We broke some plates which I'll replace. I've taken the sheets for washing. I've engaged Mrs Flynn to come in twice weekly. You can't go on living like this. She doesn't need the work, so you can cancel her if you like. Thank you very much, love, Katie.'

I went down into the kitchen and put out water for Philip. Then I went to bed.

In the morning, as I came downstairs I heard someone banging and shouting on the door which led into the garden. It was Elmira. I opened the door. 'I've been round every morning since Boxing Day,' she said. 'Didn't even get a Christmas card from you. Is Naomi here?'

'She wouldn't come,' I said.

I sat with my head in my hands at the kitchen table, waiting for the coffee to be ready.

'Did you ask her to come?' demanded Elmira. 'Or just sit there looking indecisive, waiting for her to ask you?'

'I pleaded with her, I shouted at her, and I wept,' I said wearily. 'I did everything I could.' And I told Elmira about Jessica's phone call.

'Well,' said Elmira, handing me a cup of coffee and sitting down. 'I must say even I'm surprised. What a dirty trick. What can be the secret of your strange power over women, Joe?'

'I'm a dream-merchant,' I said, feeling that I was, at that moment, dreaming myself. 'In desperate cases I'm the substitute for the priest or some pills from the doctor. The women I have no influence over are those lacking in faith, meaning the capacity to believe something you know to be untrue. I can't touch the realists, cynics, the reconciled ones, the happy ones – and those like you, Elmira, who know that generally speaking it's up to them to make their own dreams come true. But there are a lot of the others, thought of as Messalinas, but really Cinderellas, all waiting for the prince to come.'

'Well, I wouldn't worry about Naomi's cop-out in those terms,' Elmira observed. 'I think she can't forgive you for what you did, and she's scared you'll go and do it again. Well Naomi's scared, and that's the whole of it. I don't want to be brutal, Joe, but I don't think she really loves you. She probably tells herself she does but she doesn't. She's never grown up. Is that Roderick still hanging about? I thought so. I met him with Naomi by accident one night in a restaurant. Perhaps the dream Roderick's selling her is the one she wants – Sanders of the River, only there's no river any more and so no danger to Roderick, If you think you're weak, look at him. He wouldn't last five minutes where I come from.'

'I'll have to keep on trying,' I said. 'I suppose Naomi deserves a bit of fidelity after all my neglect.' Then I said, 'My father died just before Christmas. Luckily I was on my way there after a row with Naomi, so I got there soon. The funeral was on Boxing Day.'

She sighed, 'Jesus Christ. You're getting your share now, aren't you? I think I'll cook you some breakfast. I think Katie left – ah, here we are. This is what you need to set you up.'

'Put that stuff away,' I said. 'When I want my own heart attack at 9 in the morning, I'll come round and ask for one.'

'Don't get stroppy with me, Coverdale,' she said. 'How about some toast for that weak Pommie digestion? Ah, Joe, can't you see I want to do something for you?'

'Thanks, Elmira,' I said. 'Make some toast, then.'

'How's your mum?' she asked. 'What's she going to do?'

'She'll get a man in to help and carry on. But she's got my crippled uncle to look after, too. It may not work. I'll go up for the lambing.'

'About the end of March, is that?' she said. 'Well, take me with you. It's years since I cut out a dead lamb.'

'Strong enough to cut out a dead elephant, I should think,' I said.

'Come on, Joe. Do you think I've been maintaining my opulent style of life on my savings from ballet-dancing? Some hopes. Sheep, that's where it all came from. Miles and miles of them. When Dad died, Mother sold out. So I'm serious – when lambing-time comes, I'll stand beside you in the snow-drifts.'

'All right,' I said. 'Thanks.'

'Poor Joe,' she said. 'Poor old Joe. Oh,' she said, 'A little bit more cheerful news – Laura Greenwood took an overdose on Boxing Day. She's all right. They got to her in time. But there's no doubt she was serious. She'd just taken the children off for a week at her mum's. She was alone in the house and Roy was meant to be out at the Young Men's Fellowship. If the tea-urn hadn't blown-up and wrecked the lights, he'd have been away for another three hours and by then it would have been too late. He came home and found her in one of the children's beds. She's coming out of hospital today. They're going to Crete tomorrow.'

'Crete?' I said.

'Well,' said Elmira, shrugging self-consciously. 'I ran into Roy doing the shopping in Tesco's and I stood there and told him bluntly that if he didn't get his sex-life, his religion and his emotions straightened out, Laura'd try it again. He took it well, considering he was standing there next to the corn-flakes in his dog-collar holding a wire basket. I told him that I didn't see how he could expect to help anybody if he couldn't help himself. He took that straight and said he was beginning to drink too much. I said I'd noticed. Anyhow, the Church has fixed them up with help and counselling, and I've fixed them up with a holiday – it's worth a try. Obviously his job's at stake, as well as his marriage. A clergyman loses credibility if he's always pissed and his wife's always trying to kill herself.'

'You're so kind,' I said, wonderingly.

'Nonsense. I'm very selfish. What's a few sheep more or less to me? Anyway, I got promotion. I'll be dancing Giselle. Christ, have I worked hard.'

'I've decided to sell books,' I told her.

'Do you know, I've always thought of that as a tatty job for posh layabouts,' she said.

'I daresay,' I said, 'but it's what I want to do. I'm thinking of writing another book, too.'

'Books about books,' said Elmira. 'Well it's your life. I've never been very literate myself. I suppose hopping about the stage, always in pain, with your toes bleeding, wouldn't appeal to you – ' She looked at her watch. 'I'd better get going. I said I'd walk Ajax to the nursery-school he's terrorizing these days.

This is his third day and they're doubtful about keeping him – nothing wrong with his disposition, they say, but he's disrupting the others. He'll come into line. The moment the idea of being thrown out came up, I saw a reflective look come over his face.'

'I'll come round and say hullo to Katie,' I said.

As we walked round the corner and down to Katie's house Elmira said, 'And guess where the heroic Julian is now? Living with his parents at the seaside and commuting to work every day. He said that with the stairs collapsing – which they did, by the way, we were lucky there – and then Katie at her sister's and finally at your house, the situation was too chaotic for him to be able to work properly. Personally, I think he was scared. Anyway, Katie knows that half the time he doesn't go home at night. He stays with Glenda MacFarlane at her flat. That's on again.'

'Does she mind?'

'She does, I think. But not too much. Who'd miss Julian? He's got no really good qualities to compensate for his nagging and complaints. And its obvious she's better without him. She's not so rattled and shaky and things don't go wrong so much. He's one of those people who make other people incompetent so they can turn round and be superior. I'm wondering what he's going to do now the stairs are repaired – hard to find another excuse for going back and forth between his mum and Glenda.'

'Katie doesn't hold that business about Jessica against me?'

'Katie?' said Elmira. 'She worships you. She thinks you've got true grit. Well, compared with Julian, there's no doubt about it. She'll be pleased to see you. What are you going to do about Jessica?'

'Go round and tell her what she's done. Just to clear the air. My heart's not in it. How could it be? But she did precipitate my last row with Naomi. I still think Naomi would have come back with me if Jessica hadn't rung up just then. If I could only have told her about me and Jessica first and got her back to London – '

'I don't think episodes like that affect the issue in the end,' said Elmira. 'Perhaps I'm wrong.'

Ajax was swinging on the front gate as we arrived. He was wearing his coat and a red hat with a bobble on top.

'I'm going to be quieter today,' he announced, getting off the gate.

'That's right, Ajax,' Elmira said briskly, taking his hand. 'You've got to join them sometime.'

I walked up Katie's steps. A holly wreath hung on a new front door, which was covered with undercoat. The bell was missing so I hammered on the door with my fist.

'Joe!' cried Katie, opening the door. 'I wondered when you'd get back.' As we went upstairs she said, 'You're looking very thin.'

There were rolls of new carpet in the hall, which had been decorated with fresh wallpaper covered with big leafy roses.

'It'll be so nice,' she said, 'when the carpet's down. And well worth it, now even Ajax is old enough to wipe his feet on the mat from time to time. The insurance company was very generous. Look at this,' she said opening the sitting-room door. 'It was a pleasure to be blown up to get a new carpet for this room.'

Siobhan and Patrick, watching the television, looked up when we came in. Siobhan said, 'Here comes the Bionic man.'

Patrick said, 'You've been drinking my Coke.'

Siobhan said, 'I haven't. It's mine. Look – it's got my initials on it.'

Katie gave me some coffee and made me eat a slice of Christmas cake.

'It's very smart,' I said, looking round.

'Are they at all nervous after the bombing?' I asked, nodding towards the children.

'Not really,' said Katie. 'Ajax had a few nightmares, that's all. Did Naomi come back with you?'

'No,' I said. 'I wanted her to, but she'll have nothing to do with me at present.'

'Perhaps she will come – when she thinks about it. She told me she wasn't planning to come when I rang up to tell her we were in the house. I don't think she liked it very much. She said we were welcome to stay but I felt she didn't mean it. I would have gone, but we only needed another day before the place was ready to come back, so I took her at her word and hung on.'

'Thanks for what you did – the curtain and everything.'

'I hope you didn't mind about Mrs Flynn. It was Naomi saying she wasn't coming – I thought you might want some help and she said you were in Yorkshire – '

'My father died,' I said abruptly.

She said nothing, then sniffed and said, 'Poor Joe. How sad for you.'

I looked at her. I thought I could see a tear. I said, 'Thank you for the flowers.'

'Thank you for lending me the house.'

There was another silence of a kind I could not explain. It was as if, suddenly, we were in that room at night again, mist-bound, waiting for the attack.

At the back of it I heard, dimly, a drumming on the door and Katie said, 'Answer the door, someone.'

She sat and stared at her coffee-cup, while the television in the background gave out bangs and Indian whoops.

Siobhan called, 'It's the carpet-layers.'

'Tell them to start,' shouted Katie, and again we sat there while the hammering started. I could not look at her. Finally I stood up and said, 'I'd better go now, before they block the stairs with carpet. I don't want to have to make that jump from the window again.'

I was going to say something else but I lost it.

Katie smiled.

I went away.

Later that morning I went to see Crosby at the Department. I told him that I did not want my job back. He seemed sorry but unsurprised. He asked me about my wife and children. He said, 'How sad that she doesn't seem able to forgive you. I have seen this before, you know. And it's not the end of the world, if you'll overlook a platitude. Things do piece themselves together, somehow. What are you planning to do?' And in the end he told me to go and see his uncle, who owned a house near Hanover Square where the bottom two floors, formerly a shop, had just become empty due to a bankruptcy. I went to see my secretary and told her I would not be returning. 'Keep in touch,' we said. And, 'Look after yourself.'

I missed Crosby's uncle who had gone to his club, and left a message for him. Then I took a taxi to Jessica's house for the confrontation I wanted, probably, even less than she did. But I told myself that, especially if she was going out into the world, she ought to learn that if she played dirty tricks, the victims would frequently come round and shout at her afterwards.

I was let in by a new au pair, wearing the usual beginner's air of doubt about what was happening to her. I found Jessica in the kitchen making preparations for a dinner-party. She said, distantly, 'Hullo, Joe,' and went on chopping onions, very fine.

'I only came to tell you that phone call was a real bastard's trick,' I said, without preliminaries. 'I thought you ought to know that the morning before you phoned, Naomi and I had agreed to have another try and that you put paid to all that. I don't say it was entirely what you told her or how I had to tell her suddenly about our night together, but what you said certainly didn't help. If she never comes back and I lose my children, I hope you'll think about what you did.'

'You told Naomi?' she said, raising her eyebrows over the onions.

'I was going to anyway. As it was, I had to throw it at her to explain your crazy accusations. You're mad Jessica, that's the trouble.'

'Huh,' she said. 'So you threw me in to cover up your affair with Katie. You smell more charming every time.'

'Well, you are mad,' I said. 'I mean, if you still believe that then you really are mad. You're hanging on to that story about me and Katie for reasons of your own. Just to defend your own ideas of yourself. If you go on believing it long enough, you'll be able to forget you ever had anything to do with me yourself. That's what it is. Gradually you'll start to believe it really was Katie. Not that I care – in fact, I'm sorry for you. Because you're mad. But I'll never forgive you for that malicious phone call.'

Jessica tipped the onions into a pan. They sizzled. 'Naomi's well rid of you,' she said.

'You've been an evil bitch,' I said. 'That's what I came to say and now I'm going.'

'And good riddance. I wish I'd never set eyes on you,' she

retorted, taking the skillet off the stove and banging it down on the counter. If she could manage that degree of psychological dodging, I thought as I left, saving the family business would be child's play for her.

For almost two months, until well on into February, I was busy. I secured a lease on the Hanover Square shop. I put up shelves, borrowed money from the bank, decorated, cleaned and shifted in stock. I went to auctions, searched shops – in my spare time I read for my new book.

I saw almost no one and telephoned Naomi regularly. On one buying trip I stopped at Stonebridge to see the children. I avoided any opportunities for long conversations, but when I left I said, on the steps, 'I still want you and the children, Naomi. You've only to say.'

'Is there anyone else in your life at the moment?' she asked.

I said, 'No – no, I'm too busy.'

She had gained a little weight and her face was rounder. I looked at the healthy woman in the tweed skirt and sweater who stood beside me. Here she was again, as she had been fifteen years ago, during our courtship, wearing almost the same clothes, with almost the same expression on her face which was plump now, as it had been in youth. I had the sudden notion that she was deliberately going back in time to the days before I came. I did not know whether it was a panicky impulse to start all over again, wipe out what had happened completely, or whether, all the time, she had never wanted to be anything but a rich, protected schoolgirl from the Midlands and all the rest had been an interruption, a patch of extremity, something to be got over, like a war. Was that it? Had it, had I, really been so bad? Or perhaps Naomi was just resting, just pretending, for a while, that she was the same, safe girl again. Nevertheless I was frightened, for her and for myself. If she was really retreating, would she ever come back? If she had decided to be a schoolgirl for ever, how could I be her husband and the children's father again? There they were, cavorting round us, unable, I think, to acknowledge fully that once more their father was leaving. It must have been Irene's idea to buy the pretty, stupid labrador puppy who now ran over the gravel after Philip, trying to play. She had tried to replace me with a dog, I thought to myself gloomily.

'It's ridiculous, Naomi. I can't wait forever,' I found myself saying, although I had promised myself I would not squeeze her any more in my vices – my blackmailer's nagging, my self-pity.

She stared at me, her eyes completely blank. The inside of her head must have been full of mist rolling slowly over rubble.

'All right,' I said quickly. 'I'll wait.'

'Give me time,' she said, weakly.

I kissed her quickly on the cheek. I embraced the children, seeing them sag and fail as they realized I was leaving again. I drove away, a man with a dog and cartons of books in the big car, meant for a family. If things got worse these visits would soon become something to dread, a duty like going to see someone in prison – worse, because I would have to watch the children slowly grow away from me. And I would have a new life, become uneasy with them and not know what to talk about.

The days got lighter. The bookshop was painted. I became, without realizing it, fussy in my domestic habits. I watched television in the evenings, fanatical about not missing the serialization of *Daniel Deronda*. I was content and saw no one. My days of popping in, like a housewife, to see the neighbours were over, for I was an economic man again. Routine and small pleasures keenly anticipated kept me going. The wound left where my father and children had been torn away used to flare up suddenly so that for hours I would be helpless, forced to stop work and sit down suddenly on the floor of the bookshop and wait it out like someone subject to attacks of dizziness, or lie rigid in bed with the tears prickling my eyes and waves of a pain I could not feel rolling through my head. And then the tide would withdraw and I would stand up and go on with what I was doing, or get up and make cups of tea, have a drink, a cigarette, go back to bed. It was after one of these assaults of grief, which had woken me at 6 in the morning, that I decided to go out and see what books there were for me on the stalls of nearby Portobello Road market. By 7 I was walking, in a freezing east wind, up between the stalls. Old china, books, radios, television sets and rails of clothes were coming out of the backs of vans. Stallholders blew on their fingers, hung up clothes, bargained with other dealers, out early to find the treasures, if any there were in thin times and bitter weather. By a stall outside the convent walls at the bottom end of the market I saw a familiar figure raking through what looked like a tin. It was Katie Mulvaney wearing a thick black pea-jacket, mittens, and a white knitted beret on her flying, fluffy hair. Close to, I noticed that her nose was red with cold and her eyes watering.

'Hullo,' she said. 'How are you?'

'Not bad,' I told her.

She looked at me. I had a sudden vision, through her eyes, of my pale, now thin, face and dulled, if resolute, eyes. In my leather coat I must have looked like one of Cromwell's soldiers.

'I was on my way back from Mass and I saw these old medals. I thought I'd get one for each of the children.' She held out one for me. 'It looks like an Iron Cross. St Cecilia's Sunday School medal for Valour in Christ's Name.'

'Perhaps you should wear it yourself,' I said. 'I thought I saw Sean going down into Bond Street station last week.'

'It could well have been him,' she said. 'He comes round sometimes and takes the children to the pictures. I try to get him to go home, but he won't. I don't think he's forgiven me yet for what I did.'

'I expect Julian's back now,' I said.

'Oh, yes,' she said. 'He is.'

'That's the way it goes,' I said.

She stared into the box of medals. Then she picked out another, a lacy arrangement of silver and ribbon held by a rusty pin, peered at it and read out, 'Universal Grinding Company. Long Service.' She smiled and said, 'Only a few more years and we'll all qualify for that one.'

After a pause she said, 'Well, I must go now.' She paid the stallholder and left.

The bitter wind cut into my bones as I looked down at the medals in the rusty tin biscuit-box. I stared down the long vista of stalls, and the heaps of junk in the streets around them, and the chilly stallholders, and their detritus of cardboard boxes and old newspapers. But as I stood there some warmth came over me. I felt I was thawing. Half-dazed I went on up the street, looking for books and I could not account, when it began to snow, for that feeling of ease, comfort and heat which surrounded me.

I went home and phoned Naomi, as I usually did on Saturday mornings. 'That's nice,' I said to Harriet. 'I'm glad you like it. Can I speak to Mum now? – What's all this?' I said when Naomi came on. 'Harriet says they're at school.'

'Well I couldn't keep them away from school forever,' she said. 'Anyway, it's against the law.' She was on the defensive but she still sounded plausible. Nevertheless, I knew that however many times Naomi claimed to be keeping her options open, she would not have sent the children to school in Stonebridge if she had really been coming back to London soon. I felt sick, chilled.

I said, 'Does that mean you're not coming back?'

'No,' she said in the same reasonable voice. 'It means the children have to go to school.'

'Come on, Naomi,' I said. 'You don't – wait a minute. How much did you spend on their uniforms?' It was a trick question. For all I knew they did not have to wear them.

'They were certainly expensive,' she said in a grudging tone. 'But Father made a point of paying for them –' Then her voice trailed off. We both knew that she would not spend over £100 on school uniforms for the children, if at the back of her mind, she was planning to leave Stonebridge soon. Naomi was not like that. The horror of it was that she had probably not known herself, up to now, what the purchase of a few gym tunics, grey flannel trousers and navy-blue macintoshes actually signified.

'Well, Naomi,' I said, in my dreadful voice, the one which froze her, like a small child waiting for a smack, 'don't tell me now that you're coming back. If you had even had it in mind at all, you'd have put them in the state school. You know that.'

She would have talked it over with Roderick, I thought, while the waiter set fire to the crêpes at a candlelit dinner in Birmingham. Roderick would have had a hand, already, in deciding how the children would be educated and what kind of people they would become. My poor Paul, I thought, so sweet-natured and biddable – how would he survive the education of a Glennister – the half-sadistic jollying-along, the ties and caps, the hard bullying, and competitiveness? Harriet, bright and resilient, might come through toughened but with some spirit intact, but how would my Paul manage? They would kill him.

Meanwhile she was telling me in detail precisely why the local state school would not have been satisfactory. I interrupted her by saying, 'I suppose it's Roderick's old school?'

There was a silence. I said, bitterly. 'Thanks, Naomi. You've done a good day's work there.'

'Look,' she said, 'the children had to go to school somewhere. And that council school wouldn't have done. They'd have been bullied and learned nothing – '

'I went to one,' I said.

'A village school,' she said. 'That was different. St Bede's is close to home – '

'I can't listen to any more about St Bede's,' I said. 'But you'd better start wondering how long I'll take this lying down.'

'What do you mean – ?' she said. I hung up. In fact I meant nothing except to alarm her. It was an empty threat. In a fury I whistled for Philip and walked out of the back door, intending to march round the garden and either cool off or stay angry and work out something to do. I doubted if I could get the children back legally and I was not sure how sensible it would be to kidnap them and take them abroad. That seemed to be the only way open to me at present.

'Hullo,' said a voice as I stamped past.

I turned and saw Katie, digging the garden. 'It must be done now,' she said, looking vaguely at the spade. 'Go on walking,' she added, seeing my expression. 'You look as if you need to boil something off.'

Standing by her gate as she leaned on her spade in the astonishing shambles of rusting toy cars and embryo adventure playgrounds created out of planks and oil drums which she called her garden, I told her loudly and furiously about Naomi and the children's schools.

'It's terrible,' she agreed. 'But you can't do anything without taking the matter to court. Unless it's kidnapping.'

'I'm thinking about both,' I said.

'See a solicitor, then,' she said.

'I shall,' I told her.

It began to snow again. Thick flakes filled the air and settled on Katie's coat and hair.

She did not invite me in. I said, 'Why don't you come round and see me for tea next week. Like before.'

'It's not like before,' she said, knocking the spade against a stone to get the earth off.

I looked at her. 'What – ?'

'I must be careful in my behaviour,' she said. 'Because I'm now so unhappy at home.'

I was shaken.

'I won't quarrel with you,' I said. 'I've had ample experience of what happens if you aren't careful – or scrupulous.'

'I know,' she said. 'That's the pity of it.'

'On the other hand,' I said, 'how long do you intend to go on being unhappy?'

'Oh,' she said, 'I don't want to make a profession of it. I try to understand what is wrong and change things.'

I did not quite understand, even then, why I was so angry with Julian. I just said, 'Supposing the wrong thing is the whole of you?'

'That's generally the case, I suppose. I can't alter myself much but I can alter a great deal of what I do.' She paused and added, 'I think.'

'I see the same spirit at work which made you sit there and wait to be blown up,' I said. 'The notion that anyone is entitled to demand anything of you – ' I tailed off. 'I admire it, in a way. I couldn't do it myself but then I wouldn't want to, any more than I'd want to make a model of Chartres out of discarded matchsticks.'

At that moment Julian put his head out of the window and called, 'Katie – we're all wondering when lunch will be.' Then a tear slid slowly down her cheek. I think it was a tear of bereavement, for the almost irrecoverably lost. Tears of distress or self-pity might have left some room for hope. She turned round and called, 'It's in the oven. I'm coming straight away.'

I looked at my watch and it was only 12 o'clock.

'Don't you ever feel angry with him?' I said.

'I used to. Now I feel more regret.'

'That you married him?'

'For both of us. Still,' she said, brightening up, 'it can't be very good for him to know I don't like him. I suppose it's a good sign that he can't stand me talking to other people.'

'I expect so,' I said, disbelievingly.

Julian, still leaning out of the window, called, 'Are you going to stand there all day chattering in a snowstorm?'

I almost laughed. He was so odious. I shouted, 'I'm going now,' and he shouted back, 'I've got Elizabeth.'

'Elizabeth?'

'Your secretary. She's mine now.'

This soured my laughter for I had been fond of Elizabeth and Julian's gloating, half-sexual claim over her made me angry. Fortunately a moment's thought told me that however hard Julian had manoeuvred to get her, only a week of his insecurities, his use of her as an office wife and hints of obscure seigneurial rights would soon drive her away.

'Cheerio, Julian,' I called, and 'We can't keep on meeting like this,' I said to Katie, thinking to cheer her up a bit after Julian's hinting glee about my secretary. Once I had said it I knew that I wanted to go on meeting her. I actually put my hand to my head in horror, smiting an unruly brow for releasing its anarchies. I groaned, left without saying any more.

Next day, the spring came. I walked around my garden and saw buds appearing on the apple tree and the spikes of bulbs coming out of the ground. I walked to my shop through the park feeling happy, perhaps, as I had not felt happy for a long time. Happy and virtuous, I thought, for I was sticking to my bargain with Naomi and would do so, until it seemed hopeless and at that point I would sue, sue up hill and down dale, sue to the House of Lords, to get my children back. I doubted if any court in the land, least of all the House of Lords, would let me win, but I could try.

That was the day I felt ready to start trading so, even though the man painting my name in gold above the door was still on his ladder, I opened the shop.

Luckily I had already had two customers before Julian, like Dis, came in, evaporating the tentative spring sunshine and puffing dust over the shelves. He looked round with suppressed envy and said, 'Things going well?'

'Bit early to say.'

'You don't seem to have got that interesting clutter you usually find in antiquarian bookshops.'

'Never shall have, I hope. Not in that way anyway.'

'You plan to keep it going as a sort of antiquarian book supermarket?'

'With wire baskets, if necessary.'

'Always a worry – starting a business.'

'It's the least of my worries at present,' I said, and, as if God, today, was really on my side and working to put Julian's nose out of joint, a Bentley drew up outside and a wealthy lady, a cartoon wealthy lady in a fur coat with matching Pekingese, came in.

'Well, things are flourishing,' Julian said uncomfortably. But knowing him as I did I felt no ease. He always had the air of a man prepared to flatten the entire world if, in the end, he would be able to stand on the last small boulder and be larger than the destruction. Today there seemed to be extra sinews of spite coiling through his long body. The night before I had, secretly and sentimentally, gone to stand in front of his house at midnight for I did miss Katie. I had easily detected, from the disarranged curtains in front of the house, the pile of old soggy, cardboard boxes left round the dustbin to collapse and Patrick's cycle, abandoned outside to rust or be stolen, that disorder had overtaken the household in spite of Katie's good intentions. It was as if Julian could emanate enough mistrust, lack of faith, terror and greed to waft through the house like a miasma, bringing despair to all it touched.

Two weeks later I discovered what Julian's new comportment meant. Elmira, lying in bed on Sunday morning stretched and yawned luxuriously and said, 'You know what's happened – of course you do.'

'What?' I had woken to hear birds singing and had called round to see her for the first time for weeks. She had let me in, doubled up with agony after the week's work, and had hobbled off up to bed moaning, 'Make me some coffee, Joe.'

'About Julian,' she said.

'What?'

'Him shutting Katie up. What a disgrace.'

'You mean he won't let her out?'

Holding out her cup, into which I obligingly poured more coffee, she said, 'Why, don't you know?'

'Why should I? I don't believe it. You mean Julian's got her locked in the attic?'

'Well, she's shut up, eighteenth-century style. He's taken away her shoes. He won't let her near the phone. All the food's brought in by Siobhan or Patrick. I heard about it when I met Siobhan in the street on her way to the park with Ajax. She was furious – it was raining and she'd been told to take him out from under Dad's feet. I thought Katie must be ill. Siobhan's angry about the extra work, particularly as, she says, Julian makes her do it because Patrick's a boy. So she told me that Julian told her that Katie was ill and they all had to help her. But she says Katie's not ill – the doctor hasn't been called – Julian just makes her stay in bed most of the time. It seems he's been having long rambling chats with Siobhan about how Mother's been seeing too much of a certain party – what do you think of that?'

'He must be having a breakdown,' I said. 'I mean, it can't be true. I saw him a couple of weeks ago. He looked as normal as he ever is. He came round to the shop.'

'That was when it set in – oh my legs.'

She shifted uncomfortably in her bed, like a woman who has just given birth.

'Should it be as painful as that?' I asked. 'I thought you were trained – '

'Always a little extra for the performances, duckie,' she said. 'That's what does it. To think I have to get up and go down to the *barre* soon. If I don't give performances I'm miserable and if I do them I end up like this. Why don't you get into bed with me?'

'I might catch you on a sore point,' I said.

'There's someone else, then? It should be me, Joe. You know that. Our relationship is just like a ballet-dancer and a pouf – but you're not homosexual. Is there something wrong with me – it's not as if you were fussy? Christ knows, you're not that.'

'I'm keeping myself pure for Naomi. It's like a vow,' I told her. 'She left me for infidelity – then last time she wouldn't come back because I'd been having it away with Jessica. If I really want her and the children to come back, I have to hang on until she wants me. As long as I keep on offending her – '

'The worst offence is that you don't love her,' she said.

'Love – what the fuck does that mean?' I said angrily. 'Of

course I love her in some ways. And I do want my children – and her too, in a way. If she'd come, I'd try. All men don't love their wives that way or vice versa. The world would collapse if they did. But people manage. And if Naomi rang me tomorrow and said she was on her way, I'd do it and I'd do it throughly, and if it failed I'd feel I had failed too. Intention's half the battle in these things. I'm fond of her, I've lived with her for nearly fifteen years and I can go on living with her. I'd just settle down comfortably and live through quiet interludes of despair and the knowledge of something lacking. And so would she. I know how it's done – they do it all the time where I come from. They do it all over the world except in the parts where people are rich and have the freedom to make choices. And half the time that freedom just leads to more and more selfish decisions. It's like religion. The minute you can tell yourself you love God with the full approval of society behind you, then you can go ahead and do anything you like – start the Crusades, burn witches, abandon your wife and children – '

'I don't see that all that's got anything to do with you and me this one Sunday morning,' said the pragmatic Elmira. 'I think you're just wearing a hair-shirt – you're like something out of the Middle Ages yourself.'

'Shut up, Elmira,' I said. 'Or I'll have to leave. Anyway, what's all this rubbish about Julian? Hasn't anyone been round to stop him?'

'The only person allowed in that house is Jessica,' said Elmira. 'You can imagine how Katie feels about that. Of course Jessica's hand in glove with Julian – she agrees with everything he says.'

'I don't understand it,' I said. 'It's all too complicated for me.'

'Well, come on, Joe,' said Elmira. 'Use your head. Who do you think this would-be seducer is?'

'How should I know where Julian's fantasies have led him? Who – oh my God,' I said. 'You don't mean me? Jessica hasn't been round to Julian's with that tale about me and Katie?'

'Not in so many words, I suppose,' said Elmira. 'She wouldn't dare. Julian hit on you before. She just reinforces it with a few hints about the night of the bombing to keep the pot boiling. He's taken a fortnight's sick leave already and now he's starting in on his annual holiday. Of course, he'll have to give up sooner or later, or lose his job.'

'What is he doing?' I said. 'Just what is he doing? She must be complying, though,' I said, as a new thought struck me. 'After all one man can't keep a grown woman in a house, shoes or no shoes, if she really wants to get out. Katie's an accomplice – I wouldn't have thought she'd connive at her own punishment to that extent.'

'Maybe she likes it. Or perhaps she doesn't want to hurt him,' said Elmira.

'Hurt him?' I said .

'If I were you I'd go and stick a ladder up to her window,' said Elmira and there was an expression on her face I had never seen before.

'What are you talking about. You look all funny,' I said.

'Don't be a child, Joe,' she said. 'Look – Julian's right. And Katie knows that Julian's right to lock her up. Not for what she's done but for what she wants to do – there's hardly any difference as far as she's concerned.'

I stared at her feeling confused, as she went steadily on, 'She wants you, Joe, and the horror of it is – you want her. If you knew it,' she finished and rolled over, burying her head in the pillow. I wondered what she was doing. Then I heard her sobbing. Elmira – I could hardly believe it – had burst into tears. 'Piss off,' came her muffled voice. 'Piss off and leave me alone.'

'Elmira,' I said, bending over her. 'Oh – Elmira.'

'It's nothing, Joe,' she mumbled, heaving with sobs. 'It'll pass. I'm so fond of you. You're so stupid.' And after another couple of sobs she turned over so suddenly that I had to spring back and sat bolt upright with the tears pouring down her face. She cried, 'It should have been *me*, Joe.' Then, in a different tone, she said, 'Don't worry. We couldn't stand each other for five minutes in real life. I'm too big and strong and dedicated – you don't want a big, bad nigger like me. Now do me a favour and get out.'

As I went down the stairs she called, 'When's the lambing?'

'I'm going next Wednesday,' I said, running gladly back into the room. A tear was trickling over Elmira's bare breast.

She said, 'I'd like to come and help. But – well – Joe. Forget it – this.'

'I don't want to,' I said. I went over and kissed her on the cheek and left. It was better to do so.

I went straight to the pub and drank first one toast and then another toast to the pity of it all. I wound up with one of the local book-dealers and his heavily-painted wife. We took a lot of bottles home with us when the pub shut, and spent the afternoon getting drunk. 'You're drunk, Joe,' said Naomi, when she telephoned.

'That's right. I'd like to see you.'

'Who's there?'

'A book-dealer and his wife. You don't know them. When can I come and see you?'

'I hope it's all right there.'

'Naomi, I'm being true to you,' I said.

'What is all this? Is the house full of people?'

'Naomi,' I said. 'I'm being true to you. I have a business now. Do I have to join the Band of Hope as well? When can I come and see you and the children?'

'I've never stopped you,' she said. 'Ring up when you're sober and tell me.'

Ooh, she was hard. I went back into the other room and had another drink. 'Bloody women,' said I, and my book-dealer friend said, 'Cheers to that,' raising his glass. Then his wife took the glass from his hand and knocked it back, every drop of it.

'That's what I think of the lot of you rotten sods,' she said, venomously. 'And cheers to *that* as well.'

Before going home to Yorkshire I managed to bump into Siobhan and Patrick on their way home from school and, by a wealth of dramatic and gruesome detail about the births of lambs, made sure that they took home the news that I was going away for ten days. Julian, I knew could not hold out for ever, drawing on his summer holidays to make a bitter spring. Once I was gone he would let Katie out.

'I can't phone or go round there,' I said to Elmira as we went up the motorway. 'That would only make matters worse.'

'He's definitely ended it with Glenda,' reported Elmira, 'in a great big scene. He's suggested to Katie that they reform their life together – well, he's just stepped back at the right time, now life's easier and Ajax is older and Katie's not quite so preoccupied with child-rearing. I hear that's what they all do. Anyway, as a contribution to the new life, Katie suggested she'd get a job. So they'd have more money and she wouldn't brood. Do you know what he did?'

'No.'

'Threw a chair at her leg.'

'I'll kill him,' I said.

By mutual consent we did not talk about the scene between us that Sunday morning. It was, I suppose, like so many things of that kind. Either you go ahead, make love and vows, and declare later that it was the hand of fate which put you with that particular person in that place at that time, or you do nothing, shuffle away apologizing and try to forget about it completely.

It had been quiet and sad up at the farm, and in spite of my mother's suspicion of the gaudy colonial I had brought with me she and Joe were pleased to see us. It was hard work. I shall not forget the sight of Elmira, in a huge fur coat, crossing the yard in the wind at first light followed by two bleating lambs. She had a surprising knack of getting up in the morning in good spirits, for hauling out lambs and clamping them to their mothers and for detecting, early, the signs of distress. Also, she was stronger than me.

'It's not as hard as ballet-dancing,' I heard her say to Uncle Joe,' as she stretched out gratefully in front of the fire one evening.

In the kitchen my mother said, 'She's a good lass, that one.' Then she paused. In the other room I heard Elmira say, 'Come and see then. I'll get you some tickets when you come down to London.'

I took a plate and dried it and said, 'She's only a friend, Mother.'

'I can see that,' retorted my mother. 'What about Naomi?'

'I don't know. Whatever happens I'll bring the children up in summer.'

'Oh – I would like to see them.'

'You will.'

As we drove down to Stonebridge Elmira said, 'Are you going to leave those two up there?'

'I don't know. Anyway, they've got to have a say in it too. And obviously I can't decide anything at present. If Naomi comes back I don't think she'll want to look after my mother and crippled uncle.'

Elmira turned to me and said, angrily, 'If your uncle was the crippled Lord Pymme and your mother the Honourable Elizabeth, she'd do it.'

'I daresay,' I said.

Irene looked flustered when we arrived and said, 'I thought you were coming tomorrow. You should have given me warning.'

As Elmira came over the gravel towards the steps after locking the car door, Irene said, 'I didn't think you'd be bringing anybody.'

'I told Naomi all about it,' I said. 'I'm sorry if it's inconvenient – ' and it suddenly crossed my mind that Irene was not going to let me in. So I stepped towards her and she was obliged to give way. I left Elmira to go into the sitting-room and followed Irene into the kitchen.

'Who is that big woman?' she asked, buttering scones. The silver teapot was out, I noticed. And the bone china.

'I thought Naomi – I'm sure I told her – well, she's a neighbour of ours in London. Are the children here?'

'They're at school,' she said. 'It's a weekday.'

I had hoped that they would be kept back from school after lunch; I realized now that even if I had been expected, the children would still have been sent to school. Irene was obstructing me. Naomi had let confusion develop about when I was coming. I began to feel the frustration men feel when women, powerless to do any large damage, begin the guerilla war of the unbought new socks and the unposted letter. 'You said you'd post it yourself.' 'I thought you said you didn't like the socks I bought you – you'd rather get your own,' they report, with perfect truth. But surely they must have known all along, you think, that you would be late for the meeting, or in time, but wearing odd socks? Of course they did but, it is slave's war, sabotage, and you can't touch them for it.

'I wanted to talk to you, Irene,' I said. She jolted. Me talking to her was what she most dreaded. 'I wanted to ask you if Naomi had told you what her plans are. I can't seem to get much idea – on the phone – '

'You're phoning too much, Joe.' she said. 'She feels badgered.'

'If I didn't she'd feel neglected. I want her back.'

'You seem to be very confused in your mind about what you do want,' she said, but it was an old litany. It had been true, and she wished it still were. But it was not.

'On the contrary,' I said, knowing that anyone who says 'on the contrary' is normally taken to be in earnest. 'On the contrary,' I said, 'Irene. That may be what you and Naomi tell yourselves and it may be a consolation to you to think it. But you know it's not true. I've asked her for a decision – she doesn't seem capable of it.'

'Nor were you before,' she told me. 'I'm afraid you can't expect the whole world to dance to your tune, Joe.' And she filled up the silver teapot.

I took the tray from her and walked into the sitting-room. The reason for her startled greeting was there. Henry was at work, the children at school, but Roderick, good old well-set-up Roderick, was sitting there in the living-room, waiting for his tea.

'You remember Roderick, don't you?' said Naomi.

'I don't think I do,' I said.

'We met at your wedding, I think,' he said.

Irene had not followed me into the room. He said, 'Who's going to be mother?'

Or father, I thought, as I watched him hand a slice of cake to Elmira.

'How was the lambing, Joe?' Naomi asked, pouring out tea. She was at ease now, looking comfortable in a cashmere sweater and soft brown skirt. Roderick was wearing a tweed jacket with leather patches at the elbows. They made a handsome couple.

'Hard work – too many twins,' I said.

'Is it worth,' asked Roderick, 'the cost of feeding them these days?'

'Not much choice, in Yorkshire,' I said. 'It's do that or sell up. The land won't do for crops.'

'Of course, hill-farming nowadays – ' began Roderick.

'It's never been a fat living,' said I, looking at Naomi, who had her gentleman farmer at last, while she looked back at me, appealing for something, I didn't know what – rescue from Roderick, sympathy in her plight, tolerance, acceptance, or, perhaps, no fuss. Was I facing my children's new father? The thought was intolerable.

'I'd like to talk to you, when you've had your tea,' I said politely to Naomi. I saw her glance at Roderick with almost the same expression on her face. I got angry.

Elmira said, 'Roderick and I can have a chat while you're gone.'

Walking through the hall, I wondered if he had virtues I could not see. In the study I asked her, using husband's English, 'What do you see in that creep of a boyfriend of yours?'

'What do you mean – what right have you – ?'

'No,' I said in the same tone 'No. Tell me. I'm genuinely curious.'

'Perhaps he doesn't patronize me like you do,' she said in rage. 'Half the time you talk to me as if I was your dog. Also, he's not a muddler, like you. Being patronized is one thing – being patronized by a muddling, emotional fool is another. You asked me – now I'm telling you.'

'Thanks a lot,' I said. 'He lives in a simple world, your Roderick. Perhaps if it gets more complicated he won't seem so calm and clever.'

'He might make an effort to stop the world from getting so complicated,' she told me. She was just bored with me now. She had suffered and now she saw a clear, easy course ahead of her. Suddenly helped by Roderick's plain man's reading of me, she could see me as the intrusive voice on the telephone, the maladjusted, difficult fellow she had married when she had been too young to know any better, the man who had taken advantage of youth and trust to half-ruin her life. It must have been a relief to go along with Roderick's view.

I said, 'Please, Naomi. Come home with me now.'

She said, 'Can't you see I'm frightened?'

I said, 'Naomi – you've put the children into that posh school. You're sitting here having cosy chats with good old Roderick while your mother brings in the tea. Can't you see what's happening? While you keep on not making a decision, you continue to do things all the time which are bloody decisions. All you need is one thing – just one thing. You only need me to get fed up with waiting and take up with someone, however casually. If you get to hear that one woman who isn't my sister, has spent one night in the house that'll be it.

You'll have your justification. I wouldn't put it past you to have detectives watching me - my God,' I shouted, 'you have. You bloody well have, haven't you? You're having me watched. Go on –' and here I sprang towards her, 'admit it.'

Taking a step back, she said, 'And why shouldn't I? Why should I trust you? I trusted you before, for years, and look what a fool you made of me.'

'By God,' I said. 'My own wife.'

'Oh, shut up, Joe,' she said. 'Don't start that.'

'Watched,' I said, 'in my own house.'

'*My* wife, *my* house,' she said. 'You bloody hypocrite. It's all right when it's you, isn't it? All right when you can get away with it and I'm too trusting to suspect any ill and believe any lie you care to tell me – now the boot's on the other foot, and I seem to be suspecting you, we hear a different story. And my mother's telling lies about you – oh yes – everyone's against you and now, what shocking disloyalty, I've put detectives on you. Joe – one detective isn't enough. The way you've behaved in the past, the whole Flying Squad couldn't have kept up with you but now, of course, it's all right and you're reformed and you expect me – *me* who waited for years and years, me, who you lied to, me, who hung on because we were a family – to trust you straight away. And when I don't, you start acting like Jesus on the way to the cross. Joe,' she said, 'you're nothing but a joke.'

I said, 'Come home with me, Naomi. Pack up. Pack the children's clothes. It's only a hundred miles. We can be there this evening.'

She stood by the window and said, 'I can't make up my mind.'

'Well, I've made up mine,' I said and grabbed her by the arm. I pulled her into the hall, shoved her towards the stairs and said, 'Get up there and pack.'

Naomi looked at me perfectly neutrally and said, 'Don't you dare push me.' Henry, who must have been called home by Irene, at that moment let himself in through the front door to see me trying to push his daughter upstairs. Then Roderick came out of the sitting-room. I saw Elmira in there, smoking a cigarette. She did not even turn her head.

Inevitably, Roderick said, 'Take your hands off Naomi. What do you think gives you the right – '

Predictably, I said, 'More right than you, you bastard,' and hit him in the eye.

Showing no sign of pain, he grasped me by the shoulders and said, 'Pull yourself tog – ' and I hooked my leg behind his knee and toppled him over in the hall. And his head hit the carpet with a thud.

Naomi cried, 'Stop it, both of you.'

Irene came out of the kitchen and said, 'What's going on?'

Henry just stood in the open doorway. He had expected this.

Naomi cried, 'Joe!' as I kicked Roderick in the ribs. Winded, he gave a groan.

'Stop it, Joe! You're behaving like a child,' Naomi cried.

As Roderick tried to lever himself up, I saw through the open door of the sitting-room Elmira's hand, as if in slow motion, move to put out her cigarette. By now Roderick was up. He put his hand to his eye and said, 'I suppose you feel better now, Coverdale.'

Elmira suddenly there, pushed me off balance as I swung at him and I only managed to hit him on the temple. Then, as Roderick squared up she said, 'I think we'd better go, now.'

Roderick, showing his true colours, said with enjoyment, 'All right, if this is what you really want.'

'Oh – balls,' I said.

He said, 'Put up your hands.'

Naomi said, 'Father, can't you stop this farce?'

'I'm going anyway,' I said. I did not want to give Roderick the chance to hit me in a fair fight. Basically, my desire was only to hurt him when he was not expecting it.

'I think that would be as well,' said Irene.

And, as we went out, Naomi said in a vindictive hiss, 'There aren't any detectives.'

I felt better as we drove away. Twice, now, both before and after Christmas I had slunk humble, ashamed and rejected from that house and there had been no effort from their side to soften the blow to me. This time, as we swished down the drive, I felt that at least I had given him a good reason to throw me out. I had fulfilled their expectations, given them their money's worth of villainy. In return I had had the pleasure of punching Roderick Glennister.

'You hit him, anyway,' said Elmira, comfortingly.

'Next time I'll run him over,' I told her.

'I enjoyed the bit where you tripped him up when he wasn't looking and then kicked him in the ribs when he fell down.'

'Being a foreigner, you would,' I said.

'I've seen better fights,' she said.

'You probably been in them,' I said.

We stopped for tea, and Elmira allowed herself a doughnut.

'Taken all in all,' I said, 'and on mature reflection, I don't think I did myself much good there.'

'I don't think you could. They're getting nice and cosy and you're the outsider now. Still, you hit Roderick and that showed Naomi you cared. That's two good things.'

'They'll talk her round,' I said. 'She'll wind up thinking I'm uncouth and hysterical. Roderick will make a special point of my low blows and general lack of sportsmanship.'

'You fought to win,' Elmira told me encouragingly.

'That doesn't really recommend you in those circles.'

Elmira, popping the last bit of doughnut in her mouth, just smiled.

At home I sat and played some music, looked at the apple-blossom and made myself ring up Naomi.

'I thought you might be ringing up to apologize,' she said.

'What for?'

'Did I make a point of going round and scratching the eyes out of the women you slept with?'

'It might have been better if you had.'

'You're impossible, Joe. Mother was in tears after you left.'

'Fuck your mother. I love you. I want my children,' I shouted.

'I suppose you think you're being very manly now.'

'Are you coming back?' I asked, loudly and clearly.

'Give me a little time, Joe.'

'How much?'

'Leave me alone.'

'Oh, Christ,' I said and put the phone down.

All the time I knew I was forcing an unforceable issue, that I was asking for a decision in an area where decisions are rarely made, where everything depends on an inner self which makes no definitions, no decisions and no plans – which just loves, desires, hates and fears. Happy the man or woman who can dig quickly down through the layers, find that inner four-year-old, consult him or her and come up with a fast answer. In the meanwhile I could only judge the matter on the basis of what had happened and was happening. Originally, free to go to Naomi, I had not gone. Now, free to come to me, Naomi would not come.

So I worked hard, I was patient, I waited. But by now I was not hoping for much.

The next Sunday, on a bright, cold spring afternoon, I was cataloguing some books I had bought on the previous day when I heard the drum. At first it was so faint that I did not consciously recognize it, but as the beat, loud and steady, became gradually more demanding I put my head up and listened. As it got louder I heard behind it the sound of voices. Were they singing or not?

I put my cards away and went upstairs where my view out of the window would be longer, not obscured by my gate and the front hedge. A pair of motor-cycle police came past on the main road at the top of the street. Then came a large black police-van travelling slowly. Then the first marchers, a man and a woman carrying small hand-made banners, saying 'Troops out'.

I went out, and up the street. A bus cruised slowly by, and behind it, the rest of the march, about 500 men and women, singing a little, chanting. Rather tired. The men, and most of the women, were in jackets and jeans but some of the women wore long skirts. One or two had children by the hand. On either side of them, in the road and on the pavement, the police marched with them. Police motor-cycles went up and down and police-cars, travelling at walking speed, split the marchers into groups. The sunshine struck faces, pale after the winter. And the songs were ragged. Suddenly, in the middle of the march, I saw the drummer, a short man in a dark suit. Beside him, in his old tweed coat, marched Sean Green. The drum, like the sound of a beating heart, went on, but picked up speed and a few voices began to sing *The Wearing of the Green*. Then more and more voices took up the song. A police-man pushed through to expostulate with the drummer while the voices rose:

She's the most distressful country that ever yet was seen,
For they're hanging men and women for the wearing of the green.

Beside me on the pavement a woman said, shocked, 'It's an IRA demonstration.'

'They ought not to allow them,' said another. 'Come on, I'm going.' And she put her pushchair into the gutter and began, quickly, to wheel it past the marchers. The march stopped suddenly. The drummer played no more but the people went on singing. Across the road I saw a man heave his toddler on to his shoulders and walk away rapidly.

'You're only giving them what they want – attention,' a man said, too quickly, to his wife. 'Come along.'

From the corner of my eye I saw Roy Greenwood and Katie, with Julian and the three children, come up to the corner and stop. Katie's eyes wrinkled up as she read the banners. She did not seem to see Sean, who was partly masked by the policeman.

As the drummer and the policeman argued, another two policemen on motor-cycles pulled up and went to join him. At the same time someone started up the tune on a whistle, or flute, and the demonstrators sang the louder:

Then since the colour we must wear is England's cruel red,
Let it remind us of the blood –

While over the song a megaphone boomed, 'This march will not be allowed to continue unless it is quiet. Can you hear me? This march will only be allowed to proceed in silence.'

I walked up to Katie and Julian and said, 'Perhaps you should get the children home. There could be trouble.' The song had stopped. In a low voice, I said, 'Sean's here – standing next to the drummer.' There was a murmur from the crowd. I heard a voice say, 'Outrageous.' When I looked up I saw that some of the marchers had put on black berets and dark glasses. Even as I watched, another man in front of me fished in his pocket and pulled out a beret. Suddenly the drum beat a rat-a-tat and, at the same moment, the voice over the megaphone said, 'This march cannot go on any longer. Will marchers disperse. This march is over. This march is over – ' Clearly I heard the song being whistled from the back of the line.

I picked up Ajax and said, 'Come on, Patrick, come on, Siobhan. Let's get out.' The drum banged, there was a cry as I ran round the corner with the children. Then I heard two bangs. There was a scream and people began to come running towards me. Putting Ajax on his feet I said, 'Patrick and Siobhan. Run home and wait, now. Can you get in?'

Patrick nodded and Siobhan said, 'Mum – '

'The shots weren't near her,' I said quietly, as a man bumped against me. 'Stay one on either side of Ajax, in case he gets pushed over.' Then they were away, running.

I ran back. The demonstrators and the crowd were disappearing fast. The police were pushing two men into police-cars. On the opposite pavement there was a small crowd, standing round a prone figure. A few people stood, in a group by the kerb, staring, without comprehension, at another figure, a man, spreadeagled in the street. Roy Greenwood was leaning over it. There was a police inspector, a policeman coming up with a blanket and Katie, running. The inspector, moving forward, put his arm in her way to stop her. She cried out, pushed past him and threw herself on her knees, beside the body. As I went forward I heard her saying, 'No! He's alive. *Look.*' She took the hand of the outstretched man saying, into his face, 'Sean, Sean. It's Katie.' By now there was a ring of policemen around the group. I could see the bottoms of Roy Greenwood's shoes, as he knelt by the body, and Katie's face peering intently into the, to me, invisible face of her brother lying in the street. I heard Roy Greenwood say, in a low voice, 'Katie – please. He is dead. You must believe me.'

She took no notice but went on saying, 'Look, Sean. Look up at the sky, now. See how blue it is. Look at it and see the sun. Look at it. Now, speak to me Sean – ' And so her voice ran on, earnest and reassuring as a mother talking to a child, calling on her lifeless brother over and over again.

Julian came from nowhere and stood over her as she knelt there. In a shaken voice, he said, 'Please, Kate. He's dead. It's no use. It's no use. Come home with me.' A policeman hid Julian from me, all but his pale face and his eyes, which did not look at the body. At the same time I heard the wail of an ambulance far away.

'Listen to me now, Sean,' she said, and she had taken his other hand, so that now she leaned right over him, talking into his face. 'I want you to listen to me, hard. I want you to look and listen to me now. I'm calling you now. You know me – it's Katie. I'm calling you and I want to talk to you, Sean. Now can you hear me? This is Kate, your sister, Katie. I must talk to you – it's very important. Can you hear me? Sean? Sean? Are you listening to me?'

The traffic, by mistake, was being filtered through. A bus crowded with passengers came along the street, the engine noise muffled her words. On the top deck, people craned to look down at Sean's spreadeagled body, at Kate crouching over him with Julian and Roy Greenwood and the police inspector standing by. On the lower deck a woman covered a small child's eyes with her hand.

As the bus passed, I heard the inspector say to Julian, 'Are you her husband? Can you try to get her away? I can't let this go on.' The clang of the ambulance grew louder and I half-saw it pull in on the other side of the street and ambulance men going to the body on the other pavement. A police-car drew up. Two men pushed past me and, behind the cordon, flashbulbs began to go off. Crowds were collecting on both pavements, all staring into the ring of policemen. Meanwhile, between the sounds of the passing cars I heard Katie's flat, caressing murmur go on and on. 'Now I'm glad you're listening, Sean,' she was saying, 'because I have something to tell you. Are you really listening?' I saw a white Mercedes edge past the group. A pretty girl in a headscarf looked down to where Katie leaned over Sean. I saw her expression change. Apart from anything else, Sean must have been lying in a pool of his blood. As the engine noise died away the policemen in front of me, one muttering to the other, 'This should be stopped,' moved forward and I had a clear view of Sean on the ground with Kate kneeling over him, holding both his hands. His blue eyes were open and staring calmly at the sky. There was a little of his blood in the street, a small puddle showing past his coat, flapped open in the road. The photographer frowning slightly, was standing at Sean's head, holding his camera and talking to the inspector, plainly telling him to get Katie away. Across the street a second ambulance stood by, doors open, ambulance men outside. Julian and Roy

Greenwood stood beside Katie, listening, as she murmured on. 'This is Katie, Sean. Your sister Kate. I'm glad you're listening to me a little now. It's a lovely day and I'm waiting for you to take a good look at it – can you see the sky a little now?' The inspector moved over to Julian and began to say something, urgently, in a low voice. I heard Julian say, 'I can see that you have to – '

'Well, that's right, now,' Katie's voice came, encouragingly. Sean's eyes stared blankly up into the cold blue of the sky. 'Now, you can hear me a little, can't you? That's my boy, that's my Sean. You can hear my voice now, can't you? Will you make a little effort now. You're not really trying, not really.'

I could bear it no longer. I walked forward, through the policemen and said to Julian. 'Come on – ' And at that Roy Greenwood, his small face pinched and serious, staring down at Sean's dead face said, in a low, steady voice, 'He blinked.' We all looked. Katie, silent at last, looked down at her brother.

She said to him, 'That's better. There's a good boy.'

'He's dead,' said the inspector to Roy Greenwood. 'Now, Katie you must get up and let us take your brother away – ' and Sean's eyes shut, blanking out the blue. As the ambulance-men pushed forward and took Sean's hand from Katie's, Roy Greenwood pulled her gently to her feet. He said something to her. I caught the words 'done it'.

'Bit of a pulse there,' the ambulance-man declared. 'You'd better get your pictures fast.' The flashbulbs went off and the stretcher was brought forward.

'I thought he was dead,' said Julian to the police inspector. There was a touch of indignation in his voice.

'We all thought so,' he said. 'But there was no doctor present – it's always possible to be mistaken. Perhaps,' he said, 'you'd better go to your wife.'

Katie was on the other side of the street, watching them load the red-blanketed stretcher into the ambulance. A boy came up to me. 'Are you Mr Coverdale?' I nodded. 'I've a message from Olivia Lumer. She says will you look after the children?'

'Who?' I said. 'What children?'

'You know Olivia,' he told me. 'That big black girl. She got shot. Over there – ' and he nodded across the street. 'She told me – before they put her in the ambulance, "Find Mr

Coverdale and ask him to look after the children." Her dad's just left, see, and her mother's working long hours. She's afraid the welfare woman will come round and put them in care.'

I saw Katie climb into the ambulance.

'All right,' I said. 'I'll see what I can do.'

'She didn't look too bad,' he told me. 'It's just her leg. It wasn't half a mess, though. I'm going up to see her now. Can I tell her it's all right?'

'Say I'll do my best,' I told him. 'And I'll come up to the hospital later and tell her if I can sort anything out.'

'Thanks a lot,' he said, and was gone.

Julian came up to me and said, without preamble, 'He said "Mother".'

'What?' I said.

'I could have sworn I heard him mumble "Mother" as they put him in the ambulance.'

'Oh, Christ,' I said.

'Did you get the children home?' he asked.

'I put them on their way.'

'I suppose I ought to be getting back to them,' he said.

'Could you do with a drink first?'

'I'll go round there,' said Roy Greenwood, 'And babysit until you get back.'

'Thanks, Roy,' said Julian. As Greenwood hurried away, he pulled out a packet of cigarettes and lit one. He put the packet back in his jacket and said, 'Sorry – do you want one?'

'I'll get one indoors. Come round the corner and have a whisky. It can't be a long one because I've got to go down and sort out that black family at the bottom of the square. The eldest sister got shot in the leg.'

'Rotten bastards,' said Julian.

Inside the house we both drank our glasses down fast and I poured another. 'This'd better be the last,' Julian said. 'I must get back to the kids. Oh, Christ. What an awful thing. And so fast. One minute you're standing on the corner and the next there's your brother-in-law bleeding to death in the street. I wonder if it was his gun?'

'Shouldn't think so. He wouldn't shoot himself deliberately.'

'With the Greens, anything's possible,' Julian said gloomily.

'Probably one of them wanted to shoot a policeman,' I said.

'Sodding maniacs. I wouldn't be a bit surprised,' he said. 'What an afternoon's work.'

A silence fell. Finally I said, 'I thought Sean was dead, myself.'

'That seemed to be the general opinion,' said Julian. 'Greenwood and the police inspector both thought so and they must have seen a few. Still,' he said pulling himself together, 'obviously they were wrong.'

There was another possibility and we both knew it. We were like two schoolboys, alone in the woods at night, afraid of the noise of a creeping thing easing itself through the bushes, each daring the other to express the horrors they are imagining.

Julian mopped his narrow brow with a handkerchief. It would have been wicked of me to suggest to a man like Julian, whose whole existence depended on coming as close to an imagined norm as possible, that there was something uncanny about his wife. In the end he said it himself.

'The awful thing is,' he said, 'I've seen her like that before.'

'Like what?' I said.

'Intense,' he said. It was plainly something he disliked. 'You know Katie,' he said, but he was talking more to himself than me. 'Well, she's normal enough but just occasionally she – she seems to muster herself in a funny way, but not in order to do something – you see her gather herself together and then – instead of doing anything – she just goes off. It's no good. I can't describe it. There aren't any words to describe these funny states she goes into. I suppose it's day-dreaming, really. She's like a medium, you know – in a world of her own. She can't hear you if you talk to her. She blots you out completely. It's like a trance. She can't even hear the children unless one of them falls downstairs or something – then she comes to fast enough. But only for that. It's deliberate of course.' He paused. 'Perhaps she's just trying to have a rest. She's so scatterbrained. I sometimes think her head's like a badly programmed computer which can't sort the information out properly.'

He lit another cigarette and said, 'It's depressing. There's something very depressing about the way she comes and goes mentally, like the Cheshire Cat. One minute she's with you and the next she's evaporated. There's a statue in the room staring into space.' He finished his drink. 'I know people think I'm unfair to her, and it's true, but let me tell you, I've had provocation. There've been times in my life when I've been talking to her and she's gone off like that, when I could have jumped at her and strangled her. It makes you feel so small. I shouldn't say this but I used to envy you for having Naomi – a nice, normal woman, who concentrated on you and had the same ideas as everybody else.'

'That's what I used to dislike,' I said uneasily. 'It goes to show, no one's ever satisfied with what they've got. I'll walk down with you. I'm going in your direction.'

As we went down to his house he said, 'I shouldn't have said all those things about Kate.' And I liked him then, for the first time for years.

At his gate, I said, 'I think Sean was dead.'

'So do I, as a matter of fact,' he said. 'It's bloody awful.'

'Never mind,' I said with an attempt at a joke. 'Just think – if you drop dead suddenly she can call you back, too.'

He looked at me for a moment and said, 'Ah. But would she?'

Thinking about all this, I walked down to see what I could do to keep Olivia's brothers and sisters, and little cousin Leonie, out of the hands of the welfare lady.

That is all.

Now, in August, the sun beats down over our enclosed garden, the leaves are the deep, dusty green of late summer, the grass is scorched in places and large roses hang their heads in the heat.

I know that when this long summer breaks, the rain begins, the air grows less bright and the leaves fade, Katie will come to me. Julian has gone back to his parents and Glenda, where he can feel at ease. She did come once, Katie, arriving in the doorway of my living-room late one warm, clear June night. She was carrying a casserole in a brown pot and said, behind me, quite suddenly above the music I was playing, 'I'm sorry I didn't come earlier, Joe. My sister and her children arrived this morning to stay.' Then she stayed, all night, until the early birds woke us with their twittering and she went home, with the sun coming up, across the dewy grass.

So I am nearly sure that in autumn Kate will come, just as I am nearly sure that Naomi never will. She pines for me, sometimes I can hear it in her wistful voice on the telephone, but her hard memories of me and the confident voices of Roderick and her mother in her ears will make sure, I think, that she will never break the ever-thicker barrier between us now. In any case, everything I do, however natural, serves to drive her further and further away. I see now that I shall never recover from the loss of her but, like the dead, she will not be brought back.

And the others?

Olivia is out of hospital now, although her recovery, in the end, took longer than Sean's. He is back in Ireland, looking after his mother. In the odd way communities have of dealing with their own affairs, the whole episode of the demonstration and the shootings has somehow disappeared from the collective memory of the neighbourhood. It is as if certain affairs, however dramatic, have no proper significance for people, whereas others, seemingly less important, have more real relevance and are longer remembered. However, none of this stopped me from having to spend nearly three months looking after Olivia's four younger brothers and sisters, as well as their little cousin, Leonie. Eventually I invited them to move in with me because it was more convenient. This did not please Naomi. The children helped, their mother helped – although their absence from the crowded flat at the bottom of the garden was more like a holiday for her, whatever else she did – Kate helped (thus the late arrival of the casserole) and even Jessica often sent Beth round with prepared food, or a cake, or some games. She came round herself once, smartly dressed and distant. In an hour she managed to make a vegetable soup and put it in the refrigerator for next day, iron a large pile of children's clothing and spot the early signs of measles in the two youngest children. Having called the doctor she left, remote, friendly, wary.

It was at about this point that the welfare lady, already suspicious about this ramshackle situation, which depended for its continued existence on her belief that Naomi was really living in the house, became restive and probing in her attitude.

Olivia's mother, Mrs Lumer, was a nurse on night duty, and also took care of an old lady in the afternoons. With her husband gone she could not afford to pay the rent and feed and clothe the children unless she kept both jobs or went on Social Security, and with Olivia in hospital there was no one to mind the children while she worked. It seemed that the children might be taken away and, perhaps split up, put in children's homes. It was Olivia, still hobbling painfully about in hospital and threatened with a third operation on her shattered leg, who solved everything. She could sing. Unknown to me, and some of the time to her mother, she had, for a year, been singing in pubs and clubs. And in the end that voice saved the family. I am sure it will save her, too.

After the news came through she sang for me in the hospital, one afternoon. The other patients in the ward, who had been told that the black girl was going to sing to them that afternoon, had braced themselves, in beds and chairs, for the experience. Then Olivia, standing lankily in her old dressing-gown, on crutches, at the foot of her bed, sang. In deference to my old age she abandoned her normal style, which was more funky, and sang *Smoke Gets In Your Eyes.* I could not believe that Olivia Lumer could sing like that – she opened her mouth and pure sound came out. It had nothing to do with her speaking voice and I felt, as one often does with great singers, that it had nothing to do with lung or throat or mouth either. It was like a beam of pure gold light being transmitted through a wall, a stream of sound which seemed to have no connection with Olivia.

There was a silence at the end and then the women clapped. Olivia confessed to me afterwards that she was upset because the other women became colder to her. She was, remember, the ward's oldest inhabitant by then. How could I explain to her that they were frightened by her, a poor, skinny black girl, victim of an unjust accident, who had suddenly produced a miracle by means of ordinary, fleshy throat and lungs?

However, although Olivia had half-forgotten it, some weeks before the shootings she and her group had made a demo-disc for a large record company. Now the company wanted them to make the record. Olivia's share of the first payment from the company, although small, was enough to persuade her prosperous uncle in Harlesden, who owned a taxi firm, to lend her some more money. She was able to buy, at a knock-down price, the tumbledown house, crammed with tenants, in which she and her family lived. The landlord, pressed by the Council to bring the premises up to standard, was only too glad to get rid of it. How this venture will work out I do not know. What I do know is that now, before the deal is even concluded, Olivia is already trying to get sitting tenants out by unfair tactics, so that she can let their rooms out at high rents. She is making her younger brothers and sisters work like slaves at cleaning and repairing the property. They come to my house to hide from her. As I pointed out to Jessica, who approached me in the street to ask me if I could use my influence with Olivia over the treatment of the children, I doubted if the Lairds of Cromarty and Ness, her ancestors, had been any kinder to their fellow clansmen in their own day, or, indeed, to anyone else they met on the route to the lush pastures of the South, via Culloden and the shipyards of the Firth of Forth.

And as I wait the summer out for Katie Mulvaney, Jessica is, even now, beginning to prove her worth at Lombards. A genuine servant runs the household now, a competent woman who is not pretending to learn the language or be one of the family. Jessica, on a wider stage now, does not need any longer to be the star in her own home. So far she is not having an affair with one of the firm's directors, but I predict that she soon will. As Jessica affirms herself, Hugo sinks. That is the way it always goes – in a crisis the strong get stronger while the weaker deteriorate. All this augments Beth's sympathy and understanding for her father and from this will grow her own adolescence and marriage. That is how families operate. Or perhaps, who knows, later Hugo will fall in love with some young, sweet girl who will take away some of the pain caused by the cuts of sharp-edged Jessica. Perhaps she will remain forever gentle and submissive and perhaps, so subtle and undetectable are the pressures we put on each other in marriage, perhaps she will gradually become another Jessica.

I end in mid-story, really. The tale for all of us is only half-completed and will not, I suppose, be truly finished until old age and death overtake us.

Elmira blossoms, as usual. And the Greenwoods are a fighting unit again. Their house has been redecorated. Their children are happy again. Roy Greenwood has taken what seems to be the only useful course for him in our Victorian neighbourhood, where riches and poverty live so closely together. At any rate, he is now involved in local politics. Too busy, almost, for the troubles of his well-heeled parishioners, he spared the time recently to come and insist on ten pounds for a housing scheme and to suggest slyly that since Father McGrath would not be the man to ask, he might be prepared to conduct my marriage to Kate.

So shall I marry Katie, with her visions, her noisy children and her tendency to get fat? Shall I run my secondhand bookshop, live in a chaotic household, father to children not my own? Shall we invite my mother and crippled uncle to live with us, fail under the pressure, sink into ruin, quarrels and debts? Shall I begin to grab and grasp again, from necessity, becoming the perpetually tired businessman with no time or attention for anyone else? Will Kate get harassed, take a part-time job, start to talk of freedom? Can I survive? Can she? Can love itself?

I know one thing, though. We can hope to live better. We can try.